THE
ALCHEMY
OF
WINGS

Dawn Celeste McGregor

THREE THREES
PUBLISHING

To the Rebels and the Seekers....

May you always find your way to yourself.

PREFACE

Lucia's journey did not stem from carefully crafted ideas or planned storylines. She was born through the crucible of my own deeply personal and transformative awakening—a unique and often devastating evolution that reshaped my soul. As I grew, so did Lucia. Her emergence was not confined to the boundaries of fiction but was, instead, an alchemy of my experience, the Universe, and the written word. Her authenticity came alive through me, flowing from the cosmos, into my being, and onto the page.

Characters appeared as if summoned from the ether, carrying wisdom that shaped not just Lucia's story, but my own understanding of life's mysteries. As they channeled through me, they taught lessons both profound and unexpected. Authoring this novel was not merely a creative act; it was an act of surrender. It became a process of divination, where mysticism and determinism intertwined, a sacred dialogue with the Universe itself.

Lucia's story is an invitation—not for passive observation but for profound participation. It beckons readers to embark alongside her on a path of self-discovery, spiritual awakening, and humanity's reclamation. Her story resonates with the reader, creating a shared journey of revelation. This novel is not just a narrative; it is a mirror, a bond between the words, the character, and the hearts of those who choose to walk this path with her.

As I wrote, I felt the wisdom of these pages flow through me as a gift from the Divine. It arrived in transformative waves, surprising and illuminating in equal measure. The chapters encapsulate the essence of an awakened existence—stepping into the unknown, surrendering control, and embracing the mysteries of life. Lucia's journey begins in chaos—raw, visceral, and unapologetic—as she wrestles with her past in pursuit of an embodied spirituality. Her

1

lessons taught me to let go, to practice presence, and to discover the beauty of becoming.

Through this novel, I invite you to hold Lucia's hand and accompany her as she dismantles and rebuilds her world. Together, you will share her joys, her awe, and the synchronicities that define a life of meaning. May her insights inspire your spirit, and may her growth echo in your heart long after the final page.

When I first set out to write this book, I sought to create an alternate life—a vibrant world brimming with passion and authenticity. What I discovered was something far greater: a channeling of my divine energy, flowing into my consciousness and into these words. Drafting this story became an act of revelation and faith, a surrender to myself as a Microcosm to the Universal Macrocosm.

Much of my life has been defined by a mystic's quest—venturing into the dark unknown and returning with fragments of light. Within these pages, I have gathered treasures for you, each one a spark of clarity, inspiration, and truth. May you find every gem and golden nugget waiting here, and may they illuminate your journey just as they have illuminated mine.

Many Blessings and Much Love,

Dawn Celeste McGregor

Chapter One

IN THE BEGINNING, THERE WAS WOMAN

We delight in the beauty of the butterfly but rarely admit the changes it has gone through to achieve that beauty.

- Maya Angelou

Lucia wandered through a labyrinth of her mind, navigating a reality birthed from her inner workings. An owl followed her while a dragonfly led the way, its wings slicing through the fabric of existence. They guided her through spirals of energy, each movement dizzying, her stomach churning as her thoughts spun intricate webs. She searched for a safe place to land, a space to set her intention. Diving deep into herself, she shone a beacon on her darker, scarier parts. Life had dealt her harsh blows, but she had endured enough. It was time to shift her direction, time to reclaim herself.

She envisioned blood-red pigments swirling around her, attempting to loosen memories, pain, and the burden of constant management. As she ventured into the twisted corners of her psyche, her belly dropped, like plummeting on a theme park ride. Spinning sensations erupted, serial isolation, then the ride restarted, like a child enjoying an all-day pass, eager for every thrill. Lucia called herself inward, redirecting the energy she had poured into mending her heart to fortifying her inner being. She resolved to stop fixing and start being.

In this energetic flow, she found safety. The movement rocked her, soothed her, and enveloped her in a sensation of invulnerability. She imagined herself as a little girl watching her transformation into womanhood. She felt her body grow; emotions mature through years of experience. Gently nurturing herself, she rewove her past, offering the care she had always sought.

The woman emerging in her vision stood intense and empowered, less damaged. Through strength and self-sufficiency, she grounded herself. She became the earth, like an ancient oak, rooted to withstand relentless storms. Each gust pushed her toward authenticity, shaping her into a solid structure that connected to the heart of all things.

Lucia observed her face morph repeatedly into those of a child, an infant, an elderly woman, a man, and then into the manifestation of destruction and creation, Kali Ma. The Black Goddess danced within her mind, extending a sharp red tongue from her supple lips into the cosmos, reaching beyond sight. Suddenly, it snapped back, swirling around her, enveloping her in potent energy. This power held magnificence, fear, intensity, and a nurturing quality, like a mother guiding her children. Kali stormed into her psyche, ready to dismantle everything.

Fragments of Lucia's reality shattered, revealing fractals of her experiences. She witnessed her past, no longer a participant but an observer. Amidst destruction, void, and the spark of creation, her sense of self expanded beyond time and space. She listened closely as Kali Ma granted her permission to embrace the anger over her lost marriage and her lost self, releasing guilt for allowing herself to shrink into someone unrecognizable. The fierce deity invited Lucia to channel that rage, breaking down the structures that no longer served her and paving the way to rebuild her chosen life.

The tongue melted into a crimson force, surrounding her like firecracker smoke. Lucia's face shifted from fire-eyed onyx to pale porcelain. She envisioned her emerald eyes—sparkling, relaxed, soft. Her long chestnut hair flowed gently behind her, framing her form. The water on her skin enveloped her like a womb of graciousness. In that peaceful state, something inside her shattered. A single thread unraveled, releasing the tightness she'd clung to for so long.

Harnessing the crimson energy, she softly focused on the story of her past decade, battling the urge to blame herself. She noticed the tension in her shoulders as they curled inward, protecting her heart. She resisted the unhealthy constriction, forcing herself toward self-acceptance and a loving embrace. She reminded herself to avoid judging the time lost or the toll her aching heart had endured. Instead, she concentrated on the lessons learned through her responses, shaped by the limitations of her knowledge.

These reflections stirred a sense of loss within her—a feeling that lingered for too long. It was time to stop reliving the past and start transforming herself. Lucia inhaled deeply, confronting her fear of relying on others. She seized the sensations in her body—the constriction, the sharpness in her groin, the tension—using them to trace the source of her pain. She accessed the deep angst of her childhood, the feeling of being unsafe, misunderstood, and alone.

Lucia had to be in control. As a child, she lacked guidance in regulating her emotions, cultivating a fierce independence that distanced her from trust. A question emerged: What if people could be trusted? What if her refusal to let anyone in had trapped her in a cycle of self-fulfilling trauma?

"Damn it, there it is!" Lucia exclaimed, tears flooding her eyes.

She heaved and hyperventilated, pain erupting from every pore. Gradually, reality's pressure eased. Clinging to this release, she slowed her breath, drawing it deep into her belly and calming her nervous system. Acknowledging discomfort as a necessary step toward healing, she surrendered to the process.

Lucia recognized that what she once deemed a strength had become bondage. It held her back from true freedom and an open heart. With every ounce of control she exerted, she closed herself off further. An imaginary obligation to maintain tranquility in her marriage, within herself, and for her son loomed over her.

Her consciousness began to reformulate, blocking the issue from holding any power over her. She needed to unravel the tightly wound ball that compressed her potential. Stories, trauma, and past hurt no longer belonged in her present.

Everything dissolved, leaving Lucia alone in what felt like infinite space and time. She forced her lungs to take in oxygen after eons of barely surviving. She had hyperventilated for years, breathing just enough to endure.

Suddenly, a warmth surged through her body, overwhelming her system and igniting a forgotten spark. Fear tried to smother this warmth, whispering that it might fade. Lucia clung to it, refusing to let it go. The more she embraced it, the brighter her inner light shone, a glow no one could ever extinguish again.

This imagery sparked a deep need for substance in her physical form, an affirmation of her reality, a sign that someone recognized her existence. Yet, she understood that she must embrace disconnection in this moment, as if her mind floated like a balloon, drifting away from Earth, past the clouds, into outer space. Deep within, a fear whispered that she should not linger in this void; a sense of purpose tugged at her. What was it she needed to accomplish? She pondered, perhaps she didn't need to do anything at all. Perhaps choice lay before her; perhaps she could guide herself.

Lucia quickly justified taking a bite of this liminal space. When the call beckoned, she could return to the world, recalling the binding weight of obligation and the tranquility found in serene emptiness. In this lack of projection, she glimpsed divinity. She perceived truth as the canvas onto which everyone projected their narratives. This place held everything. So did the world, if only she could remember to stop imposing her story upon it.

The urge to dissociate reignited images of scarlet light swirling and pulsating around her. This energy moved with intent, communicating that the sacred resided within her humanity. Its vibrant presence sparked her skin, awakening every point of contact—her emotions, thoughts, and fears. She hesitated, wanting to cling to the ethereal. Finally, she felt the inevitable pull to release control over every desire to remain in the abstract, to flee a world distorted by her projections. She knew she must allow herself to flow with this force, with whatever felt utterly right in each moment.

An inner knowing of impending change had drawn her into this matrix. For at least a year, Lucia oscillated, yearning for a unique perspective. Confused about how to shift, she resorted to the only option she could envision—meditating in the bath.

The crimson energy and Kali's support infused her with the strength to navigate the pain of her marriage. Lucia sensed the potency of this work; her heart thumped like a drum, louder until it nearly overwhelmed her. This rhythm breathed life back into her.

As she continued this exploration, Lucia felt a newfound fortitude in her skin, thicker and stronger than before. Transformed and bare, wrapped in love's embrace, she experienced a rebirth. For the first time, the Universe enveloped her, revealing who she could become.

She marveled at her own capacity. Her insides felt solid yet pliable. After years of struggle, she finally recognized her beauty—not dependent on anyone else's gaze, but a flame ignited from within. She embraced the flow of her pain, grateful that it no longer stagnated in her aching body. Finally, she acknowledged it as part of herself, able to exist within it without detachment, feeling completely relaxed.

Lucia lay naked in the bathtub, steaming pink flesh surrounded by lavender vapors and flickering candlelight. The vessel cradled her like a womb of heated liquid lifeforce. Water became the sanctuary for her body, a realm where transformation and healing thrived. The steam lifted the heaviness she had carried for over a decade. Lucia felt her body lighten as if she might float away. Something within had shifted. Ready for anything, she watched the fear of consequences and the weight of concern for others dissolve, realizing it was time to prioritize herself. At last, she awakened from someone else's dream.

Suddenly, the music echoed in the background, "You must wake up…Wake up, Child, pay attention…Wake up, Love…" Kate Bush's Waking the Witch rouses Lucia back into reality. As the music wrapped around her, she gathered her senses and embraced her body entirely. She had spent too long trapped in chains of her own making. The healing she discovered in that steamy bathroom provided the catalyst for her self-actualization.

A tapping interrupted her thoughts. At first, she believed her heartbeat synced with the rhythm, but soon realized someone knocked, pulling her from the solitude of her awakened mind and goddess guide.

"Hold on!" she mumbled as the knock grew louder. Clarity washed over her in those moments as she remembered the need to lead her life. With a firm resolve, she vowed never to forget herself again. She promised to seek her truth, pursue meaning, and chase what ignited her spirit. She rose, emerging from the warm reservoir of transformation, her skin glistening as if a fire had smoldered out, and the smoke whispered memories of the past. After blotting her hair, she swayed toward the door.

Opening it, naked and radiant, Lucia faced her friend Sherry, who stared in awe. Ignoring the sight before her, Sherry said sternly, "Why aren't you ready, Lucia? We're supposed to leave in ten minutes." Lucia nodded, shutting the door after assuring Sherry she would be ready in twenty, planning for a thirty-minute delay. "Sherry, there's white wine in the fridge! Why don't you chill out for a bit?" she sang through the door.

Standing before the mirror, she saw herself for the first time. Her shoulders pulled back; her spine straightened. Her electric gaze pierced her reflection, reading her future. Confidence surged within her, stronger than ever before. The prospect of the evening settled in; anticipation bubbled for the party Sherry had coaxed her into attending. Sherry thrived in the sex-positive community, and Lucia had hesitated about joining this gathering. Now, certainty embraced her choice. When nervousness threatened, she reminded herself that no one expected anything from her—she didn't have to participate. Empowerment coursed through her; she could choose her path.

The party promised kink and allure at their friend Sam's vibrant home in Seattle's queer Capitol Hill. Curiosity ignited within her, free from the compulsion to rush. "It's fashionable to be late," she mused, despite not fully embracing that mantra. A giggle escaped her as she considered fashion's fickle grip; she had long abandoned societal expectations.

Lucia craved two to three hours to revel in the party, knowing ample time remained. She continued to bask in the afterglow of her meditation, moving through molasses as the thick summer air wrapped around her. Muscles relaxed, she focused on each micromovement—every sensation against her skin, every joint grounding her as she assembled herself. She wanted to feel everything.

Sherry had attended parties like this many times and understood the rhythm; there was no rush. But once she decided to leave, Sherry would always get neurotic about getting to the destination. Lucia knew her friend could stand to chill; it would not kill her. Nothing could persuade Lucia to quicken her pace anyway.

Sam intrigued her. Since the divorce, Lucia craved complex personalities. She found fascination in chaos, though she constantly reminded herself not to take on the role of fixer. This understanding freed her, allowing her to enjoy passionate souls without losing her essence.

Her years with Arlo had blurred the line between excitement and dysfunction. She had reveled in the fires of a turbulent relationship but wanted no part of the wreckage it wrought. Prioritizing freedom was her pathway to well-being; thus, she gladly embraced a hiatus from romance.

Lucia yearned for an exhilarating life, one untethered by others' dramas feeding her need for control. She adored creative, emotional, and intense souls, cognizant that she had to establish boundaries to prevent slipping into her regulatory tendencies. A sex party beckoned as the perfect setting to practice this balance.

Her thoughts drifted between the possibilities of the party and her meditation, and she felt a stronger, grounded strength than before. The image of the Black Mother, Kali, lingered in her mind. This powerful Goddess imparted comfort during her transformative journey.

Years ago, she had encountered Kali through a witchy friend named Raven, a woman who navigated the realms of dark and light with entrancing grace. Raven captivated Lucia, exuding an otherworldly allure with her black hair and dark eyes. Through Raven, Lucia discovered a vibrant world rich with magic, passion, and the divine. Raven's work with Kali, one of her most cherished deities, taught Lucia about embracing all aspects of the self. Eager to learn, Lucia immersed herself in the mythology of the primordial Mother Goddess.

Lucia felt unafraid of her own darkness or Raven's. She sought intimacy with her shadow self, believing awareness was the key to preventing it from gaining control. This meditation illustrated how she could transform her less desirable traits into sources of power.

Envisioning herself as Kali startled her; this figure embodied the destruction of the old to forge something new. This transformation aligned with her desires, yet the intensity frightened her. The uncertainty of what might crumble loomed large. Anticipation coursed through her body as she contemplated the wild ride ahead. The urge to surrender to chaos enveloped her once more.

Before marriage, she had embraced that facet of her sexuality. Years earlier, she had dated a captivating man named Gabriel, whose charm and passion ignited her desire. He had repeatedly tied her up and used dildos and vibrators on her without hesitation, pushing her limits through her body. He used pain and pleasure together, sending her into submission and euphoria. She reveled in the experience; bound yet free, she surrendered control completely. But that chapter of her life closed when she met her husband. At that instant, she accepted the change. Arlo had attempted to tie her up a couple of times, but each instance only fueled her irritation. She couldn't trust him in everyday life, and the thought of being bound by him felt entirely wrong. Every movement he made while she was restrained intensified her unease.

Arlo embodied fun, eager to try anything in the bedroom. However, he possessed a side that did little to ease her sense of control. She missed the peace that washed over her in moments when she could nurture her kinky side and didn't have to make every decision. The upcoming party at Sam's excited her; fellow attendees would delve into scenes, all desiring to relinquish control.

After about 45 minutes, Lucia gathered her tipsy sidekick. They admired their reflections—Sherry's striking blonde bob framed her face, paired with a sparkly mini skirt, while Lucia donned a flowy, sheer blouse that highlighted her black bra. Together, they stepped out into Seattle's tender darkness, heading towards Sam's house.

***

When they arrived, a few people stood outside, smoking. Lucia lingered, eager to chat before heading inside. Meanwhile, Sherry rushed past her, searching for a play partner she had met at a party a few weeks prior.

The smokers welcomed Lucia into their conversation about consent, a topic that consumed them since a community member accused someone of violating her boundaries.

Lucia's new friends described the situation as an issue arising during the pre-play discussion, as a woman they knew had declared a hard limit on sex. Her partner, however, had touched her taint with their hand. They interpreted her limit as a prohibition on penetration only, while she intended to include any touch to her genitals or areas in between. The group wrestled with whether this counted as a consent violation, especially since she hadn't used her safe word or voiced a desire to stop.

Most participants in the conversation concluded that the issue stemmed from communication failures. Some argued she should have invoked her safe word, while others insisted her partner should have sought clarification before approaching her genitals at all. The core debate focused on the offender's accountability amidst the unclear communication.

Lucia thrived on conversations like this. Open and honest, she reveled in the freedom to use words like "taint." She wished for a world of uninhibited minds. Yet, she recognized the challenge of her hope for an open-minded, non-judgmental, sex-positive society. Everyone embodied unique perspectives, and she respected their differences. Still, she craved the company of those who embraced this way of speaking. She found joy in engaging with diverse individuals, knowing that each interaction offered insights into the richness of humanity. She yearned to grow, expand, and evolve through every experience, transforming her bullshit into wisdom.

Lucia had tried radical honesty with her husband, and he had reluctantly accepted it. Each time she expressed her thoughts and feelings without a filter, Arlo grew disrupted and emotionally reactive. Over time, Lucia realized that she didn't need to voice every feeling. Spewing her truth onto him without considering the consequences felt selfish. She decided to communicate with compassion.

Lucia found a balance between expressing herself and embodying compassion. Reflecting on her growth, she understood that though the negative aspects of her marriage persisted, she became more attuned to her emotions and capable of self-expression.

Living within a whirlwind of emotions, heartbreak, jealousy, anger, hate, had shocked her. These feelings once seemed superficial, mere surface reactions, insignificant. So, she dismissed them, pouring all her energy into caring for her surroundings and ignoring her inner turmoil. This neglect seeped into her relationships, especially with Arlo. The emotions she ignored transformed into an overwhelming need to control what she could.

Recognizing this, she began to embrace radical honesty, striving to bring buried feelings into the light. This step proved crucial, yet she knew she needed to balance self-exploration and expression while honoring others' autonomy.

She hoped to meet her own expectations. For now, she needed to resist the urge to restrict herself. She would focus on silencing her overthinking and fully engaging in the moment.

Lucia excused herself from the smokers and stepped inside to grab a drink. She paused at the doorway, inhaling the rich musk and leather that filled the air. The majestic sight of a naked woman wrapped in rope being led around the room by a hot, chiseled leather daddy caught her attention.

In the corner, two women interacted on a red velvet chair, their joy echoing in the soft fabric. One stood exposed, her eyes hidden by a black satin sash. The other woman hovered as she sported lace stockings, spiked heels, and encased her torso in a leather corset with elbow-length gloves. Feathers adorned her hair, adding a wild touch to her striking ensemble. The extravagant woman whispered into the naked woman's ear as she used a riding crop to spread her legs wide, causing evident goosebumps from head to toe. Her shaved vulva glistened from her excitement. Lucia knew she would fantasize about this moment for months, perhaps years. Heat radiated off them, intensifying the air between their bodies. Lucia caught her breath, breaking the trance these women had put her in.

As Lucia strolled toward the kitchen, she brushed against a man who echoed Gabriel. He wore shoulder-length, wavy blonde hair and intense cobalt-blue eyes. A black suit jacket clung to his frame, and he gripped a briefcase that mirrored the one Gabriel always had at his side. Lucia recalled that Gabriel's case always contained handcuffs, a ball gag (which Lucia never let him use on her), and dildos of varied sizes and shapes. She imagined this gentleman's bag had similar contents.

She figured she would ask him later but was on a mission to get a gin and tonic. Lucia cradled a G&T in her hand, settling into a solo spot where she could go back to watching the two women in the corner. She had not attended an event like this since meeting Arlo, and the vibrant atmosphere pulled her in. The moment absorbed her while watching the scenes that unfolded. She saw the naked one quiver, instinctively trying to close her legs, while the one in lace swatted her thigh, leaning in to whisper again. Lucia imagined a sweet hiss that included that everyone was looking at her exposed, that she was a dirty girl, and that her wetness dripping down her legs showed everyone how much she liked it.

Lucia enjoyed the thrill of the moment, savoring her drink while maintaining her composure. Surrounded by such openness, she felt a rush of excitement. Participating didn't matter; simply witnessing the scene fulfilled her. She thought, "Everyone should go to a sex party if they just want to learn what they like..." She felt her desires expand as she encountered new possibilities. It empowered her to realize she could pursue anything she wanted as long as she expressed her needs clearly and respected others' boundaries.

Continuing her scan of the room, she locked her gaze on two men standing in the doorway. She watched as they cupped one another's asses, seeming to swallow the others' tongues in a passionate embrace. They both wore leather pants; one sported a vest, while the other proudly exposed his erect nipples. Lucia pondered whether they had just met or shared years. She couldn't tell.

Her thoughts drifted from the room back to her meditation. She wondered how long Kali would guide her. Lucia knew much about gods and goddesses, holding a particular affinity for Hindu deities. Their raw essence struck her as they embodied every facet of human nature.

Taking Kali Ma's cue, Lucia decided not to let fear dominate her anymore. She refused to allow it to drive her life. Fully aware of her mission to discover herself, she vowed to shed her bullshit and embrace her truth.

Lucia approached her work with Kali intentionally, knowing destruction would follow once unleashed. Yet she felt ready. Yearning to incinerate her old self and break free from destructive patterns. She had grown weary of playing nice with stories, traumas, and conditioning. Tired of the weight bearing down on her, she desired lightness, sensing it within her gut, urging her to commit to well-being, care, and self-awareness.

Lucia sought freedom. She yearned to embody her true self, the self she chose, not what others or society dictated.

As she contemplated the scarlet energy enveloping her, she recognized lingering attachments to childhood experiences. Finally, a readiness surged to release them.

Suddenly, a tall, sharp-featured woman with short blonde hair approached. The Goddess of War was draped in a red latex dress that clung to her body and cascaded to her knees, red spiked heels clicking on the floor, wielding a cat of nine tails.

"I'm Alyx with a Y," she said. "It means defender."

Lucia leaned in; her curiosity piqued. "Do you think I need defending?" she asked, trying to flirt.

Alyx, with a Y, met her gaze. "No, you look like the only person you need defending from is yourself."

The poignant words sliced through the air, sending a shiver from Lucia's belly to her fingertips. They radiated out to her toes, then spiraled upward, igniting every inch of her being. Alyx's challenge wrapped around Lucia, both exhilarating and intoxicating. In that brief exchange, a connection sparked; she would have followed this enigmatic woman anywhere.

They chatted in sultry tones until Alyx reached for Lucia's hand. Silence enveloped them as their eyes locked. In perfect harmony, they floated into a private room to delve into their desires, set boundaries, and define hard limits.

Lucia did not say touching her taint was a hard limit, nor did she say sex was off the table. One thought consumed her: she wanted to avoid making decisions and detested the idea of a gag silencing her. Lucia craved the freedom to express herself. They chose safe words—red, yellow, and green—for communication if necessary. She insisted on using no additional phrases; relinquishing control excited her, yet she understood she could halt everything whenever she wished. Whipping thrilled her, and pain play intrigued her, but Lucia made it clear she disliked pain near her vulva. Alyx nodded, then guided Lucia into the hallway, where they passed Sherry fucking a cute, petite, red-headed lesbian from behind.

They entered a room draped in red scarves, the lights casting shadows that danced across the walls. A massage table stood in the center, surrounded by candles flickering in every corner, creating an intimate glow reminiscent of an old Cinemax soft porn film. Alyx laid a clean sheet on the table, her fingers deftly unbuttoning Lucia's blouse, revealing her skin beneath.

The angelic mistress pulled down Lucia's skirt and underwear, slithering them off her body as if she had done it a million times. Alyx helped her onto the table, removing her boots with tenderness and care. The Goddess sparked with fire in her eyes as she untied Lucia's laces, loosening them until they slid off her feet with a graceful ease. Running her persistent hands down Lucia's legs, exposing her supple skin. Alyx kissed her, coaxing her tongue into a sensuous dance, coaxing a serpent of heat through her. Lucia's breathing deepened as minute moans escaped her throat, directing Alyx to keep going.

Alyx enveloped Lucia's large breasts, devouring them. Her chest quivered as she busted out through her black lacy bra, still partially covered by the satin blouse that hung over her shoulders. Lucia slid her hands over Alyx's latex-covered body. Her hands seemed to have a mind of their own, tracing her muscles through the glossy veneer. She couldn't fathom how smooth it felt, how the definition of Alyx's form penetrated through the softened rubber dress. Lucia gripped Alyx as though she might die if this moment ended.

The dominatrix took Lucia's hands and put them above her head as she slid her shirt up and over her obedient body. Alyx released Lucia's breasts from her bra in one sweeping motion. It happened so quickly that it took Lucia a moment to realize her full nudity. Lucia stood bare, the warmth of the candles enveloping her skin. The flickering flames danced, casting shadows that accentuated her vulnerability. In that moment, she felt the weight of exposure, both intimate and raw, stirring a complex mix of fear and awakening within her. A twinge of shame jabbed her heart. In that breath, Alyx locked eyes with her and declared her beauty and perfection. The sharpness of shame softened, melting into Alyx's words of affirmation and genuine adoration.

No one had ever taken her clothes off with such consideration, Lucia swooned. Heavy and rhythmic breaths awaited Alyx's next move. Lucia embraced her raw powerlessness, feeling nurtured and supported. Warmth spread through her as her skin flushed and glistened. She relaxed into whatever would unfold next.

Alyx guided Lucia to the end of the table, instructing her to lie her upper body across its surface. She took Lucia's arms and wrapped them in soft hemp rope, tying them to the table legs in front of her, with her ankles spread apart on the floor. Lucia found herself bent over the table and unable to move with her legs wide open. Alyx placed a satin blindfold over Lucia's eyes, plunging the room into darkness. The absence of light intensified every touch, and the warmth radiating from Lucia's blushing body filled the air with an electric tension. She prayed that no one would walk in and catch her like this. Nervous about the exposure, she felt an equal surge of exhilaration.

Alyx touched every inch of the longing flesh before her. Lucia felt sharp sensations, as if Alyx slid a knife's tip along her skin, followed by soft fingers easing her distress. The sensations shifted from pointed to gentle, flowing back and forth, an endless cycle. What seemed like a hand slapped her ass hard. Then kisses. Another slap, more kisses. Every bite of pain carried a sweet, soft pleasure that lingered insistently. Lucia's energy surged as heat enveloped her tender skin, igniting every pore.

Lucia felt the soft leather tickle her from head to toe. Then, the sharp stings of the implement struck her back and ass repeatedly. The motion pressed on, teetering at the edge of Lucia's endurance. Pain surged through her, both fierce and electrifying. She sensed she had reached her limit, yet a part of her yearned for more. But she couldn't bring herself to say "red," and Alyx pressed on, swinging harder with each strike.

Lucia's body screamed for rest, yet her mind pushed her onward. She fought against surrender, determined to keep moving and refuse defeat. Lucia's vision flooded with crimson light as her vulva pulsated and dripped hot juice down her thighs. Suddenly, her head cleared, and she felt as if she floated, recognizing the Universe within and around her. Lucia experienced a profound unity with her divine self and humanity, a state even more intense than her earlier meditation. No thoughts or specific feelings occupied her mind; only pure spaciousness filled every expansive element. It felt divine.

Alyx ceased the flagellation and ran her intuitive hands over Lucia's body, then wrapped her body around her tenderly with her total weight. Alyx tugged at the stagnant energy trapped in Lucia's supple form. Waves of tingling surged through her bones, spiraling outward until Lucia transformed into the air, filling her lungs, then into the clouds hovering over the house, the city, the ocean, and the mountain peaks. She drifted beyond, merging with particles of the galaxy that spark life on distant planets.

Moving her determined hands up Lucia's legs, inner thighs, and around her soaked, heaving pussy, Alyx had embodied Athena. She fucked Lucia from a thousand years of sacred experience, wielding strength, and wisdom to create a fluid cycle of time. Lucia shuddered as each nerve in her skin ignited. Powerful waves surged through her hips, spread into her chest, and pulsed from her heart, repeating in an unyielding rhythm.

Alyx read her like a familiar novel, with a keen intensity, searching for cherished passages to revisit again and again.

Somehow, Alyx understood how to handle Lucia's body; she was an arrow homing in on its target. At last, Lucia could no longer endure. Tightness and a tingle surged inside her, climbing to her stomach, radiating into her limbs, and bursting through her head, unleashing energy from her crown. Orgasmic pulsations squeezed and massaged Lucia's life force out of hiding and thrust it into her consciousness forever.

The energy surged to a powerful crescendo, overwhelming all her senses. Bright light flooded her vision, each color flashing like an echo in her mind. The warmth engulfed her, sending a rush through her limbs and forcing a cry from her throat. Lucia's body melted; her legs trembled as she fought to stand. Before she could crumple, Alyx gently untied her and laid her on the table.

Lucia couldn't think or speak as she felt Alyx's lips draw closer to hers, parting them with her tongue. Their soft, flushed lips pressed together, a passionate exchange that captured the intensity of everything that had just unfolded.

When Alyx untied Lucia, she freed her from more than just physical restraints. Lucia's mind spun from the intensity; she could hardly move or find the words to express herself. Alyx whispered that Lucia was remarkable and pressed a soft kiss to her forehead. Once Lucia wore her clothes, Alyx wrapped her arms around her, inhaling deeply. Their hearts synchronized, beating in rhythm with one another. They entwined for what felt like an eternity while an electric tingle surged through Lucia's chest, leaving her open, safe, and tender.

Alyx pressed her lips to Lucia's forehead once more, then grasped her hand, guiding her out of the room. In the front room, Sherry discussed local restaurants, her laughter brightening the air. Spotting them, Sherry waved. Alyx led Lucia to her friend and settled her beside Sherry on the couch. She shared a deep kiss with Lucia, filled with warmth, then turned and strode back to the playroom to tidy up.

"Are you ready to go?" Sherry asked. Lucia nodded, still in a daze, and linked her arm with her friend as they walked to the car. Sherry inquired about Lucia's well-being, but Lucia could only nod and offer a thumbs-up. That was all she could muster

As they navigated the misty streets, Lucia replayed the events of the night in her mind, reflecting on her journey to this extraordinary moment.

She fell into memories of meeting her ex-husband, Arlo, in her twenties and marrying him after just four months. She recalls how his honesty, charisma, and humor captivated her. Their intimacy felt adventurous and devoid of stigma, and he made her laugh, allowing her to embrace her silliness. She knew that what held her there was that he adored her and devoted himself to her comfort. For a time, these qualities filled her with happiness.

Yet, his struggle with alcohol soon surfaced. Despite this, his humor and affection made the problem easy to overlook. Lucia loved him deeply. However, his reverence for her set an unsteady pedestal, leaving her to shoulder the responsibilities, especially for their son. Their relationship revolved around her efforts to shield them from his reckless, drunken choices. Each time he stumbled into regret, the allure of his charm pulled her back, making life without him seem unimaginable.

Arlo believed he possessed the spirit of a rock star, yearning for a life of unfettered revelry. He mistook his brilliant personality and talent for a free pass, disregarding the consequences of his actions.

But while he embodied the essence of a dreamer, reality often betrayed him.

Lucia traced her story, recognizing the pattern of attracting people who needed care. As she followed this feeling through her past, she uncovered markers in the emptiness where nurturing should have existed. Insecurity with others had always defined her relationships.

The orgasms had softened her as much as the meditation had. She saw the past fade into a blur, realizing she had nowhere to go but up. She began to release her burden of holding the world, allowing herself to rest in her own support without the weight of guilt.

An intense certainty pierced her. That night, Lucia ignited her journey. No obstacle or person could divert her path. She embraced who she truly was becoming.

Chapter Two
THE UNRAVELING

Don't compromise yourself. You are all you've got.

~ Janice Joplin

For days stretching into weeks, Lucia couldn't shake the experience with Alyx. Sensations rippled through her body, steady and insistent. She also reflected on her meditation that night, feeling its deep connection to her encounter with Alyx.

For months, a euphoric high lifted Lucia through daily life, feeling lighter yet strangely more grounded than she had in years. She watched the world with a relaxed attitude that shielded her from stress. As she awaited each subsequent step, she remained self-contained, embracing the calm within her.

***

Sherry had committed to Sarah, the woman she had played with at the party. Lucia felt joy at her friend's happiness. For years, Sherry lived as a solo poly, longing for a person or people she could rely on; someone to settle into as a nesting partner. None of her past partners provided her with that stability.

Sherry confided in Lucia her longing to dive deep with someone, to explore the darker aspects of herself that remain hidden without the reflection of a person willing to understand her. Unfortunately, those she had engaged with remained tied to others, draining her time and energy, leaving Sherry with a void where depth should have thrived. Those interactions had offered playfulness, a welcome distraction, yet failed to provide the space for her to voice her innermost feelings and wildest dreams.

Lucia had always seen Sherry as a good soul. This sweet, loving woman represented the best thing that could happen to her. Lucia recognized that Sarah brought out the best in her friend, offering her the freedom to explore connections with other partners. Their relationship thrived on love and empowerment, lacking any controlling dynamics.

The joy she felt for her friend's happiness invigorated her. She thrived on witnessing the people she loved experience good fortune. Unfortunately, this generosity of spirit seemed rare in society; too many had tried to diminish others' successes, fearing it would reveal their shortcomings. Lucia, despite her past struggles, cherished her achievements and celebrated others' victories, knowing their accomplishments didn't erase her own. While she recognized the ease of falling into jealousy amidst life's disparities, she refused to let those toxic influences into her circle. For her, expressing her truth mattered more than letting envy dictate her relationships.

Lucia's struggle centered on her feelings of inadequacy as she watched others thrive effortlessly. She wished for their blessings yet craved them for herself. She often felt excluded from substantial rewards, such as a supportive family to turn to during tough times. This sense of exclusion fueled her envy, for despite her relentless, arduous work, she never sensed true success. Lucia pondered whether her family's refusal to support her when she became a young mother deepened her feelings of isolation and frustration.

Lucia felt overwhelming guilt for her envy, acutely aware of her privilege as a white woman—a privilege that women of color and other marginalized communities lacked. Despite her absence of financial support or connections to nurture her talents, she never feared for her son's life during a routine traffic stop or struggled to claim her right to exist in a world that so often denied it to others.

With those reminders, she gained perspective on her hardships. She saw the blessings in her life more clearly and recognized her privilege, understanding how to use those benefits to help others rise from struggle. Lucia resolved to listen to the needs of those who faced systemic racism and bigotry. She refused to get lost in her turmoil, determined not to forget how society built itself around suppressing people of color and marginalized communities. Recognizing her struggles and those of other women stood central in her battle against the patriarchal structure. Yet, she acknowledged the countless individuals who faced far more challenges beyond their control than she ever would.

She often pondered how to leverage the privilege of her birth to create more equity in the world while also transforming her fate. She craved visibility, sought opportunities, and wished to feel worthy of success, humility, and empowerment. Driven by these thoughts, she contemplated how to embody these ideals—how to remain socially aware of her advantages, assist others, and fulfill her destiny, embracing the worthiness of a rich and meaningful life.

Lucia packed these thoughts with her as she knocked on Sherry's door, carrying a root vegetable medley she was fond of making for gatherings during the fall. When Sherry opened the door, her beaming smile and radiant charm lit up the space, her blond curls tumbling over her freckled face. Sherry enveloped Lucia in a warm embrace, her energy overwhelming in the best way. With an enthusiastic gesture, she pointed toward the kitchen, indicating where Lucia should deposit the vegetables. Lucia nodded, stepping aside, and moved in the direction Sherry had shown, just as more guests arrived at the house.

This party marked Lucia's first social gathering since the sex party. She felt surprised by her unease.

Strangers populated the halls and the front room. Lucia navigated the narrow hallway to drop off the tepid dish. She discovered the oddly placed kitchen in the quasi-Victorian house, its steep stairs leading to a yard shaped like a slice of pie. As she wandered through, she shyly smiled at the guests she passed.

Overwhelmed by unfamiliar faces, Lucia battled her instincts to disappear. She often considered herself an extrovert, thriving among friends or in conversations about topics she loved. Yet here, engulfed by strangers, she felt like a little girl trapped at a gathering of adults.

There was an internal push for connection that drove her. She approached a woman with trendy, short black bangs, and a gothic edge, hoping for a spark of interest. Nothing. Next, she tried striking up a conversation with a handsome hipster at the drinks table. He interrupted her so often that she turned away in frustration. Finally, she found a middle-aged physics professor, hoping he would engage with her. Each time she initiated a conversation, it felt like she had to draw him in, yet he offered little in return.

She listened intently to their stories, and they responded enthusiastically. Yet, the moment she shared anything about herself, their eyes glazed over, or they quickly redirected the conversation back to their lives. Not one of them showed any interest in her, which puzzled her.

This disconnection drained her energy, leaving her with a sense of dysregulation. She had always forged connections with people, but this time felt different. Lucia questioned whether her recent awakenings caused her odd energy that was creating these responses, or if she had awoken to what had always been there. She wandered through the crowd, her smile shy as she hoped to encounter at least one person open to a genuine conversation.

Confused and frustrated by her inability to connect with others, Lucia tried to understand the disconnect. She sensed she could see through these people's egos; this skill had accompanied her throughout her life, but now it felt thicker and more entrenched. People usually revealed their deepest selves to her quickly, making her presence alluring. Yet tonight, that openness slipped away. In the past, many queer individuals had confided in her within minutes of meeting, sharing secrets she never sought. She knew she inspired this vulnerability in others, but not tonight, as now she realized how one-sided it was.

Lucia had grown accustomed to this kind of interaction—people eager to share their own stories while neglecting her deeper layers. Loneliness often wrapped around her, a familiar cloak that she accepted as part of life. But tonight felt different. She observed these people clearly, yet something held her back from opening up. She couldn't bear her soul as she once did; she had reached a tipping point. She finished surrendering herself.

The past few months had turned intensely introspective for Lucia, especially since the night she met Alyx. That encounter freed her from burdens she didn't realize she carried, clearing space for her own thoughts and feelings. She found no room for the emotional baggage of others, unwilling to bear their loads any longer. Helping those struggling to lift their own burdens felt rewarding, but the days of shouldering others' weight had ended. This realization explained her inability to connect with the crowd at Sherry's house.

Lucia left Sherry's house feeling heavy-hearted and jumbled inside. After taking an Uber to the gathering, she decided to walk and clear her head. She would call another Uber when fatigue set in.

The frigid air kissed her face, misting gently as she navigated through the dark Seattle neighborhood. The droplets awakened her senses, grounding her in the moment as she paused to observe the trees and buildings.

Her steps crunched on the ground, and giant burnt umber and butter-colored maple leaves drifted slowly from the branches, floating down to the earth. Under a streetlight in the grass, she spotted a plate-sized vermilion red mushroom with white spots, a sly reminder of Alice in Wonderland. She chuckled, imagining where the chartreuse caterpillar, smoking a hookah, might hide. Recently, she had read about these fungi, notorious for their powerful hallucinogenic effects, capable of sending anyone down the rabbit hole with a single dose. Temptation flickered within her, but the thought of diving deeper into her awakening terrified her. Discombobulation already shadowed her mind.

Lucia often reflected on her hallucinogenic experiences, pondering whether she might have blended better into society without them. Certain complexities emerged from her early awakening, yet the possibility of her innate nature lingered. She bore witness to truths others shunned—people's worst fears and undiscovered potential intertwined with her ingrained conditioning to care for others.

Some labeled Lucia as empathic. She absorbed others' physical and emotional traumas, and sometimes their joys, into her spirit. An ardent desire to provide comfort fueled this connection. Frequently, she questioned whether her heightened sensitivity would have evolved without the influence of hallucinogens. Walking down the narrow street, glancing into lives illuminated through open curtains, she felt bewildered by how her functioning might shift without the barriers she had built. The world revealed itself anew—brighter yet darker—and she pondered the depth of that contrast.

She touched on self-pity as she thought about her isolation. Misunderstanding wrapped around her like a heavy cloak, and loneliness seeped into her very being. Logically, she knew most people faced similar feelings. Yet, she longed for exposure, desperate to be seen after years of watching others. Her mind echoed with a childlike plea, "I want to be seen, too."

Since the night of the party, she faced a stark reality: her social safety net had vanished. The urge to please others faded, replaced by a self-centeredness that left her intolerant of shallow exchanges. At this point in her journey, she found no alternative. She consciously rejected guilt for focusing on herself.

For too long, she had nurtured others. Now, her pendulum swung toward necessary selfishness, a means to restore balance, at least, she hoped. Life had become both secure and uncertain, a contradiction that unsettled her yet felt strangely acceptable. She embodied a walking conundrum, one that seemed pointless to unravel. Deep within her heart, an undeniable certainty lingered: somehow, it would all work out.

Kali Ma entered Lucia's psyche with relentless scrutiny as she walked through the misty evening. The Goddess's presence overwhelmed her. Destruction, creation, destruction, creation echoed in Lucia's mind as she watched leaves drift from the branches, contemplating how death can cradle like a falling leaf or rage like a glorious blaze, consuming us to the bones.

Lucia had always longed to experience a shamanic death-of-self ritual. She ached for all her bullshit to be stripped away so she could shine in all her universal brightness. There was a hunger arising to be exposed. Deep within her soul, she sensed that by opening and expanding, she could align entirely with the universal flow. Throughout her life, she had explored this idea, but only recently had it transformed into her primary focus. She felt this might mark the beginning of her death. She prayed to Mama Kali, hoping the deconstruction would soon turn merciful, for it certainly felt harsh now.

She longed for the palpable energy she had felt with Alyx. That connection grounded her, making her surrender and trust in her own capacity completely. In that heightened orgasmic state, she experienced something new. She realized it wasn't just about seeing Alyx again; it was about unlocking a part of herself. Since then, she felt a vibrant sexual energy coursing through every inch of her body. It neither dissipated nor overwhelmed. Instead, she recognized it as an erotic life force, a steady hum vibrating within her.

Lucia sought to replicate the intensity she experienced with Alyx, dedicating herself to harnessing the magic that had swept through her. Deep down, she felt confident that this powerful moment wasn't a fleeting peak but something she could recreate. It didn't have to be Alyx who guided her to that second act. Although she cherished the warmth and kindness Alyx had shown her, Lucia accepted the unlikelihood of crossing paths again. Strangely, this realization brought her peace. She smiled at her strength; she hadn't clung to Alyx despite the life-changing connection they shared.

Lucia recognized Alyx as an open invitation to explore another dimension of herself, serving as a catalyst for her awareness. Alyx possessed an uncanny ability to tap into precisely what Lucia needed, a significant revelation that sparked transformation within her.

Lucia walked, absorbing the details of the trees against the skyline. Leaves fluttered down, crunching beneath her feet. Vines shifted from rich jade to stunning shades of cardinal red, bleeding into carnelian and delicate peach. The vibrant climbers clung tenaciously to buildings, embracing the intricate designs carved into the stone foundations. She gazed softly at the water on the windows, which cast a gentle glow around the shapes of the lives within.

As she walked, Lucia listened to the car motors passing her by while overhearing muffled conversations outside little bars that she had no desire to join in on.

She couldn't help but revel in the city's sudden vibrancy, alive with a rich rumble of creativity and expression that had just moments ago felt dormant. Each sound pulsed through her, revealing a lively tapestry of life unfolding all around. The streets bustled with energy, and the air was infused with a sense of possibility that made everything seem brighter. It was as if the city had taken a deep breath and was now exhaling a chorus of voices, laughter, and music that intertwined in a harmonious rhythm. Everywhere she turned, there were colors and flavors, stories waiting to be told, each corner a canvas painted with the essence of its inhabitants. It was this spontaneous eruption of life that made the city feel truly alive, a beautiful reflection of the unique fusion of nature and human spirit.

Finally, as the evening had become closer to daylight than dusk, Lucia started to get tired. Although she had walked for what seemed like hours, her house was still miles away. As her thoughts solidified, there was a recognition of a need to write them down; in that thought, there arose a sudden desire to hurry up and get home. Hailing an Uber, she was home within fifteen minutes, something she never took for granted about living in a vibrant city.

She crept into her sanctuary and made some jasmine tea, hoping to warm up. Lucia began to think about her journey and who she felt she was, what sang to her soul, and how she could describe herself. The images were plentiful of her, and they swam around in her head as she thought about what resonated with her the most. The images began to feel fluid, forcing their way to the service of her fingertips. She knew there was no way to put her finger on what to do with everything she was going through, but it was necessary to get a minuscule piece of her mind out of her and onto the paper. Gradually, the symbols and metaphors formulated into something that felt true to her, and she found her words.

> *My soul is colored with crimson, emerald, cobalt, and rich purples, and my heart beats with hard bass lines and deep, thrumming drums. I dream in kaleidoscopes and mystic ruins, wishing I could show others how they live among us. My eyes shine with the ocean tides, high and low, seeing the Universe in the sacredness of the world. I am the cell that rides the flow of lifeblood, always ambitious, leaving no possibility of stagnation in the body of all that is.*

> *As I sit on the edge of the world's fishbowl, I watch, dipping my toes in the water and occasionally diving in for a swim. I long to feel complete in every part of myself, as my heart continues to ache when I pay too close attention. While playing hide-and-seek with mushrooms under the ferns, I ask the leaves for their secrets. I paint my darkness with puddles of color as the rhododendrons drip their hues onto the earth.*

> *My thoughts resemble gemstones, each a speck of light emerging from the darkness, diamonds in the sky. Today, I remember myself. I recognize that everything flows with light, yearning for us to reclaim its sacredness.*

Lucia performed a spell beneath the full moon's glow filtering through her third-story window. She concentrated on shedding whatever had restrained her from becoming her best self. Blocks tightened around her body and mind, a fist squeezing her spirit until she uncovered the secret password. With fervent desire, Lucia longed to utter the right words to free herself from the grip of that tension. Deep within her, a fierce yearning arose, guiding her to discover her purpose: to find what ignited her passion in this world. This journey felt vital, promising to weave sacredness into every choice she made, every action she took, and every moment she experienced.

She anointed a black candle and a white candle with dragon's blood oil, infusing strength, power, and intensity into her desires. The candles urged her to embody the interplay between positive and negative. The black candle served her need to banish the stories she no longer wished to inhabit, carving a path toward a life forged in authenticity. She aimed to sever the ties to the aspects of herself that stifled her true essence. The white candle became a pathway for Lucia's radiated light, beckoning forth the latent potential within her while purifying her intentions.

Lucia remembered how Kali Ma gripped her hand, guiding her since the night of the party. She had lost her need to control the world; her illusion of power faded, leaving an emptiness that made room for something new and genuinely powerful. The dismantling of her identity disoriented her. The absence of a foundation unsettled her because what had once felt real no longer did. She began to rebuild, aware of the complications ahead. She accepted the challenge, knowing it wouldn't unfold smoothly.

She floated in nothingness, unable to grasp anything to stabilize herself. Her heart raced, and panic welled within. The living room spun, illuminated by candles and the moonlight. Her psyche struggled without the constructions that had anchored her, the beams of societal expectations crumbling around her.

She analyzed her turmoil. When feelings grew too strong, she often left her body, retreating into a mental realm where she felt safe. Yet she knew the answers lay in the discomfort, not in escape—it would take courage to change this pattern. She had to rest in her emotions and sensations, anchoring herself in her physicality. She reminded herself to breathe, to return to her body. With intent, she reached out, touching her feet, legs, stomach, neck, and arms, grounding herself in her material existence, refusing to disassociate.

Incense burned, curling into tiny smoke rings that carried messages to her higher self. The Universe pulsed through her veins. She sat enveloped in silence, tuning into the sensations within her body, heart, and spirit. Uncomfortable and insecure, she let each thought rise like cresting waves, then settled into the calmness of glassy water. Finally, she surrendered to the only comfort left—an unwavering belief that deep within, she walked the right path.

Months earlier, she joined a group meditation at a Buddhist temple where she learned that thoughts would come, but the secret lay in not attaching herself to them. The peaceful yet powerful female monk explained that clearing the mind did not mean expecting everything to vanish when we closed our eyes. Instead, it meant allowing and releasing every thought to float by, letting it happen without trying to control it. She repeated the mantra, "It is what it is."

She learned to acknowledge her attachment to ideas throughout her life. Having recently mastered the release of attachments to food for comfort, relationships, and material possessions, she recognized that her ideas continued to constrict her. While attending the class, she prided herself on her disconnection from material things. It shocked her when the monk revealed that attachment to ideas held the most power over people. The monk helped her realize that the stories she clung to about what should happen formed the most problematic barriers to break.

Lucia shed weight by releasing her attachment to food and quitting smoking. Yet, she created a new way to control her body. After her divorce, she disconnected entirely from her ex-husband and most material possessions. Over the years, her devotion to things shifted from needs to mere wants. Still, the ideas she clung to remained stubbornly sticky, making her struggle to let go. She yearned to embrace everything while also maintaining boundaries. Despite her efforts, balance eluded her. There remained a continuous inquisition about whether she would ever find that sweet spot between will and surrender.

When Lucia meditated on her attachments, countless thoughts and feelings overwhelmed her, and she felt like she was drowning in them. She craved a tether, something familiar and stable amid the chaos. Lucia began to realize that she had always defined herself as a friend, daughter, and wife, and there was a need to release those identities. That thought stirred a throbbing tightness in her womb. Flashes of expectations surged forward—images of her as a savior, needing to prove her worthiness of love. This internal storm blinded her. She always had to be the best, to support everyone while neglecting her own needs. The "bratty teenager that was too much to handle" label from her youth haunted her, driving her to chase balance so she wouldn't make life difficult for everyone else.

Each day felt like a monumental climb, and she doubted her readiness for the journey. However, she forced herself to refocus on her rituals, determined to unravel the rubber band ball of tension tightening within her.

As Lucia restarted, she carried the lessons she had learned and those still waiting to unfold regarding attachments. She no longer judged or sought proof of others' worth; she naturally offered them her adoration and respect. Yet, there continued to be an internal battle to extend that same unconditional kindness to herself. Why did she find it so difficult to embrace the same grace that flowed so freely to others? Why did she feel compelled to earn the positive attention she generously bestowed?

Untangling this pattern became essential because it remained insistent. That meditation class merely scratched the surface of Lucia's journey. She began to recognize her attachments to beliefs about her role in the world, her connection with others, and her sense of self. These attachments painted a picture of how she believed life should unfold. The layers of her perspective began to peel off like the skin of an onion. She fought to open her eyes to the burdens she had carried her entire life. And it was a struggle.

She began to recognize the details of the idealistic viewpoints she clung to, questioning their validity and scrutinizing whether they still served her life. Surprisingly, most had outlived their usefulness, binding her for years. These thought patterns had barred her from embracing her worthiness, deepening relationships, and experiencing life as it was rather than through her skewed imagination.

She focused intently on her self-judgments, aware this journey would demand years, perhaps a lifetime, of self-awareness and effort. The weight of that realization felt overwhelming at times. Months ago, a meditation class had gifted her this insight, but it also left her feeling raw, vulnerable, and adrift in an uncertain void, untethered to anything solid.

She transformed her patterns and attachments into clouds, which she'd learned to do. Gradually, she sensed her energy strengthening and becoming less chaotic within her body. In mind's eye, she envisioned a vibrant red glow radiating from her vulva at the base of her spine, swirling and expanding to envelop her pelvis.

Through six months of confronting her fears and desires for control, she had familiarized herself with this color. She dismantled much of her old structure, knowing she needed to experience the absence of form before rebuilding a more solid foundation. The process would unfold over time, but at least it had commenced. Lucia reminded herself not to judge the time it had taken. Instead, she practiced offering herself grace, repeating what she often told those she believed deserved compassion, "It is a process. You are exactly where you need to be. Give yourself grace; you deserve it."

The red energy surged, then transformed into a blinding white. The energy surged through her organs, limbs, fascia, and crevices, filling her and expanding outward into a radiant light that pierced her vision and reached the Universe's hidden corners. She felt supple, yet understood it was time to focus on healing other parts of herself. Detached from the outside world, she recognized the moment to reconnect with her creative spirit. Determined, she focused her energy upward into her uterus. White light gathered, transforming into a hazy tangerine orange from her womb, a muted hue signaling a need for attention. Instead of dwelling on that recognition, she shifted her focus to the power surging within her. She opened her eyes and inhaled the incense smoke, filling her lungs, and gazed deep into the flickering candle flames. Then suddenly, she opened her mouth and heard a voice booming and commanding come out of her body:

God, Goddess, All That Is, I humbly ask for your assistance in clearing all that blocks me from my true self. I draw into me the strength to confront my darkest parts while always remembering my light. Fill me with the power to deconstruct the parts of myself that no longer serve me. Make available the wisdom that lives in me to see the truth in myself and others through this time and forever. Thank You, God/Goddess, Universe, All That Is! Blessed be!

Lucia bowed her head in reverence to the Divine and blew out the candles. It was time to release her incantation into the Universe and let it go. She savored the ritual's energy, a fullness she hadn't felt since that night she met Alyx. A whisper of potential beckoned her from the future. With a smile, she snuggled under her soft blankets and cool sheets atop her billowy mattress.

Lucia slept soundly that night. In her dream, she roamed a sprawling house she had inherited, its walls stretching broader and higher with each room she entered. Each space overflowed with treasures, inviting her to explore their depths. The dream's exhilaration lingered for days, leaving her with a sense of wonder long after the visions faded.

***

Since moving to Washington State, Fall has become Lucia's favorite season. She appreciated the trees and vines bursting with vibrant colors: deep reds, brilliant pinks, bright mandarin, and rich pumpkin tones, all mingling with flashes of translucent salmon peach—a gift from the Gods. Dark, blood-red leaves clung to the cobblestones, pierced by the cold, crisp air, while vivid fire engine leaves would compete with the stubborn chartreuse, determined to last another day. The colors had a way of finding a balance between blend and contrast, forming a mosaic alive with variations of yellow and gold that would glow against the misty gray sky, representing nature's neon sign to mark the point between life and death. Mushrooms were sprouting everywhere; diverse types, enticing smells, and intriguing textures littered the Pacific Northwest. Lucia felt that Fall embodies growth emerging from death, incorporating a harsh transformation distinct from spring's creative metamorphosis.

Lucia has been obsessed with mycology since her first Autumn in Washington. She wandered her yard, picking and identifying mushrooms, feeling as if each day revealed a new treasure. On strolls around the waterfalls, she uncovered mushrooms nestled beneath bushes and trees, a source of immense joy. Her passion for these extraordinary organisms, straddling the line between plant and animal, consumed her. She immersed herself in their study, captivated by their mysteries and beauty.

Something resonated with her about mycology—a magic that deepened with each new discovery. Her learning uncovered the marvels of the mycelium, a sprawling web beneath the earth that fuels the growth of mushrooms, connecting trees and enabling their communication. She discovered that this network fosters forest growth and cultivates symbiotic relationships, allowing trees to work together for the nourishment of the entire ecosystem.

Lucia quickly became immersed in the world of medicinal mushrooms, learning to create tinctures and gaining the confidence to identify safe varieties for cooking. Her observation skills had even sharpened, and she developed the ability to research any mushroom that might grace her path. Through this journey, ways to heal herself and engage with the natural world emerged. Each step connected her more deeply to the pulse of life around her as she embraced the intricate dance of creation.

Lucia would miss her treasure hunts after the first freeze, knowing the season would soon end. She would shift her focus to the delicate patterns of frost on spider webs and the glow of holiday lights twinkling through icy windows.

***

During winter, loneliness seeped into her soul. She grappled with her desire to understand herself, searching for the blocks that kept her from moving beyond mere survival into her true purpose.

Unsure of her path, she decided to focus on the moments in her life that sparked joy. She thrived as a student, immersing herself in the mystical, exploring philosophy, and unraveling the patterns of the Universe.

To regain equilibrium, Lucia sifted through memories filled with love and passion. She pondered what constants remained within her throughout her many transformations, searching for the fire that kept her alive—what continuously ignited her spirit. It was essential to her to examine the sources of these feelings. As she explored, she realized many interests had faded away.

Ultimately, she settled on her enjoyment of contemplation. And in that moment, she found peace. She didn't need to pinpoint the specific passion shaping her path; she could savor its essence without rushing to consume it. She embraced the uncertainty, accepting that her true purpose had yet to emerge and that forcing answers drained her energy.

As she headed toward a period of discovery, the calm, introspective winter provided her a sanctuary. She recognized the loneliness that loomed ahead; few could grasp the weight of her journey, and most seemed disinterested in the alien process consuming her. She made peace with her solitude, understanding that this path must unfold within her.

Resolving to embrace the disconnection, she delved deeper into her art. Brushes danced across canvases, jewelry took shape from natural stones, and meditation guided her toward surrendering to the creative force. She anchored herself in trust—trust in the unfolding process, trust in her inner knowing, and trust in the Divinity that thrived within. She sat with these thoughts, allowing them to swirl around her.

Loneliness wrapped itself around her soul, a sensation unlike any she had known. She hovered at the edge of the fishbowl, captivated by the vibrant fish gliding effortlessly through their world, yet she could not immerse herself in their lively interactions.

She occasionally ventured into the world, observing others and studying their movements. Finding herself analyzing how they connected or repelled each other like opposing magnets. In her observations, she saw swirls of light that pulsed between them, ebbing and flowing, expanding, and contracting in tune with their personal traumas. Her heart often ached for them as she witnessed these interactions, sensing their struggles and wanting to urge them to pause. It was clear to her that so many people allowed trauma to dictate their actions, often without realizing it. Each impression deepened her exploration of how her burdens obstructed her path to living fully.

The awakened part of her grew more substantial, yet she understood this relationship with her awakening would endure as long as she walked the earth. Tempted to spiritually bypass the human experience, she resisted that drive. She committed to immersing herself in it all, even when she felt more like an observer than a participant.

It felt as if she spoke a different language from those around her. Lucia questioned whether her story fueled her sense of difference. She wondered if she could stop feeling like an outsider if she kept seeing reality the same way. Inside her tender heart, there was a clinging to the hope that another path existed, as something within her yearned for acceptance as her true self. "Is that even possible?" she asked herself sharply.

This question plunged her deeper into her turmoil. She felt isolated, alone. Although she had friends, family, and potential partners with whom she could share some thoughts, none seemed genuinely interested in her inner journey. She recognized that her mindset bred isolation, deepening her disconnection, but changing it eluded her.

Relying on her bond with the Universe, she embraced this necessary period of evolutionary darkness. She chose to walk this path alone, armed only with the Divine's support. Her connection to humanity could wait.

***

The experience of Lucia feeling lost dismantled any sense of normalcy, brick by brick, devastating her ability to connect with others and ask for support. She longed for nurturing, like a neglected infant yearning to suckle the tit of the universal mother. Her aching heart craved an embodiment of the Goddess to pet her head and assure her that everything would be okay. In those moments, a tangible form to hold her close and soothe her felt impossibly distant. She struggled to find it and doubted anyone enough to offer comfort through this agony. She fantasized about a big, round-bellied woman cradling her head in warm, soft flesh, caressing away the burdens of years spent overthinking. The woman would whisper that this hardship would not last, urging her to journey through the void to reach the life she deserved.

Someday, love will envelop her wholly and unconditionally as she proves to herself that she is extraordinary. Lucia's heart sought reassurance from the world, yet she continued to rely solely on herself. She felt responsible for her emotions, readily absorbing others' pain but struggling to share her own. Vulnerability eluded her; the thought of asking for help filled her with dread. She often avoided her friends during tough times, waiting to connect only after she resolved her struggles. Intuitive friends sensed her distress and reached out, but she crafted excuses to deflect their concerns until she restored her equilibrium.

In the cocoon of her plush protection of blankets, she often cried in solitude, wrestling with her thoughts until clarity emerged. Lucia recognized her loneliness but recoiled from dragging others into her turbulent mind. Although she consistently felt distrustful of anyone lifting her burdens, her heart started to ache for the soothing touch of connection.

She convinced herself that asking for help felt impossible. She feared rejection or guilt over making it solely about her. Worst of all, she imagined others resenting the very act of supporting her. She justified to herself that they needed nurturing, too, and how could she accept support while they suffered? She knew no one could fix her; she alone held responsibility for herself. Yet, something was shifting and opening inside her. This time felt different from before.

Lucia couldn't recall a single moment of selfless nurturing in her childhood. She learned to give care but couldn't think of a time when someone offered it to her without expectation. A few memories surfaced of her family providing support, yet those moments lacked emotional depth in her recall. No cellular memory lingered in her psyche, although she questioned whether her mind had resisted the idea of actual nurturance, as it was deemed illogical that no one gave her that. As she considered this, Lucia abruptly realized that she had pushed people away her whole life, denying them the chance to support her. In doing so, she had isolated herself from the possibility of receiving help.

The memory of organizing a Native American conference in Colorado surged in her mind. During that conference, a sweat lodge offered a space for healing, and the Lakota elder who led the ritual directed the focus toward the womb and the nurturing essence of a mother. Lucia cried throughout the ceremony, her tears streaking her face as her chest felt like it was caving in. Her overwhelming sense of emptiness and grief surrounded her inability to envision a nurturing mother's womb as Mother Earth cradling her.

Lucia could not remember anything before second grade when her aunt died unexpectedly, and her mother sank into devastating grief. She never discovered why her childhood memories slipped away, so she learned to accept the absence, complicating her healing.

A deep ache pulsed in her soul, craving nurturing, yet there was always a struggle to conceive what that even felt like. Asking for care felt impossible, and she sensed no entitlement to encourage tenderness. Her mother was not wicked but rather profoundly wounded. She questioned whether love had surrounded her in the early years; it must have, she thought. But now, in this dark night of the soul, that warmth eluded her as it had during the sweat lodge twenty years ago.

This raw longing approached intolerable levels for Lucia in these moments. For years, Lucia had coated herself in strength and arrogance, allowing her to navigate life's difficulties. Now, that strength was waning, and the pride in her resilience faded like a distant memory; she felt like there was no defense against the harshness of the world.

She slipped into fantasies about being in a loving partner's embrace, searching for a reprieve from her yearning for unconditional healing and support, and her chaotic psyche. Yet, the thought of judgment or competition paralyzed her. She needed someone who understood that her desire for support stemmed not from weakness or inability to solve her problems but from the immense effort it took to let others witness her pain.

Desperate for emotional, energetic, and physical healing from her deep loneliness, she imagined someone would come and soothe her wounds with a magical, healing tongue. The thought thrilled her, promising any respite from her pain. Yet, despair clung to her, intensifying her sense of isolation. She recognized the futility of seeking this relief; no one could give her what she truly needed.

Lucia settled into her soft blankets, shutting out the world and confronting her winter despair. Finally, one night, amid the darkness, she slipped into meditation, hoping it would ignite a cascade of changes in her perspective. She recognized her need for a break from inner turmoil, a need for peace and hope.

She decided to spray herself with cotton candy perfume, the sweetness of which had always invoked pure joy in Lucia's heart. The scent did its job by lifting her spirits, prompting her to light Nag Champa incense. As the smoke curled around her, she ignited pink candles, inviting soft, loving energy into the space. Disrobing, she nestled under the cushiest blankets she could find, crafting a matrix of comfort. In that serene moment, the call for nurturing enveloped her once more.

The desire clawed at her core, each pang urging her to shut down. The ache tethered her to those feelings, yet pushing through felt necessary, if agonizing. She summoned a sliver of strength to remain present, tracing the source of her need within her body. Though discomfort spread throughout, a subtle movement flickered inside her, hinting at something more profound.

The intensity peaked as her womb began to pulse, resonating like a cello string stroked by a bow. The sensation escalated to a point that churned her stomach. Nausea surged through her spine, creeping upward until it gripped her head. For minutes, it held her captive, a storm raging within. Then, just as abruptly as it began, the wave of aversion receded, leaving her in a profound silence.

The reverberation continued unabated, growing more insistent. Lucia felt her uterus swell, expanding as if it might burst, like in a horror film where a woman carries something otherworldly, clawing for release. In her mind's eye, her lower belly glowed a vivid neon orange. She questioned whether she needed to decipher this sensation. The moment the thought struck her, a loud voice boomed in her head, "NO! Just feel it!"

Loneliness twisted and expanded inside her like a full-term fetus after a caffeine jolt. Finally, when the emotional agony reached a breaking point, a pressure bubble burst, unleashing a wave of unfathomable relief. Lucia's body relaxed, and for the first time in months, she recognized the tension that had gripped her.

She felt the orange light seep through her system, sparking a flicker of hope. Yet, with no other choice, she surrendered to exhaustion and confusion. Her consciousness, tightly wound for too long, finally unfurled. She lay motionless for a few minutes, then blew out the candles and slipped into a deep rest.

In her dream that night, a woman with dark hair and deep eyes appeared. When they touched, rainbows of light danced between them, revealing the Universe woven into their connection. Upon waking, Lucia recognized that this woman had come to help them both shift the mourning they held. Their bond illuminated for Lucia how the Universe thrived in human connection. In this dream, for the first time felt what it was to embrace the vulnerability of asking for nurturing, unconditional love, and nourishment.

Lucia felt she had experienced the most beautiful dream of her life. She named the woman Aurora because her image filled Lucia with flashes of color and light amid the darkness. This woman showed her that unconditional support would emerge once Lucia embraced her worthiness. Deep within her being, Lucia felt the truth: this person existed somewhere, and they had shared lives before—many lifetimes ago. Pure magic and joy surged in her heart at the thought of this dream. She clung to it like a lifeline, drawing her back into the world.

Kali had helped Lucia purge her life in countless ways, and, as she feared, it came not from a gentle flow but from a devastating fire that consumed everything. But after the tangerine bubble burst in her belly and the dream of the mysterious woman, a shift occurred within her. For the first time in months, she felt a spark of openness in her heart. Yet, this openness exposed her to emotions that had long simmered, allowing a path forward that would indeed boil over.

***

Lucia had always worried endlessly about her husband, her child, her friends, and her family. This has caused her existence to lean heavily into survival mode for most of her life. Now, her child had moved on, no husband needed her care, and her friends and other family members pursued their own lives. For the first time, she found herself free to care only for herself. And when she invited Kali in to help her release her pattern of control, she finally recognized her ability to break free from the overwhelming sense of responsibility for others.

As that feeling subsided, she grappled with defining her true self. What did she honestly want? How could she even know? Buried emotions, long suppressed while nurturing everyone else, resurfaced. She recognized that her yearning for authenticity outweighed the fear of confronting the void. Summoning the Goddess of Destruction had carried its risks, she learned quickly.

"You get what you ask for," she reminded herself as she chuckled over the difficulty she had recently been through with herself.

Months passed without contact from her son. She reached out, but he remained silent. This behavior felt typical when life got busy; communication had never been his strength. However, it baffled her how a mother so affectionate and open-minded could have raised someone so distant. Yet, she admired his brilliant mind and unmatched self-motivation.

The weight of his silence pressed on her. This time, she chose to confront her pain differently; she reached out to her friend, seeking solace amid her turmoil. Over coffee, Lucia opened up to Sherry, unraveling her tangled feelings about motherhood. Lucia explained how guilt wrapped around her heart as she recognized how often distractions pulled her away from him. Each choice she made reinforced the sense that he felt unloved, and that realization stung deep within her.

Lucia explained to Sherry that she believed she made healthy choices for her son by moving to the middle of the ocean and letting him live with his grandmother because that was what he said he wanted. She hesitated to uproot him to an island with her and Arlo, having witnessed kids taking wrong turns when they felt trapped. At 15, her son stood on the cusp of adulthood, and she felt pulled to follow her dreams to paradise. Lucia trusted his grandmother to care for him and emphasized to Sherry that she always prioritized flying him to visit as often as possible. She filled their conversations with warmth, attempting to create fulfilling memories during his time in Hawaii. Yet, he was just like any teenager, craving the company of his friends over spending time with his mother.

Lucia justified herself by explaining that each time she sensed his frustration with her presence, she felt a sharp pang of guilt but pressed on, driven by the only instinct she understood.

Lucia recounted that when she returned to the mainland, he moved to the Pacific Northwest to be closer to her and Arlo. After five minutes together, it felt as if no time had passed. Unfortunately, he only lasted a year in Washington with her before he and his girlfriend decided to return to his hometown.

With no more visits, communication dwindled from his side. That was his nature, but it only thickened the ache in Lucia's chest. She worked to express that her fierce love for her child allowed her to express a nurturing instinct that the world largely denied her. She explained that she felt his absence keenly, longing to shower him with affection, but understood that as he had begun to carve out his own identity, she knew her space for closeness had shrunk.

Lucia recalled their bond when he was little, how he clung to her side. In those days, he was safe miles away at his grandmother's. Lucia turned wild when she would drink and revel, trying to reclaim fragments of her youth in the fleeting moments between motherhood.

When she spoke to Sherry about this, tears streamed down her face. Guilt engulfed her regarding motherhood and her choices. She always aimed to prioritize her child and make the right decisions for him, yet she questioned her effectiveness.

She believed her son would feel a deeper connection if she had done more to keep him near. If she had stayed by his side until he graduated from high school, he might have considered Hawaii as an option if she had found a way to support him as he stepped into adulthood. They might have forged a stronger bond if she had made different choices.

Lucia grappled with deep angst and sadness, her heart heavy with guilt. That night, she bellowed cries that surged from her core, aching for her past decisions and the mother she yearned to become. If only she had embraced a different path, if only her relentless urge to travel hadn't consumed her.

Sherry stood by, granting Lucia space to confront these painful feelings, wrapping her in a comforting embrace as she mourned the life she had never lived. Sherry held her tight until tears dried and the heaving ceased.

"You know," Sherry said, recalling her aunt's words, "Guilt arises from the certainty of the past. It drags us into a realm of 'what if,' where we believe everything will improve with different choices. Our hindsight reveals potential paths that could have enriched our lives beyond measure.

"But we fail to see that different decisions might have led to an uncertain future filled with unimaginable pain and suffering. Perhaps those burdens would have crushed us in this lifetime. Guilt confines us to harsh realities; it offers no magic or expansion. It chokes us, making breath feel impossible. We must release it because only by accepting our mistakes can we find freedom."

Lucia grasped at the wisdom in Sherry's words, offering a deep sigh and a faint smile in gratitude. Her friend's support had lifted something from her, something she couldn't carry on her own any longer.

Lucia fell into a dark, endless sleep that night. She plunged into the vastness of the Universe, floating in nothingness. Upon awakening, life resumed. Her son visited, and it felt as if they had never parted. Each goodbye shattered her heart a little less.

Chapter Three

EXPANSIVE CONNECTIONS

Being a strong woman is very important to me. But doing it all on my own is not.

~ Reba McEntire

Lucia began to release her guilt while energetic healing surged through her dreams and meditations, opening doors of connection. She felt less isolated in her heart and mind, and she actively sought to share her complex feelings with others, just as she had done with Sherry.

Lucia felt vulnerable and self-conscious. Allowing Sherry to see her like that, to be perceived as less than perfect, drained her strength and exposed her fears. Yet, deep down, she knew this exposure would heal her; showing herself to another soul became essential. She immersed herself in the memory of Sherry's nurturance—how her friend stood by her, not making it about herself but offering love and wisdom. Lucia replayed this support in her mind over and over, sensing its pulse within her body. The constrictions in her chest loosened as she relived those moments filled with understanding and encouragement. Her heart began to unravel the tightness woven since childhood. She recognized that her long struggle to express feelings stemmed from being silenced in her youth. Finally, she acknowledged the knot inside her required practice to loosen. Staying open became her commitment.

Lucia understood this journey demands consistency and awareness to discern what needs addressing and what can fade. Each encounter would challenge her, often shattering her composure. Still, she dedicated herself to these repetitions, determined to ease the burden over time. By accepting her circumstances, her life transformed into a shaken carbonated bottle, the cap finally loosening and letting the pressure hiss away.

Her revelations and new ability to connect with others genuinely led her to date someone she genuinely liked. She embraced new experiences with this fascinating man in her life, and these moments reignited her sense of wonder.

His name was Michael, and they had been together for four months. When she met him, he practiced polyamory, managing five other girlfriends. This fact didn't bother Lucia; she felt no need to be his sole focus. She lacked the time for a boyfriend, demanding constant attention anyway. As she prioritized her own growth for the first time, she recognized how this relationship nurtured her development. Lucia also dated other people periodically, a choice she had embraced over the past year.

Regret washed over her for having been convinced to stop seeing others when she met Arlo. Committed to her flexibility in relationships, she vowed to remain open, at least for a while. She absolutely refused to lose herself in someone else and stray from her chosen path.

All the men she had been serious with wanted her to save them, and she slipped easily into that role. She swept them off their feet, nurturing their hearts, exploring her sexuality, and offering a uniqueness no other woman possessed. In her past relationships, when someone desired her, they demanded all she had to give. Now, she refused to fulfill that expectation. She felt no urge to fix anyone but herself. Her relationship with Michael was a whole new playing field, and she wasn't secure with how she could balance being caring while also prioritizing herself. She was concerned about seeming selfish or cold, aware of her tendency toward black-and-white thinking.

Lucia found Michael spiritual and profound. He managed himself well and didn't require Lucia to have all the answers. Michael had been deeply enmeshed in the sex-positive community for years and had recently reemerged as a kink guru. He pursued her for months, revealing a sincere desire to know one another honestly. This prospect excited her, promising growth in unexplored ways. His commitment to understanding her felt like a balm to her soul after her recent disconnection. Best of all, he didn't seek rescue or need her to take charge of his life. He commanded his own life and relationships, expecting her to do the same with hers.

They spent time together regularly, exploring their burgeoning connection. Despite the strong chemistry vibrating between them, they had yet to share a bed, even with their overflowing sexual energy. They consciously chose to savor this wave, embracing the opportunity to embrace the other authentically.

***

One muggy summer evening, the air felt thick and heavy, demanding each breath. Michael invited Lucia to an art studio event featuring performers, drinks, a hot tub, and a fire pit. Eager to flex her social muscles, Lucia donned her flowy, alluring attire and painted her face.

She draped herself like Soleme, poised to reveal layers of illusion to anyone watching. Lucia aimed to illuminate rather than conceal her imperfections with makeup. She thickened her eyeliner, framing the transparent windows to her soul. The soft leather corset highlighted her voluminous chest while billowy handkerchief sleeves cascaded past her wrists, casting a graceful shadow over her arms and milky shoulders. Emboldened by the essence of the Goddess Aphrodite, she prepared to step into this unknown world.

They climbed one of Seattle's many hills to a large studio adorned with wall-to-wall paintings of naked humans in all their imperfections and glory. The scent of red wine and musk wrapped around Lucia as she moved forward with her hesitant body. Her heart thumped in her chest. She steadied herself, inhaled deeply, and placed one foot in front of the other. After Michael introduced her to a crowd with striking yet friendly facial features and extravagant clothing, she began to absorb her surroundings. The art radiated rawness and truth, showcasing people of all shapes and sizes in radiant beauty. Rich red velvet curtains shrouded the corners, and beams holding hidden treasure lined the ceiling. This vibrant place pulsed with life, while the images on the walls felt like guardians, watching over and protecting all who entered.

Lucia spoke with a model featured in one of the pieces hung in the main space. They discussed the studio's dual purpose as a spa by day. The woman introduced Lucia to the artist who owned the space. They explored the healing properties of art and the importance of embracing every facet of oneself. Lucia remarked that the figures in the portraits resembled gargoyles, standing sentinel to ensure safety and care for everyone. The artist beamed at her observation, realizing he had created these custodians of his community. It stunned Lucia that he had never considered that connection before.

Suddenly, silence engulfed the room as a large metal hoop descended into the center. It towered eight feet above the floor, suspended by a thick silk cord. A stunning red-haired woman stepped through the hoop. Black lace clung to the lower half of her body, intricate patterns dancing across her skin, showing glimpses of her nudity underneath. Her breasts were bare, perfectly round, and supple. Her nipples protruded into sharp little points from her soft, pale skin. Her auburn waves cascaded down her back while her smile ignited the warmth of the candlelit room.

A muscular man lifted her by the waist as she reached for the ring, pulling her up to sit at its center. Everyone held their breath, waiting to witness the magic about to unfold. Lucia felt mesmerized; her heart raced, and warmth surged to her cheeks with excitement. The artist vanished into a corner with a grand piano, and suddenly, his fingers danced over the keys, coaxing a classical piece to life. She twisted and turned, navigating the ring with a skill that defied belief. The music flowed with her graceful movements, a perfect match to her extraordinary agility and immense strength.

Lucia had never experienced anything like this—beyond even the Cirque du Soleil. This performance reverberated with erotic energy and personal intensity, far surpassing any choreographed show. It stirred something deep within Lucia, igniting the essence of her soul that felt like home. When asked about her thoughts afterward, words escaped her. The experience transcended expression: it forged new pathways in her imagination. Beauty washed over her, both familiar and exotic, enthralling and deeply moving. The studio rumbled with palpable energy. Participants radiated electricity, sparking unexpected connections. A warm, interconnected atmosphere enveloped Lucia, a phenomenon she had never witnessed in a gathering before.

As the group scattered after the aerialist's final act, Lucia slipped away to the restroom, seeking a moment to gather her thoughts. She sat on a plush bench, tears welling in her eyes, overwhelmed and bewildered. The performance unearthed something deep within her—a stirring she couldn't yet name but recognized as essential.

Lucia freshened up and gathered her wits after the transcendental experience by imagining her feet sinking into the ground below her. She envisioned her strength shaping her body into that of a goddess, calling forth the priestess of the Divine that lay dormant inside her. She saw the hidden essence, adorned and radiant, waiting to emerge in a blaze of light.

As she walked through the crowd, Lucia found Michael gently placing a hand on his back. Warmth radiated from her touch, and he turned to her, half-smiling with an understanding gleam in his eye. Just then, a tall, handsome man with wavy blond hair and a chiseled face approached them. He introduced himself as Brian and informed Lucia that he would pose for everyone in the room tonight to paint. He spoke with confidence, revealing this wasn't his first time, and embodied pride that the artist had called him back to model again.

He explained he would stand nude in the middle of the room while everyone received paint and brushes to decorate him. Then, he boldly asked Lucia to join him as the other model. The question caught her off guard; she had never envisioned herself in such a role nor considered what it meant to be seen like this.

Lucia glanced at Michael, who beamed with delight. He nodded in approval as a rush of thoughts flooded her mind. Fear gripped her at the idea of exposing her body to strangers. She couldn't hide her flaws; they stood bare for all to see. Stretch marks and scars invaded her thoughts, and she worried about a pimple on her backside. She anticipated the judgments that those imperfections would incite.

Recently, Lucia shed about forty pounds—a source of pride—but the thought of being naked felt daunting. She perceived her skin as saggy and dimpled, and shame crawled up her face. Yet, in that moment, determination ignited within her. The constriction around her shifted toward a determination of action. She said to herself, "I will not let shame control me. I must do whatever it takes to feel free." And she agreed.

Before she could hesitate, Brian whisked her to the changing room and handed her a white robe. As she peeled off her clothes, tremors coursed through her body; heat flushed her cheeks, aflame with feelings of fear and shame. She stepped out, gripping the terrycloth robe around her tender, vibrating skin.

With a few swift movements she was lifted onto a pedestal she hadn't expected as part of the deal, as it placed her a foot above everyone else in the room, even Brian, who seemed not to be elevated at all. She handed her robe to the man who had guided her out, standing before over thirty people without an ounce of clothing. Brian sat a few feet away on a stool that spun, allowing artists to paint him from different angles.

Lucia acknowledged the tension in every muscle of her body, recognizing that the shame she carried served no purpose in that moment. It would only wound her further if she allowed it to take hold. With every conscious breath that arose heavily from her trembling chest, there accompanied a fight to believe that this was her chosen path and that running away wasn't an option. She wanted to focus on the sensation of each soft brush on her skin as an effort to absorb everything unfolding around her.

A fleeting thought crossed her mind that no one would choose to paint her and that everyone would gravitate toward the hot, muscular blonde man perched nearby. She felt a single drop of sweat stream down her forehead and onto her flushed cheek. An intense angst surged from her belly, a reminder of childhood rejection. She clenched her fists, struggling to breathe, searching for Michael's warm smile in the sea of people poised to grab the brushes laid out.

Not finding him, she took a determined inhalation and inwardly resolved that it was what it was.

The masses approached her with paint, intent, and gentleness. They selected their favorite parts of her body, sweeping brushes in smooth, cool strokes of adoration. A line formed, eager to reach her. Doubts crept in—did they judge her cellulite, her sagging breasts? But soon, she recognized the truth: she judged herself harshly and all they wanted was to celebrate her bravery. They smiled, ready to revel in her flawed body, witnessing only its beauty. At that point, she transformed into living art. Love and electric energy flowed from them to her, healing old wounds of criticism and correcting illegitimate media images of perfect women. She felt each soft brush, every breath against her skin, saw admiration in their eyes, and heard appreciation in their words. This awareness liberated her, and she relaxed in her skin for the first time since she was a child.

All of the shame that had burrowed into her collected in the core of her being. She squeezed it through her toes and plunged into the floor, down, down, into the earth's center, where Mother Gaia transformed it into self-love. In the blink of an eye, Lucia recognized the spell cast on her as a child. Memories of every harmful, broken word resounded in her brain: every mocking television show, every perfume ad, and even every female superhero with society's perfect measurements. Suddenly, shattered projections of society's expectations that had pierced her innocent psyche were broken by those heart-led paintbrushes and adoring faces. Not just in her body but throughout her entirety. Lucia heard a familiar echo in her mind, "There is no room for shame when finding one's true self." Huh, "Well shit," she thought. "I didn't see this one coming," she laughed aloud, her shining face grinning as others looked up at her in wonder.

Lucia vowed that from here on out; she would eliminate any shame that crept up in her during her darkest moments. She realized that shame stemmed from a decision about how she believed others wanted her to be. It shackled her for years, preventing her from discovering her true self. Determined to rid herself of its toxicity, she began to dismantle its grip on her being. A seed of rage was rooted within her as she recognized that society's unreasonable beauty standards dictated every little girl's worth.

As her body transformed into a canvas of incredible images, the group began to wander in different directions. Michael approached her, asking if he could take some pictures. Lucia hesitated, her nerves colliding with curiosity at the thought of seeing herself so exposed, the same way these people had all witnessed her.

He led her away from the pedestal and asked how she felt. "Vulnerable and powerful," she replied. He nodded, warmth in his gaze, and asked what she needed. At her request, he guided her to the fire pit outside.

She declined the offered robe, opting instead to wear only the paint, embracing the shamelessness that finally washed over her. She settled in with a circle of people, their warmth enveloping her bare skin as the paint cracked in the heat, creating sensations of tightness and freedom. The others, dressed but unfazed by her nudity, maintained a strangely relaxed atmosphere around the fire.

Eventually, Brian stepped outside and asked if Lucia would like to shower and remove the paint. She agreed it was time to melt all the colors and let them be carried away into the pipes forever, leaving only a lack of shame and a few photographs behind.

He took her hand and led her to the shower. They scrubbed together, and as he watched her, he got erect, which she noticed but ignored. Brian asked her to wash the back side of him and offered to clean hers. He rubbed against her as he ran his soapy hands over her paint-muddled body.

She felt a jolt of surprise that she had never considered this possibility. Lucia was confident that Michael wouldn't mind if she let Brian fuck her as per his statements in their pre-party boundaries conversation. Michael had emphasized he wouldn't control her choices but preferred to discuss them first. He asked her to inform him if she wanted to explore intimacy with someone else. And she hadn't done that, caught off guard by this unexpected turn. Yet, the likelihood that Michael would understand the situation was high.

There was no doubt he was turned on, and his hard cock rubbed her, trying desperately to slide between her legs. Her body wanted him as she imagined him inside her. She even considered bending her over in that shower and him fucking her until they both exploded with ecstasy. The feeling of this chiseled man's desire for her and his stiff, soapy muscles were turning her on beyond measure. Yet, unease gnawed at her, a tension coiling tightly around her gut since she hadn't spoken to Michael. Moreover, an inexplicable sensation lingered, a presence that she couldn't shake—something just felt off.

She turned toward him and said she was with Michael and that it felt inappropriate. Brian winced and argued, claiming she had ignited his desire, and it was cruel to leave him hanging; his words doused the flame. In an instant, the fire between her legs was extinguished. She imagined they might unite later, but then he brought up blue balls, revealing his selfishness around his unmet needs. She stepped out of the shower, gratitude washing over her for heeding her intuition. The realization struck her: her passion for him thrived on false anticipation. She paused, recognizing the strength in her hesitancy, and offered a silent thanks to herself for listening.

Lucia wrapped a towel around herself and returned to the fire pit. Michael laughed and chatted with a few newcomers. He opened his arms as she nestled against him. Relief washed over her as she shifted from passion to logic, recognizing Brian's self-absorption just in time. She thought about how natural it felt with Alyx; even having just met her, Lucia had not hesitated for a moment.

She recalled her lovers since the divorce, noting their palpable passions that echoed her connection with Brian. Yet, none had stirred that same red flag feeling. Finally, she understood the importance of listening to her instincts and acting on them, regardless of the excitement stirring within her.

They chatted outside for a while, then slipped into the hot tub with some flirtatious, friendly folks. Lucia savored the freedom to choose her path and the power she felt in deciding how intimate to get and with whom. This journey awakened a more profound sense of empowerment around her sexuality, illuminating options and choices like never before.

Thoughts swirled in her mind about how society taught many men to claim the female body, manipulate it, and exploit it for pleasure without considering the humanity of the individual. For the first time, Lucia embraced a profound sense of ownership over her body. Deep within, she understood she alone held the power to choose her sexuality.

***

Michael leaned in close and asked Lucia if she would enjoy a full-body massage. She replied with enthusiastic consent, almost as if an invisible force drew her into his embrace. He poured her a glass of wine, turned on soft music, and guided her to a plush chair. "Give me a moment to set up," he said, disappearing for about ten minutes.

When he returned, he wore a satin robe, his eyes shining with excitement as he took her hand.

Michael led her into a room alive with the glow of twenty flickering candles. Nag Champa filled the air while soft, deep chanting flowed from the speakers. He slowly peeled away her clothing and asked her to lie face down on the massage table. Nervousness tightened Lucia's chest, but she relaxed as his hands began to move over her skin. They had only ever made out, an odd situation considering they faced no barriers to having sex. She understood the problem they faced would lead to sex, and she desired it.

He poured warm sandalwood oil into his strong hands and swept them over her skin, the scent enveloping them both, filling the air with an earthy richness. His fingers glided, tracing soft curves, igniting sensations that flickered like embers. Each touch spoke of connection, a tangible thread woven between them, stirring the atmosphere charged with intimacy. Gently taking his time, he moved into a deep penetration of her musculature, the rhythm shifting, oscillating between gentle caresses and stark contrasts. His touch buzzed with intensity, electricity coursing through him and igniting a fire within her. The force surged through her, each touch igniting her senses. She embodied every moment; her entire being, a responsive mechanism, reacted to the sensations. Her heart, mind, and spirit united as one.

He worked her every muscle and knot, kneading, sliding, and stretching her. Without thought, she responded to each intoxicating motion as if her essence might drip off the table in answer to his magic touch. No shame, no hang-ups, no insecurities, no past, or future only that single moment held her.

He signaled her to turn over and lie on her back. She hesitated. In an instant, he leaned over and kissed her, a spontaneous act driven by an unspoken connection. Deep and lovingly, his potent tongue parted her flushed lips, opening her. She shifted beneath his hands, resulting in a fluid movement that had her lying on her back. She was exposed fully before him, open and unguarded, her heart free from fear, stress, or shame. Lucia found herself moaning deeply as his hands enveloped her soul through her skin. She expressed gratitude to the Universe for this shift, embracing the comfort she had finally found inside her flesh.

Lucia experienced unexpected nurturing. She felt unrestricted and malleable, her body finally resonating as her own. For the first time, there was a sense of unity among her body, heart, mind, and spirit, dissolving the separation that had long defined her. Empowered and fully attuned to the flow of erotic energy, she embraced this new, vibrant reality.

After Michael massaged her breasts, his hands glided over her stomach; she recalled her lifelong self-consciousness about this area. Yet, she lay there, open, and fully aware of her vulnerability. A sense of wholeness enveloped her as she embraced the moment. Michael rubbed her belly, each stroke deep and methodical. She felt energy flow from his heart into her; a sensation of building and expanding. The power filled her core, holding it there before it would be released outward into the world. A tingling sensation reverberated through her as he poured his life force into her. She opened her eyes briefly, taking in the soft glow of orange candlelight that enveloped the room, grounding her and wrapping her in a cocoon of safety.

The buzz under her skin became more potent, clenching her center, spreading into her vulva, and then through all her appendages as an intense flood of full-body orgasm overtook her. Moans rumbled out of Lucia's throat, unwittingly simultaneously raising her hips off the table.

In one swift motion, Michael coasted down her stomach and cupped her drenched vulva. Gasping, he made a circular motion, and she felt him palpate her clitoris while descending his fingers deep inside her. She writhed as pressured flesh moved in and out of her. He cleverly positioned his head between her legs. She spread wide before him, riding the orgasm she released as his tongue and fingers coaxed every last drop of her juices from her swollen pussy.

Minutes felt like an eternity as her body released an ocean of pent-up pleasure. Wave after wave overtook her as Michael delicately continued to touch her tender, purring pussy; each time the orgasm relaxed, he'd start the process from gentle to intense, coaxing another crescendo.

Lucia had always stopped after the "big one." Instead, she embraced a full release and squirted fluid all over him as if she were his personal water fountain. Not caring whether she embarrassed herself, what juices had drenched him, or if her body did other not-so-sexy things, it just didn't matter. She craved the power surging through her veins, electrifying every thought and movement. Nothing would stand in her way.

Michael met her sparkling gaze, his pulse quickening as she gasped, "DON'T STOP!" He charged forward, a Cheshire grin spreading across his face, daring her body to keep pace with him. Every ounce of pleasure she had ever wanted to feel was being extracted from her.

Lucia contorted and bellowed, "MORE!" She couldn't help but entangle herself in her robust lover, grasping him and then relaxing into every single orgasm without hesitation. She felt power pulsate through her and fill the room; a force more vibrant than she had ever known. The erotic energy coursed through her, surging with remarkable intensity. In that moment, she recognized that this feeling embodied Divinity itself.

Eventually, she had wrung out every last particle of longing, her limbs heavy, sliding off the massage table. With tears glistening in her eyes, she collapsed into oblivion. Michael wrapped around her, holding her tightly as she wept with the intensity of release. She sensed the Universe within her, the energy of not only him and her but everything.

Lucia suddenly found herself uncontrollably sobbing, unleashing the sadness she had carried for so long—the loneliness, the yearning for understanding, the ache of invisibility. Michael wrapped his arms around her, his presence a steadfast shield.

She immersed herself in the flood of tears, each drop a testament to the disconnection that had haunted her all her life. Mourning arose from every pressured sexual experience, and every fuck was not enjoyed but continued anyway. Her heart shattered into a million shards of light, and in that moment, she understood she had merged with the web of life. A profound sense of belonging filled her; she would never feel alone again.

Michael gathered her clothes and led her to his room. They entwined in each other's arms, drifting into a peaceful slumber until the morning light stirred them awake. The pair devoted the next couple of days to exploring each other's bodies, hearts, and minds.

***

After physically connecting, they spent every moment they could together. Lucia reveled in how Michael's body responded to her touch. Through him, she unearthed the potential of energy manifesting in their deliberate connection. This experience pulsed with a potency beyond any meditation or introspection, brimming with an inexplicable life force. She had finally awoken to primal erotic energy as electrical sensations coursed through her entire being, illuminating her own sense of Divinity. In that moment, she vowed never to feel separate from herself again, for within her lay everything she had always longed for.

Chapter Four

TRANSITIONS

Knowing yourself is the beginning of all wisdom.

- Aristotle

Lucia and Michael maintained an open relationship. They enjoyed each other's company without imposing boundaries that restricted their individual experiences. Their connection deepened more than Lucia had intended, and embracing polyamory became increasingly challenging as they grew closer. Yet, she refused to sacrifice her freedom. She remained open to whatever life might introduce. Neither felt the urge to pursue others without the other present, but Lucia treasured her ability to explore connections with anyone who sparked her interest. Nothing held her back from responding to those moments.

For months, I worked a lot, laboring tirelessly, and embraced every opportunity to be with Michael. The couple started attending erotic parties together. They discovered the mysteries of bodies intertwined beneath dim lights, and whispering secrets danced in the air. Each gathering was charged with anticipation, igniting desires that flickered like candle flames. Couples and strangers explored boundaries, their laughter mingling with soft music, creating an atmosphere charged with electric tension. In these spaces, freedom thrived, and Lucia lapped it up. She experienced her inhibitions fading, revealing raw, unfiltered passion. She was entranced by witnessing the conversations, which ignited like sparks as connections formed in fleeting glances and lingering touches, weaving a tapestry of shared experiences that left an indelible mark on their souls. They started to tie Lucia up in public, testing her limits and pushing against her edges. Michael discovered her tendency toward a certain cat-of-nine-tails and took advantage of that when he had her immobile. She challenged her previous limits, embracing the thrill of knife play and the sharp sting of thumpy implements. Each touch ignited an exhilarating blend of fear and desire, pushing her boundaries further into uncharted territory.

She uncovered clarity and empowerment through BDSM, diving into an exhilarating balance of pain and pleasure that expanded her consciousness. Every time she found herself naked in front of others, old conditioning crept in, but she rejected it fiercely. With each encounter, the weight of that conditioning vanished more swiftly as she embraced her vulnerability. The more complex types of play allowed her to search for the remnants of shame and insecurity buried deep inside her. With each act of submission, she squeezed out those lingering doubts, uncovering the raw edges of her vulnerability. She found that in her vulnerability, she wielded control like never before.

The pain tore down the walls she had built around herself. It became a brutal therapy, forcing her to confront her deepest insecurities. In that raw space, she discovered a way to dance with her shadow, using it as a tool for growth rather than allowing it to dominate her. She relished the openness and freedom within the sex-positive community, a massive leap in her spiritual and emotional self-awareness. The experience felt like flooding sunlight pouring through the windows of her mind, illuminating corners she had never explored.

Michael held a special place in Lucia's heart. She viewed him as a guide, showing her how to trust her own body. His strong character and commitment to personal growth inspired her. Respect for him allowed her to open up, let him lead, and embrace vulnerability. She trusted him for this and what she saw through his activism and meaningful friendships, as he consistently demonstrated a genuine desire to change the world for the better. She admired him; he respected her self-awareness, spiritual depth, and intelligence, as well as her embodiment of these qualities. Her newfound sexuality transformed her, but she cherished how their connection sparked further growth in both of them. Their shared commitment to personal evolution reshaped her in profound ways.

Since she met Michael, she began to see herself as Humpty Dumpty—an egg hurled off a wall, reveling in the sensation of being cracked open. At last, the shell shattered, revealing her true self: the shiny, sparkly depths of her soul, with intense, powerful nooks and crannies. Each time she shed a piece of the shell, she felt vibrant, alive, more authentic, more like herself. She fell in love with the goo that spilled out—a blend of strength and power.

***

Lucia chose to take on an extra job and had been called to plan a solo trip to swim in the ocean and explore sacred sites. She felt the importance of embarking on this journey alone, a challenge to practice her hard-earned lessons. Bringing someone along would threaten her focus, and there was a keen recognition of the risk of slipping into codependence with Michael. Despite her deep care for him, she reminded herself to prioritize the distinction of her path. The romance that enveloped her often clouded her thoughts, filling her mind with fantasies and idealized endings. When those thoughts surfaced, she would scold the societal narrative that romantic love represented the ultimate fulfillment. So, she centered her attention on organizing a trip to southern Mexico.

The elimination of shame awakened a keen internal compass she had never known. Lucia aimed to harness that intensity and drive. Fortunately, this newfound energy surged through her body and mind, fueling her willingness to work tirelessly. Stamina blossomed within her, feeding her dreams and igniting excitement for the discoveries that awaited in the world. She channeled that vitality into crafting an adventure.

When she shared her plans with Michael, he expressed sadness at her decision to leave for months. He offered to join her, but she firmly asserted that this journey had to unfold on her terms. Determined to safeguard her independence, she blocked out thoughts of experiencing the trip with Michael. Each time those thoughts intruded, a commanding voice echoed in her mind, urging her to remain free and attentive to her inner guidance. Michael acknowledged her needs, showing respect for her choice.

***

It took her six months to save money for the trip. She scrimped, saved, and moved in with a friend to cut costs. Finally, she bought her ticket, gave notice at her job, and crafted an official game plan. She didn't care if she had a job after returning, knowing waitressing jobs always awaited her if she couldn't find something in her field right away.

Lucia trusted it would all work out. Michael assured her she could stay with him as long as necessary when she returned. The thought felt risky yet somehow liberating. Excitement mingled with fear, but she refused to dwell on it. She acknowledged those feelings and let them drift away, imagining her fear as clouds dissipating under the sun of her motivation. She reminded herself of the challenges she had faced and conquered, knowing she could do it again.

She sat in the golden energy radiating from her core. This life force inside her emanated importance while it quietly demanded her focus. She had unleashed it through intimacy and energy play with Michael, but it had morphed into a fierce zest for life. Every part of her recognized this power as hers alone, untouched by anyone else.

***

Lucia and Michael embarked on a trip to the Olympic Peninsula and the Hoh Rainforest before she departed for Mexico. They sought solitude in nature and glimpses of the ocean, relishing each moment together.

They drove for hours, weaving through patches of traffic, pausing at striking landmarks, singing along with the radio, and engaging in endless conversations about the joys of life in the Pacific Northwest. They contemplated the confines of Seattle life, recognizing how other parts of the country imposed their limitations. They marveled at the vivid landscapes, a tapestry of greens and blues, and searched each stop for heart-shaped rocks nestled among the stones.

They arrived at their cottage near dusk. Michael asked Lucia to give him a little time to set up their room for their first night. Agreeing, Lucia considered how blessed she was that Michael put so much thought into the settings of their lovemaking. Lucia sat outside and listened to the ebb and flow of the ocean waves breaking on the rocky shore. They had chosen a cozy cottage on the coast, featuring a hot tub on the porch that overlooked the sea, nestled within the native village of La Push. As the sun dipped below the horizon, the jagged rocks emerged from the water, their outlines stark against the darkening sky, while the dense forest loomed behind her, a silent guardian. A delicate crescent moon ignited the night sky, and stars twinkled above her, wrapping her in a cosmic embrace. Completely immersed in the magic surrounding her, she drifted into a state of peace and gratitude.

Michael startled her when he opened the door, jolting her from her immersion in the millions of sparkling beacons above. She looked up at him, her loving gaze making him blush. Smiling, he invited her to join him in the cottage. The world around her buzzed, and lightheadedness swept through her; she wobbled when she stood. He caught her, steadying her as laughter bubbled from her lips. This beautiful place enveloped her, urging her to stay present, to feel every moment.

The room glowed softly in amber light. Michael took her hand and guided her to the bed. She quivered as he undressed her, each touch igniting electric reactions in her muscles, goosebumps rising on her sensitive skin. He seated her on the bed and offered her a sip of white wine while gently placing a soft blindfold over her closed eyes. He whispered into her ear, urging her to lie down. As she sank into the soft blankets, something light grazed her thigh, tickling her just enough to send a ripple of sensation across her body with a single touch. Michael's tenderness stirred her senses. It felt as if he reached into her essence with a soft touch, barely grazing her with pressure or intensity.

A multitude of sensations washed over her naked body. Softness transformed into sharpness, then shifted to a delicate wistfulness, yet never approached pain. Her skin resembled the evanescence of champagne, bubbling with frolics of delight. She moaned and sighed, fully immersed in her physical form. Each cell of her being danced, every molecule, both physical and energetic, aligned with the rhythm of their motion. He continued to touch her from head to toe as she rode the waves of stimulation for what seemed like hours.

An altered state of consciousness enveloped her, and she clung to it for as long as possible.

Her energy surged and ebbed within her. She pinpointed the exact spot where it began and traced its movement through her body, recognizing she could concentrate this current on a specific area. She gathered every ounce of erotic energy and released it through her chest. Bright green light flooded her vision, piercing through the darkness of the blindfold. Healing washed over her as she melted into the bed. With her heart wide open, she surrendered to the swirling green light that enveloped her.

Michael removed her blindfold and wrapped his arms around her, whispering sweet, comforting words that echoed in her mind. He claimed she was everything he had always desired, that she stood out among all, and that he could not imagine life without her. She felt a wave of love for him, but she also recognized that his sweet words lacked substance, leaving an emptiness unaddressed.

She gathered herself, threw her hair into a clip, and purred as she pleasured him until he collapsed. They nestled in each one another's arms as the forest serenaded them to sleep.

***

That night, she slept soundly, dreaming of a journey through a nebulous void where life brims in swirling gases, light, and form. Images poured from galaxies into Mexico. Visions flowed, mutating rich landscapes, revealing a woman with onyx hair in the midst of the swirling atmosphere. They locked eyes, the magical creature swaying gently, her golden-brown gaze piercing through the mist. Lucia recognized her; a warmth of familiarity rushed through her as she studied the dissolving form, the image slipping away as another dream surged in.

She woke to the sound of the ocean. Slipping out of bed while Michael slept, she dressed quietly and walked along the beach, watching white crests crash against far-off rocks. They sang deep tones like bass drums; the rhythmic beating of the waves on the rocks expressed resilience and synchronicity. Seabirds soared around the monstrous stones jutting from the water as the sun began to peek behind them.

The sunrise ignited the sky with crimson, carnelian, and burnt umber, transforming it into the most passionate place on Earth. Lucia breathed it all in as the fire in the sky fueled her spirit. The ground beneath her pulsed with a heartbeat in sync with her own, cradling her close to its bosom.

She sat in silence for over an hour before Michael emerged. Enjoyment of this solitude washed passed her. His presence felt welcome but not necessary. This appreciation for being alone hasn't always existed. Loneliness once gnawed at her, making each moment without stimulation feel challenging and uncomfortable. But once she discovered the alchemy of her inner world, the joy found in her own company intertwined with peace. Enduring her dark night of the soul for those many moons led to healing within solitude, where a deep embrace of self and clarity thrived.

She understood why solitude once felt unbearable. In the past, she had drifted far from her true self. No comfort existed in her interior life during those dishonest times. As authenticity seeped into every area of her existence, the chasm between her and others widened, leaving her feeling isolated. However, Lucia had traversed the shadowland of her being and emerged from that chaos, facing the demons of her mind with courage. Now, only angels occupy that space.

***

Michael grasped her hand as they strolled through the lush rainforest that misty morning. Moss draped overhead, creating a canopy of ancient wisdom. In this magical realm, whispers of fairies and gnomes filled the air. Trees took on the shapes of ancient beings and fearsome monsters, remnants of long-lost epochs. The spirits of the woods danced playfully, inviting the couple to seek their presence and engage with the enchantment surrounding them.

Exploring that enchanted place filled both of them with giddy excitement. They resembled children in a fantasyland of mythical beasts and talking plants. They ventured deep into the deserted forest, discovering a bubbling creek that sparkled under the sun. Turtles and tiny frogs emerged, sharing wisdom about patience and flexibility within the gurgling water.

The dragonflies hovered, slicing through reality with a winged ballet. Their razor-sharp tails and translucent prisms tore through the veil, translating magic directly into the world. Bright red bodies settled for mere moments on the back of a turtle or a log jutting out of the water. Then, they zipped through the air, cutting through illusions crafted by humanity.

For Lucia, dragonflies exuded mystery, serving as guiding spirits. This connection grew so intense that during summer phone calls with her Mom, they gathered around as if drawn to the conversation. When her Mom announced their return, Lucia smiled, whispering a silent thank you.

The forest ignited silliness and laughter in Lucia and Michael for the rest of their trip. Michael sang and danced while Lucia clapped her hands in delight. Giggles and grins filled their days as they chased, caught, and played in the elder woods of the Pacific Northwest.

Lucia had never recalled childhood, yet wonder blossomed within her, revealing a capacity she never knew she possessed. Freedom surged through the ethereal land, close to home, drastic and expansive.

The pair hovered in the space between forest and water, thriving on the powerful balance of both. The ocean pulsed with the Earth's heartbeat, emanating lifeblood and rhythm. Lucia began to breathe in sync with the waves. La Push mesmerized her with its beauty, a place where she felt ready to burst into a million butterflies. Peaceful spirits of the native land whispered through emerald forests and roiling, rocky beaches. Sunsets transformed the sky into a canvas of purples and pinks, framing the majestic silhouettes of rocks jutting from the water.

On their way home, they discussed Lucia's trip. Michael's playful spirit faded as he somberly explained his deepening attachment to her. He offered to sacrifice all his other relationships for her sake, emphasizing his desire for her commitment in return. Passionately, he expressed his love, revealing an unsettling truth: life without her felt unimaginable.

She sat, absorbing his plight. For the first time in all her relationships, she recognized his words for what they truly were. He wanted to keep her. Freedom beckoned her more powerfully than romance. A fierce desire surged within to exist and act on her terms. Love for him remained strong, yet a bond felt suffocating. Time and energy spent on self-discovery anchored her resolve; no one would sway her from that path. A commitment to honoring herself pulsed in her heart, guiding every decision in her ongoing evolution.

Love fueled his intentions, yet efforts to shape the narrative clashed with her boundaries. No conscious aim to control her existed; instead, a conflict arose from passion meeting resistance.

In the past, profound love swept her away, prompting sacrifices for a fairy tale. Romantic gestures, once intoxicating, drew her from her essence. Society preached that love eclipsed all else. Considering this, her reflections flickered—how many women surrendered their identities to love stories? How many channeled their divine sparks into others instead of nurturing their own souls?

The belief persisted, shared widely, that romantic love represented life's primary pinnacle. Perhaps a magical illusion convinced those souls that self-sacrifice for another radiated beauty and peace. Yet, Lucia did not want to live in illusions any longer.

"Michael," Lucia began, her voice soft yet resolute, "I need to tell you about my journey. For so long, I dedicated myself to raising my child and trying to save his father. I've had to confront a painful truth: I've often placed myself on the back burner." Michael looked at her, concerned but attentive.

"But now," she continued, her eyes lighting up with newfound passion, "there's a life blossoming within me—one filled with adventure, freedom, and self-exploration. I've discovered a purpose that drives me. I have this urgent desire to touch divinity and reveal my best self. I want to carve a path toward actualizing my potential."

Lucia paused, searching his eyes. "I see how strong your love for me is," she said gently. "You work so hard to make me happy. I want you to know that I've never had a lover like you. You've opened me in ways that I never thought possible. But," she added, as she held his gaze, "I also realize you're not thinking about what's truly best for me. I understand that you want guarantees that you want me to promise we'll be together. But I can't give you that right now. I have so much I need to do on my own." She took a deep breath, trying to convey the weight of her words. "I do hope that you'll be in my life for a very long time. Right now, though, I need space to explore everything the Universe puts in my path, without any restrictions.

"I understand," he said, his face dropping as he spoke. His voice cracked slightly, betraying the sense of resignation he felt. Lucia saw his urge to give her an ultimatum, and also that he stopped himself before he said it. Instead, Michael rumbled, "I just want...want all of you. But I'll respect what you need to do for yourself."

Michael hesitated, and in those spaces between his words, Lucia assumed that he was afraid to push her away entirely if he said more. She pressed her hand against his, conveying love through a gentle squeeze, while her gaze held him steady as they listened to music during the drive home. "I'm here with you now, and I see your heart," she whispered as a soft tune emerging from the stereo enveloped them, creating a cocoon of warmth.

Every note resonated with the unspoken connection between them. Lucia ached with the desire to soothe him, to share in his turmoil, yet she remained committed to her path. This moment belonged to both of them. Soon, an imminent flight would pull her toward a different reality, where uncertainties awaited. For now, she savored their time together, embracing all the feelings that flickered in the air.

Catching his eye, she added, "wherever I am, know that I love you." The sincerity in her voice wrapped around them, a quiet promise binding their hearts even in silence.

***

Inside Lucia, a fierce battle raged: prioritize Michael's feelings or choose herself. She recognized her need for freedom, yet words like villain, selfish, cold, mean, and cruel bombarded her thoughts.

When self-doubt crept in, she turned to a Rumi quote for solace. Each quote became a lifeline, grounding her as she wrestled with the choice that would define her. "If you catch a fragrance of the unseen," she whispered to herself, "you cannot be contained. You will soar across the empty sky."

As the words settled in her mind, she felt a spark of hope. "Any beauty the world offers—and all its desires—will easily come to you," she continued, envisioning the possibilities stretching before her.

"The mirror reveals a clearer reflection," she reminded herself. "Live profoundly in the heart." At that moment, the light caught the edges of her understanding. "When you realize God resides within, anxiety about losing anyone or anything vanishes."

Lucia saw the shadows of human difficulties loosening their grip. "You're here," she declared, voice steady. "That presence lives through you."

And with each repetition, the fragrance of strength wrapped around her, urging her to embrace the beauty of existence.

Michael drove Lucia to the airport. Before this transformation, she would have spent hours reassuring him of her return, nurturing his heart, and pouring every ounce of energy into easing his pain. This time, Lucia remained silent. Instead, Lucia gazed at him with love, fully aware of his suffering. "I'm not forgetting you, you are important to me, you know," she finally said, her voice steady.

He looked away, pain etched in his features. "It's hard to think about that now."

"I understand," she replied, her tone firm yet gentle.

His silence spoke volumes, an unspoken plea hanging in the air. Lucia turned her gaze to the passing scenery outside, each blurred tree and building crisscrossing memories of their time together. The weight of his ordeal pressed against her, but for once, she refused to shoulder it.

The airport loomed ahead, its busy energy palpable. "Take care of yourself, Michael; I love you." Leaving him with a final note of tenderness infused with resolve.

"I love you, don't forget me..." he murmured, and Lucia offered nothing but a loving smile.

With a meaningful breath, she prepared to step into her new reality, leaving behind sacrifice, obligation, and self-minimization.

The airport came into view rapidly. In an instant, Lucia kissed Michael goodbye. His mouth pressed against hers—passionate, deep, and lingering. The kiss conveyed the plea: "Do not forget that I'm here." It coaxed her to return, but above all, it whispered, "Don't leave me." Beneath the surface, she sensed the abandoned little boy in him, yearning for her to stay by his side forever.

"Please, don't go," he murmured, a tremor in his voice.

"I have to," she replied, though her heart ached.

His eyes reflected a longing that pierced her resolve. "You promise you'll come back?"

"Always," she said, though uncertainty loomed. The weight of that promise settled between them as she turned away, each step echoing a silent farewell.

Yet he said nothing as she turned away. Grateful for his stoicism, she didn't want to comfort him, explain, or justify anything. Instead, she longed to envelop him in her love, to leave him drenched in its warmth. No words could achieve that—only feeling. Tired of tending the wounds of men in her life, she realized how often she had shielded fragile egos from the sting of her needs.

"Fucking hell, this is tougher than I thought it would be," she murmured to herself, the weight of her feelings for Michael pressing down.

She felt the familiar pangs of her conditioning to soothe him, to bend herself to his needs, to be the only one he ever wanted. Yet, today, she resisted those impulses and continued forward.

Choosing this untraveled path, the road belonging solely to her, pulled Lucia away from pangs of discomfort and into the embrace of her true self.

Her heart stung with every step; love for him weighed heavily as the thought of his pain knotted in her chest. As she crossed into the airport, the doors shut behind her with a finality that echoed. She focused on her feelings, acknowledging and releasing them, a quiet ritual of acceptance and presence.

A conscious shift into the moment enveloped Lucia as she chose to embrace the adventure unfolding before her. After years of growth, change, and inner turmoil, she sought to find her way into the sunlight of a new culture.

Security flowed, a hazy silhouette of interactions beneath the rhythmic beat of the music coming from her earbuds. She tapped her foot in time, swaying slightly to the bass thumping in her chest.

"Hey! What's the vibe tonight?" a voice shouted over her shoulder.

She glanced up, a smile flickering across her lips. She responded to the playful soul behind her, "Electric! Just let it wash over you!"

The beats pulsed, wrapping her in a cocoon of sound. As bodies moved mechanically through the lines, the energy surged like a mighty tide, swallowing her whole. A swirl of colors flashed around her, each note igniting shadows and memories.

The outside world faded, security's presence just a murmur amid the symphony of life. She scanned the crowd, taking in the characters before her—some lost in thought, others struggling under heavy bags. Where were the smiles? With a wide grin, she flashed spontaneous smiles at strangers, embracing those brief connections. "Why not?" she mused. "A smile costs nothing."

A man nearby chuckled as she nodded at him and grinned happily. He exclaimed, "You must know something we don't." Lucia simply shrugged and kept moving.

Around her, the atmosphere shifted. Each smile ignited a spark, lifting burdens and turning heaviness into lightness. Laughter bubbled up as strangers exchanged glances, the weight of the day, lightening just a little.

Lucia always saw airports as vibrant hubs of energy, a chaotic symphony of intersecting lives. She embraced this chaos, choosing to float rather than resist.

In the swirling tide of movement, an older man, frazzled and juggling a coffee cup, caught her eye. "This place always feels like a moment frozen in time," he said, nostalgia threading his voice. She nodded, grasping the weight behind his words.

Echoes danced around her in the vast expanse of the airport, each one promising untold stories. No destination loomed overhead, and no agenda pressed against her. The marvel of the space enveloped Lucia; it felt both open and contained. As she surrendered to it all, a deep peace emerged amidst the whirlwind. Even in the midst of urgency, beauty blossomed in each fleeting interaction.

Lucia made eye contact with a musician outside a bustling coffee shop in the terminal. This person defied conventional gender norms, prompting Lucia to hold no assumptions. Their unique voice soared with beauty and soulfulness that compelled Lucia to reach into her pocket and give the last of her American cash remaining after the currency exchange. The musician smiled and nodded as Lucia, entranced by their talent, radiated awe. After a minute of watching, she turned and moved toward her gate. "What a treat," she mused.

People in the terminal always captured her interest. "They are the epitome of the human experience," she thought. Loving embraces, dancing alongside frantic races to catch their flights, form a vivid tapestry of human emotion. Attendants and pilots strolled confidently with rolling carry-on bags, navigating the vast terminal spaces like seasoned experts. Airports consumed a third of their lives, and they maneuvered through the chaos with practiced ease. These professionals sought to control the disorder, relying on social bonds as their foundation.

Lucia arrived at the terminal and spotted a rocking chair. Strangely, it mirrored the type of chair from her childhood home. Drawn to it, she sat and rocked while rummaging for a quick snack. Each gentle sway offered a therapeutic balm to her inner child. Music flowed through her, harmonizing with the experience, like a cat responding to a gentle hand.

The world pulsed around her, vibrant with life's rhythm—heartbeats, whispers, and an independent cohesion. No other place felt as perfect as that moment. Pieces of existence clicked together in a synchronistic puzzle, and Lucia became part of that intricate machine.

When the time to board arrived, Lucia rose and joined the cattle line. Faces of fellow travelers passed before her as a moving canvas. A child wailed ahead as a mother struggled with a stroller while holding her baby. Lucia stepped forward, offering to help by holding her child so the Mom could gain her bearings. The mother sighed with relief as though teetering on the brink of a breakdown. Handing over the baby, calm washed over the little one almost instantly. Stress melted from the mother, easing with the support of an unexpected ally.

As the mother positioned herself to reclaim her child, she spoke with urgency. "I'm heading to a funeral," she said, her voice steady and slightly louder than necessary, conveying the weight of the situation. "My spouse is already there. It was my parent who passed unexpectedly," her voice trailing off.

She glanced at her child, the little one cradled in the stranger's arms. "My wife has been on a business trip, or else we would have traveled together. Never would I choose to journey alone with a nine-month-old if it wasn't the only option."

The child gurgled, oblivious to the gravity surrounding them. The mother brushed a loose strand of hair from her face, revealing the determination in her eyes. "It's just the two of us for a bit," she continued, her tone softening as she looked at her baby. "But I promise we'll get through this."

A nearby observer caught Lucia's gaze, nodding in empathy and approval of her assistance. Lucia's heart ached, not just for the mother's loss but for the challenge ahead.

The mother inhaled deeply, steeling herself a moment to prepare for the difficult hours ahead. Lucia rested a hand on the mother's shoulder, applying a gentle squeeze. A wave of relaxation washed over the weary woman as she whispered, "Thank you." With a calm child by her side and a subtle smile gracing her lips, she moved forward into her seat.

The flight felt delightful as Lucia gazed out the window, watching the landscape of clouds. She imagined swimming through the sweetness of fluffy cotton candy mountains and marshmallow fluff unfolding below. Tracing forms with her mind, Lucia drifted into every soft curve and puffy blanket.

Awe and wonder filled her as she realized the extraordinary chance to witness these clouds from such a unique vantage point, at this precise moment, in her own body. Once, this experience seemed impossible, yet now, the splendor of the sky enveloped her.

Lucia contemplated how freedom sprang from surrendering to herself. Embracing the adventure the Universe offered and fully submitting to her essence, revealed the divinity inherent in her being. She anticipated opportunities to deepen this relationship for the rest of her life.

Trust grew as she recognized no separation between herself and the Universe—merely a microcosm within the macrocosm—everything connected, access to any part. It's really within reach at any moment. "Quite exciting," she said to herself. "So many possibilities await me." Understanding dawned: life expresses that divine connection, both within and around. Releasing attachments to expectations allowed the essence of all that is to permeate every cell of her being.

Sitting silently, surrounded by souls, she saw it. She saw it all.

Suddenly, the plane began to shake violently, jolting her from her trance. The unexpected turbulence sent ripples of anxiety through the cabin. Wide-eyed passengers exchanged frantic glances, their faces painted with fear, while others gripped their armrests so tightly that their knuckles turned white. The muffled sounds of gasps and murmurs filled the air, punctuated by the low hum of the engines struggling to maintain their steady roar.

She observed the scene, finding it oddly symbolic of human existence —a collective experience of uncertainty and vulnerability. Amid the chaos, she observed the contrast between the serene overhead lights and the frantic energy of the people below. The giant metal box soaring through the sky behaved like a living organism, vibrating and jerking as it fought against the elements, desperately trying to maintain its course through the clouds.

At once, she felt a profound connection to her fellow passengers, all adrift together in this airborne capsule, drawn together by a shared fate. The thrill of the ride transformed into a meditation on the fragility of life, reminding her that, like the aircraft navigating through turbulent skies, everyone must grapple with unpredictability and find the strength to soar despite the storms that arise.

Lucia's body buzzed with curiosity and the unknown; she trembled yet felt no terror. Something clicked within her, a deep understanding that her presence in the now held purpose. Immense peace enveloped her, anchored by the knowledge of her inability to control the unfolding events. She surrendered completely to the experience. A fissure in her heart widened as she nestled into the Universe's embrace, filling the gap with a profound sense of belonging. Trust surged through her, contrasting sharply with the pervasive fear surrounding so many souls on the plane.

After a few minutes that others might label it as a nightmare, the plane finally stopped shaking and found its equilibrium. Lucia scanned the cabin, noting expressions of relief and shock. When gazes met hers, confusion flickered briefly before shifting elsewhere. In those primal moments of insecurity stripped everyone bare, revealing raw emotions at the thought of the potential death.

The mother Lucia had encountered earlier cradled her baby tightly, radiating gratitude. Any trace of earlier stress and irritation vanished as she held her child, fully aware of how close they had come to saying goodbye. Appreciation for life blossomed among all passengers, a powerful and beautiful transformation that lingered for the rest of the flight.

Lucia found it striking that this encounter with death occurred on this particular day. She planned her first stop in Mexico City, where a bus would take her to Teotihuacan, home to the Pyramid of the Moon and the Avenue of the Dead.

A fascination with philosophical theories surrounding death and pain had always drawn Lucia in. At age 14, she spent four months on a ranch in Wyoming with her friend's family. Early in that time, a sheep faced dire circumstances; a pregnant ewe had prolapsed. The ranchers faced an agonizing choice: sacrifice the mother to save the lamb, knowing no vet could reach them in time to offer alternatives.

They had to give the ewe a c-section, and as they cut her belly open, Lucia held down one of her front legs as she was instructed to by the rancher. Lucia felt attuned to the mama sheep as they did this, and after the first cut, the animal didn't move or flinch. The ewe seemed absent, as if she had detached from her own body. The pain must have coursed through her, but she lay utterly still.

Lucia marveled at the sheep's stillness; its silence was as striking as the pain that seemed to envelop it. The birth unfolded quietly, and a healthy lamb emerged, drawing its first breaths as the mother endured the procedure. It pained Lucia to remember that in spite of the ewe surviving the ordeal, they ultimately shot her to ease the inevitable suffering that loomed ahead. Grateful for her shield from that finality, Lucia carried the weight of what she had not witnessed.

This experience transformed Lucia's relationship with pain and death. Fear had gripped her until that experience, and that is when everything changed. A light bathed her childhood nights in fear of the unknown, but not any longer. After the ordeal, that kind of fear vanished.

Through trauma, Lucia unearthed an inner strength that allowed her to confront pain head-on. Her mind brimmed with untapped potential, a depth beyond anyone's understanding. Pain no longer held sway, and death lost its terror.

As the flight settled into a quiet hum, passengers reflected on their gratitude. Lucia immersed herself in her book, savoring white wine and small plates of tapas. She dozed, drifting into dreams filled with silhouettes of distant places and faces yet to be encountered— shapes hazy and incomplete. For the first time, uncertainty about the future wrapped around her like a warm blanket, offering comfort in its formlessness.

Chapter Five
FINDING LUCIA

Blessed are the curious, for they shall have adventures.

- Lovelle Drachman

Lucia inhaled the thick, warm air as she walked through the tunnel connecting the plane to the airport in Mexico City. The scent of roasting peppers and distant chatter enveloped her like a familiar embrace, stirring a sense of homecoming within her. She stepped forward, anticipation blooming in her chest. A smile graced her face as she navigated the airport, noticing that more people returned her warmth than she was used to in the United States.

In Seattle, her smiles often drew confused looks, like the anxious faces she saw during turbulence. It struck her as odd how the fear of death and the fear of connection shared the same expression. When she smiled and made eye contact back home, she felt foreign among her own people. Yet here, the faces looking at her felt familiar and welcoming, as if she belonged.

A tingle of recognition and excitement resounded in her chest, radiating warmth through her breasts and toward her belly. It was a new sensation—sweet, soft, and alive. She knew this feeling emerged from the kindness surrounding her, fostering a soothing expansion within her soul.

Catching a cab to the hotel, the driver practiced his English with her. They laughed and joked as he described in broken phrases which restaurants to try and which clubs to avoid. He showed a kindness that felt protective, mispronouncing words or using phrases in a way that made her chuckle. Each correction turned into a moment of shared laughter, their voices echoing through the streets.

His name was Edwardo, but he insisted she call him Eddie. He leaned slightly toward her as they navigated the bustling streets, his voice firm as he advised her to stay alert in the crowds and stick to busy thoroughfares. She nodded, feeling the warnings in his words. "My father taught me to be smart, not afraid," she replied, her voice firm. "I promise I will be careful," she clarified.

Eddie smiled, the kind of smile that carried a hint of understanding as if he had learned the lessons of the city the hard way. They disjointedly chatted about life, considering the little joys and the unspoken fears that lurked in shadows, sharing snippets of their worlds between stops at busy intersections. With each passing block, the noise of honking horns and lively conversations faded slightly into the background, replaced by the comfort of connection.

As she stepped out of his cab, a warmth settled in her chest. The chaos of the street buzzed around her, but it felt different now; she just didn't feel like another face in the crowd. Eddie's kindness became the sun after a long winter. She glanced back at him, a silent promise forming in her mind. In that fleeting moment, she sensed she had made a friend for life.

Lucia had finally arrived in the Centro Historico district, excitement bubbling within her as she looked up at the art deco hotel nestled among vibrant taquerias, cafes, and stunning architecture. The hotel staff greeted her warmly, their friendly demeanor matching that of the cab driver. They provided helpful recommendations for nearby dining options and shared details about the hotel's offerings, gestures, and gentle tones, creating a sense of safety amid the city's bustle.

Once inside her room, Lucia barely registered the surroundings before shedding her clothes and collapsing onto the bed. She surrendered to exhaustion, drifting into a deep sleep that stretched from day into night. With the hotel serving delicious food and coffee, she felt no urgency to explore just yet.

She slept for at least thirty-two hours after her arrival, only waking to eat. When she finally stirred and peered out at the street, a sense of restfulness washed over her, rekindling her desire to leave the hotel's comfort. After freshening up and shaking off the travel fog, she stepped out, leaving her haven in the heart of the city behind.

Everywhere she wandered, kindness and joy surrounded her, wrapping her in a feeling of belonging in this foreign land. She explored the bustling streets for the rest of the day, making her way to the nearby bazaar. As Lucia came upon the outdoor market, rows of vendors buzzed with energy and hard work. She was led by spices, fresh produce, grilled meats, and the fiery aroma of tortillas mingled in the air, drawing her into every stall she passed.

The air filled with the wafting scents of chilis, herbs, and the sweet stickiness of fresh fruits. She sampled grilled cactus, savoring each bite as she drifted from food to crafts, marveling at beautiful jewelry, vibrant clothing, and lovingly crafted souvenirs.

Each artisan display revealed intricate, affordable craftsmanship. Lucia admired the silver work, drawn in by the talent of every artist she encountered. She felt a twinge of regret for not being able to purchase something from each of them.

As she continued to navigate the lively streets, she absorbed the pulse of the city—people working, tourists exploring, and others preparing for the evening rush. At a tourist stand, she secured her bus ticket to one of the pyramid sites for the following day, her anticipation growing.

Lucia decided to try the restaurant Eddie had recommended for dinner. As she wandered through the streets, she became a bit lost. She approached an older man in one of the small shops, asking for directions. Though he spoke little English, he took her hand and led her down the street and around the corner. He pointed to the restaurant half a block away, smiled, and walked off, leaving her to continue on her own.

When she walked through the door, a wave of unique spices and the sound of lively music enveloped her. In the corner, a man in a dark cowboy hat with soulful eyes sang and played guitar, his presence suggesting a life filled with both loss and love. Lucia settled at a table near him and glanced at the menu.

She savored a delicious shrimp dish with garlic and grilled veggies. As she listened to the ballad playing nearby, she recognized the significance of the restaurant's name, La Serenatas. A smile crept across her face as she thought about how the Universe had been serenading her since she arrived in Mexico just days before. So much kindness surrounded her; the beauty of the people and the richness of each moment dripped with deliciousness throughout her journey.

Lucia felt a surge of exhilaration as she anticipated her visit to the pyramids the next day. She sensed something spectacular awaited her there, drawn to the allure of ancient wonders. As she savored the vibrant atmosphere of the eatery, she allowed that thrill to wash over her, fully immersing herself in the moment.

Every aspect of her experience in Mexico City thrilled her. Though she had wondered about safety concerns, having heard tales of crime, her caution rarely morphed into fear. Lucia focused on embracing every moment with awareness of her surroundings, grateful for the richness of her journey, and determined not to allow other people's experiences to overshadow hers.

***

The bus the following day teemed with tourists. Lucia had never liked being labeled a tourist. While it was true, she resented being grouped with travelers who acted entitled to the places they visited. Lucia craved genuine connections with the locals and wanted to embrace the culture and feel the pulse of the place rather than tick off another location on her bucket list and display it on social media. She sensed others on that bus shared her sentiment, but the crowd made it hard to connect, forcing locals into quiet corners.

The ride stretched on, and Lucia tried to find a sense of ease as she hummed softly and gazed dreamily at the landscape passing by. Although she unwittingly noticed an unexpected anxiety tugging at her, a feeling that something significant loomed, though she couldn't pinpoint what it might be or whether it would be harsh or uncomfortable. She felt unsettled by these sensations, especially since she had felt so in tune since stepping onto the airplane.

Lucia let the feeling wash over her, allowing it to flow without clinging to her resistance to it. She had practiced this technique in her mindfulness and meditation sessions, focusing intently on her breath and the sensations within her body, especially when she was uncomfortable. Each moment of stillness allowed her to reconnect with herself, fostering a more profound sense of awareness and calmness in the face of an impending unknown.

Although anxiety had shadowed her during her marriage, her persistent optimism couldn't completely silence the occasional unease when it randomly struck. The moments of anxiety had been minimized, which was her goal, yet each resurgence brought the fear that it might impede her experience.

She recognized that the unsettling buzz stemmed from thoughts about the inevitable future her clairvoyance revealed, filled with uncertainty about how it would unfold. In the past, she experienced these feelings when she strayed from her true self, while others seemed to be driven by hormones, which felt beyond her control. Since this sensation hadn't surfaced with the new experiences in Mexico, she suspected this specific feeling signaled something significant and uncomfortable on the horizon. As she clung to the window of the old bus, she fought the urge to focus on the tension in her shoulders and the churning in her stomach.

Lucia felt a weight pressing down on her, an unsettling sense that something significant loomed ahead. It echoed the moments before she left her husband, infused with a mix of dread and hope. She longed for something good to arise from this foreboding, sure that she was where she needed to be. Yet, her thoughts spiraled out of control.

When she recognized this unhealthy pattern, she closed her eyes and breathed deeply, steadying her racing mind.

Old wounds resurfaced swiftly; memories of unraveling times, of loved ones' battling illness, and moments when she faced hardship so intense that one more push might have sent her over the edge.

Lucia recognized the rabbit hole she teetered on; what haunted her was past trauma, not the present moment. Distinguishing her fears from her intuition often blurred that line. Her body sometimes sent up unnecessary red flags. Even when external circumstances appeared calm, overwhelm would wash over her. She sometimes struggled to separate the two.

To find clarity, she focused intently on the present, allowing it to unfold naturally. One truth anchored her: everything eventually revealed itself. The more she spiraled, the harder it became to navigate the depths of her emotions, and she knew that. She resolved to redirect her mind, to shift away from obsessing over unshakeable dread, and instead invite a different narrative into her thoughts.

Lucia shifted her focus, envisioning the pyramids and wrapping her thoughts in stone and magic, pondering how ancient societies lived. This imagery eased her anxiety, but it wasn't enough. Then she remembered an effortless way to break free from her restless thoughts. An idea sparked—she turned to a child sitting behind her and offered a piece of the snack she had brought. This gesture drew her out of herself, shifting her attention to the joy of serving another. Soon, giggles filled the air as the child pointed out the goats grazing in the distance.

The bus rolled to a stop at the pyramids, and everyone shuffled off, drawn together toward the ancient landmarks. Lucia's trepidation faded as the place's powerful energy enveloped. She walked toward the stones in a daze, feeling their magnetic pull beckoning her closer. Suddenly, she recognized the temple of the moon vibrating before her, its ancient structure gleaming under the light. Her hands ached to touch the warm stone, and she surrendered to the overwhelming urge, gently caressing its surface as the world around her faded away into silence.

In an instant, she found herself transported to an unfamiliar civilization, one filled with vibrant colors and distant sounds. The heat in her lungs transformed into the gritty dust stirred by ancient carts and bustling merchants, their voices blending into a lively symphony as she took in the sights and smells of this old world.

As heavy drumbeats filled her heart, pulsating in rhythm with the ancient echoes of shamans and medicine people, the atmosphere seemed to vibrate with an intensity that transcended mere sound. It didn't swing between dark and light; instead, it emanated pure power and profound awareness, wrapping around her like a protective shroud.

She sensed the collected energy of souls who had lived and died in that sacred place; their stories etched into the very ground beneath her feet. Imprints of suffering intermingled with moments of thriving surged around her in vivid flashes, each one a testament to the resilience of the human spirit.

In that moment, she felt their simple extravagance and grace, the deep connections forged through shared experiences—joy and sorrow, life, and death—beyond the constraints of time. Warmth enveloped her as if she were being cradled by the collective embrace of those who had come before her.

Fear had no place here; instead, there was a profound understanding that this world constituted just one part of their existence, a fleeting chapter in an ongoing journey through the cosmos. The power of their legacy resonated within her, urging her to remember and honor the lives that once thrived in this space.

Lucia sensed the delicate balance that these Indigenous people maintained between realms, existing fluidly in both the physical and the metaphysical without any sense of separation. They had thrived in this life, unburdened by fear of the unknown, their existence interwoven with the rhythms of nature. Amid the images of the community's fervor, she recognized their hearts and boundless souls, vibrant like the colors of the earth and sky around her.

The vision darkened suddenly, revealing a tumultuous time when greed and sacrifice invaded their once-peaceful existence. A new tribe arrived, hierarchical and controlling, imposing their will on the land, and altering its natural rhythms, steering the once-harmonious settlement toward patriarchy. As generations passed, this tribe gradually lost its sense of unity, tragically exchanging the magic of the elements for blood worship and sacrifice, veiling their lives in shadows.

A few resilient families managed to escape before the city's eventual destruction, scattering too deep into the jungles and distant mountains. Some carried fragments of the old ways deep within their bloodlines, but this heritage was often shrouded in secrecy for the sake of survival. This lineage, revered yet haunted, bred fear and confusion.

Those who fled worked tirelessly to reclaim their identities, fervently preserving the power of their ancestors for future generations, even as the weight of history pressed upon them. Lucia felt in her very bones that traces of this lineage survived beyond the present. She pondered their whereabouts, hoping that someone might still reside near their ancestors' sacred lands, maintaining the thread of lost culture.

Suddenly, her thoughts jolted her from the trance, pulling her back to the present moment as she quickly took in her actual surroundings. Determined to get a better vantage point, she began her ascent up the temple of the moon, climbing one block at a time. With each step, her mind cleared, fully present in her body, focusing on the cool stones against her palms and the sting in her thighs. The sensation was grounding. At last, she reached the summit—aching, panting, sweaty, but ignited with an inner fire that seemed to flicker in sync with the temple itself. She stood tall, arms open wide, welcoming the energy around her.

Gasping, she took in the sprawling ancient complex from her newfound perspective. Below, tourists moved about, and as in her trance at the pyramid's base, they began to transform before her eyes into the lost culture that had once thrived here centuries ago. The electric energy of the place flowed through her veins, overwhelming her senses. She sank to the ground, unable to stand, feeling as though she might be swept off the sacred spot and into the sky, mingling with the spirits of her ancestors.

This intensity surged within her, starting at her core and rising through her belly, growing larger with every breath. Lucia felt the accumulated force explode from her chest, reaching out into the lush green jungle beyond the roads, deeper toward distant lands yet untouched.

She felt her consciousness plunge into the trees and roots, descending deeper into the earth, bridging the past and present. At last, it reached the molten lava at the center of the world, perhaps even the Universe itself, guided by this profound power radiating from her heart and her womb, a connection that transcended time and space.

Suddenly, a large hawk screeched above Lucia's head, jolting her from the center of all things. The powerful beat of its wings surged her unease. As she watched the hawk circle before diving toward the ground, it snatched a mouse in its talons, capturing the poor creature near the forbidden grass.

Lucia stood in reverence as nature unfolded before her, the hawk soaring close to the crowd. She scanned the faces around her, searching for anyone who shared her fascination. A dark-haired woman caught her attention, her expression one of admiration as she watched the bird of prey disappear with its prize. This goddess, stationed at the temple's base, seemed to embody the moment as much as Lucia. Moments later, the woman shifted her focus back to a cluster of tourists, and Lucia guessed she was selling something.

As Lucia made her way down the stone steps, she realized the woman was indeed selling vibrant beaded jewelry and appeared to be a local. A shock pierced her chest, just above her sternum, as the woman met her gaze. By the time Lucia reached the bottom of the pyramid, the woman had vanished.

Lucia searched for the bead seller throughout the morning, but as the sun beat down, she surrendered to the heat. Finding a patch of shade, she settled down to eat, seeking to ground herself after such overwhelming visions.

Closing her eyes, Lucia rooted herself into the earth beneath her, asking her life force to connect with Mother Gaia. In her mind's eye, she envisioned herself as a tree, strong and stable, sending roots deep into the soil. Suddenly, the scene shifted from her mind to her heart, where bright green energy pulsed within her chest. She yearned to surrender to it, yet something held her back.

Pain clutched at her, blocking the green wisps of light from expanding. Each attempt to amplify the glow met resistance, snapping back to its smaller size repeatedly. A realization dawned on her: she was avoiding something within her heart.

Lucia knew she needed to confront the pain and uncover its nature. No visions offered insight into the secret her heart guarded, leaving her at a loss about how to rid herself of it. The heaviness sparked an immediate sense of loneliness, perplexing her after two days of feeling so connected to the Universe. The earlier anxiety transformed into a premonition, resounding with past fears. Yet, she tried to remain open-hearted. She had shed much of the shame and guilt that had burdened her, reclaiming her power over the past few years. The need for control had faded as she finally embraced a flow and appreciation she had longed for all her life. So, why did she suddenly feel so alone? What blocked her heart? She felt good about her progress. What the hell was happening?

These emotions threw Lucia for a loop, spawning deep existential angst that lingered for hours. It wasn't the feeling she wanted in this sacred place. And yet, perhaps she was experiencing a little death—maybe that was appropriate.

Random pangs coursed through her as she walked around the complex. Each shock in her chest served as a reminder of her blockage, breaking her focus whenever she tried to move on. It hurt physically, but she knew nothing was wrong with her. In response to the pain, anxiety swelled again within her, manifesting as a sharp panic that took over her comfort. This sensation insisted something was wrong—urgent or dangerous—filling her with discomfort and leaving her at a loss for how to mend it.

Lucia couldn't take it any longer. She recalled her earlier decision to seek a focus beyond herself. Spotting a few travelers with relaxed demeanors, she approached them, introduced herself, and asked where they hailed from. Stewart, Clara, and Max, all in their thirties, mentioned they were from London.

The group engaged in lively conversation throughout the afternoon, settling into their spots in the welcoming shade as they awaited the much-anticipated sunset. Their excitement buzzed in the warm air, especially with the full moon approaching; they knew the landmark would remain open to the public that night to celebrate this beautiful monthly phenomenon. As they chatted, their discussions meandered through varied topics, touching on American and British politics. They reached a consensus that both governments felt outdated, failing to address fundamental human needs and dignity effectively.

Their conversation then shifted to more progressive nations like the Netherlands, Sweden, and Canada, where they noted policies that seemed more attuned to the welfare of their citizens. Each member of the group underscored the importance of upholding human dignity, emphasizing that it should be respected regardless of nationality, race, religion, sexuality, gender, ability, financial status, or belief system. This sentiment brought a sense of unity and shared purpose as they engaged in deep reflections about what it means to prioritize humanity in an increasingly complex world.

Lucia loved discussions like this. They didn't always agree completely, but as they engaged with each other as adults, challenging opinions while honoring them.

Max added relationship models to their list of things deserving of respect. Lucia agreed but asked why that mattered so much to them. Max explained, "All three of us are in a relationship together."

Lucia raised an eyebrow. "Really?" That had never crossed her mind.

"Yeah," Max continued. "Stewart and Clara have been dating for a while and kept things open. Stewart has been seeing a few women and a man, and we joked that Clara didn't know what she wanted back then."

"Then you showed up, right?" Lucia smiled, trying to grasp the dynamic.

Max chuckled. "Exactly! Clara realized she wanted to be with both Stewart and me. We struggled at first since I wasn't interested in being intimate with Stewart. They teased me about my queerness, and Clara joked that my preferences were perfect for her."

Stewart seemed untroubled by this. "I'm the emotional one of our group," he said with a grin.

Lucia admired Max's confidence in expressing their non-binary identity and noted that they seemed to navigate the complexities of their relationship with grace.

They took turns explaining that, eventually, the three of them worked out their relationship hiccups and grew remarkably close. They even moved in together and began discussing the possibility of starting a family. Clara planned to have Stewart's child, but they wished for Max to have parental rights, too.

"Is that even possible?" she asked curiously.

"Sadly, no," Clara replied. "There's no legal protection for families like ours, just like there was no protection for gay and lesbian couples for so long."

Lucia could feel the weight of their reality. It was a conversation that held both hope and frustration, the kind of discourse that left lingering questions about love, identity, and the laws that shape their lives.

The triad shared about their recent eviction, forced out of the flat after the landlord uncovered their relationship. Stewart faced disownment from his parents for the same reason. Max's liberal family embraced their lifestyle, but Clara grappled with revealing the truth to hers, who had often stepped in with financial help. They believed they were supporting her and her boyfriend, unaware that Max was not just a roommate. The trio felt a looming threat to their safety; losing Clara's family's support had dire consequences, as the backing had been their lifeline since the eviction.

They grew somber as they discussed how the world perceived their relationship. Discrimination weighed heavily on their hearts, and tears welled in their eyes. Lucia admitted she had rarely considered these issues before. While she was a part of Seattle's sex-positive community and practiced polyamory with Michael and others, she had not delved deeply into the social challenges surrounding these types of experiences.

Seattle had its bubble of liberal ideals that enveloped Lucia. Yet, as she reflected, memories surfaced of a friend who lost her teaching job for living in a polyamorous household.

Lucia yearned to change societal attitudes. To her, love should cause no harm, and it mattered little who or how people chose to love. Her observations suggested that these relationships often appeared healthier than many monogamous ones she had witnessed.

Max kissed Clara gently on the forehead and reassured her that everything would work out. The warmth of that moment filled Lucia's heart, and she realized the ache in her chest had vanished since meeting her new friends. Instead, a lush warmth flourished within her, as if a vibrant jungle grew between her breasts. Their genuine affection and easy-going nature lifted her spirits, replacing her pain and anxiety with safety and joy.

She spent the remainder of the day and evening with this sweet and thoughtful triad, wandering around the pyramids doing little rituals every time they felt drawn to a space. They would release the negative attachments of the spirits and fill the environment with love. They noticed that every time they did this and moved on, people would flock to that spot after them. People's reactions made them all giggle with delight, and their joy was contagious.

Lucia felt a profound sense of community with her new friends, grateful for the companionship that alleviated her loneliness, even if only for a time. She understood that much of this trip would unfold alone, yet these individuals had helped her regain her balance. Surrounded by their authenticity and seamless flow of unconditional love, she discovered a renewed resilience within herself.

The connection between her companions and her own sense of equilibrium intrigued her. Reflecting on her past, she recognized the patterns that led to those moments when she felt ungrounded, often aligning with the people she surrounded herself with. She noticed a tendency to gravitate toward those burdened by addictions or emotional struggles that dominated their lives. This unhealthy pattern was not what she encountered with this group. They seemed emotionally mature and grounded, although they consistently encountered ignorance about their lifestyle.

Lucia had long told herself that she was drawn to people's creative, passionate sides. The truth was that she felt safe revealing her darkest parts around people who struggled to survive life; she knew they embraced and celebrated her shadow self because they recognized it.

It finally occurred to her that they seemed to derive some twisted pleasure from her struggles, feeling somehow diminished when Lucia radiated light. She recognized it as a kink feeding on darkness, as it brought forth a strange thrill to be in these unhealthy relationships.

Deep down, Lucia realized this pattern trapped her in a role that undermined her personal power. It had become a defense mechanism that no longer served her.

While this tendency helped Lucia embrace her shadow self, it kept her rigidly stuck in it. She awakened to the truth that difficult moments weren't permanent fixtures in her soul to endure. Instead, her shameful parts were mutable, capable of transformation only when exposed to light. By refusing to hide them from herself and others, she finally stepped into this novel approach. She no longer clung to her shadows as lifeboats amid pain. Instead, she acknowledged them, worked through them, and let them dissipate.

Lucia shared her journey with her new friends as they were each expressing their personal growth experiences. She tried to be more specific, explaining, "I understand now that patterns change and evolve with us," she said. "We can confront our darkest parts without judgment. This doesn't mean shadows vanish; they shift, like shapeshifters, taking on forms as we face new challenges. If we haven't fully addressed something, it returns when life triggers it again, giving us another chance to engage. Each time, it emerges differently, shaped by our past efforts and the relationships we navigate."

Lucia reflected on her attachment to her negative qualities as if they were a family member she had no choice but to live with. She recognized the necessity of engaging with this part of herself. Aware that ignoring her not-so-pretty parts cluttered her life by unexpectedly surfacing to disrupt her peace. But she hadn't fully realized that this family member changed each time. Sometimes, they felt less complicated, at other times, more so. The more she acknowledged them without clinging, the less they ruled her existence.

In various moments of her life, Lucia had clung too tightly to her darkness, allowing anxiety, anger, and fear to consume her. She hesitantly admitted that, at times, her self-protection led her to manipulate and control others, convincing herself that no one would truly celebrate her.

Finally, she understood that these shadows didn't define her, nor did she need to hide from them. Each aspect demanded her attention, not her embodiment. These shoddy parts weren't her entirety; it became evident that once she integrated them, she became more available to herself. Lucia explained that once clarity about these things emerged, she began to actualize her world.

Lucia started to perceive her negative qualities as fluid, shifting in and out of her life, reflected in her relationships with others. She realized she didn't have to cling to them. They weren't more integral to her identity than any family member with whom she needed to navigate a relationship. They existed, but their presence was her choice. Just as in any relationship, her shadow parts could grow and evolve if she allowed them.

As Lucia explored this significance with her new friends, she gave them an example. Lucia explained that quitting smoking reflected a deeper understanding of these principles. She detailed that the allure of positive associations with tobacco always pulled her back, while knowing its drawbacks never broke the cycle.

She needed to analyze why she always returned to it, pinpointing her infatuation with the image of smokers. Characters in movies—the creative, rebellious souls who spoke their minds—resonated with her. They embodied a brooding depth and a fearless engagement with darkness.

Smoking had woven itself into her identity; each time she quit, a vibrant part of her life felt stripped away. Inevitably, she returned to it, drawn to the very shadow she tried to escape. The last time she quit, she confronted the truth: it was all bullshit. The positive associations no longer held weight, and dismantling the warped romanticism became essential for her liberation.

She embraced the reality that plenty of her friends didn't smoke and that being a smoker had nothing to do with being a creative or rebellious person. After slightly reminiscing about the smokers' corners and the rare occurrences she encountered outside parties like the one at Sam's, Lucia couldn't help but smile. Missing those moments of camaraderie, she realized that countless opportunities for profound discussions waited inside. Fewer people smoked, and the cool conversations in smoky back alleys were fading into memory.

"Smoking was just a crutch for me," Lucia continued, her voice steady. "I had this unhealthy relationship with my shadow, and breaking down those positive associations shifted everything for me. It's how I've started dismantling other patterns in my life—the dark parts I clung to for far too long."

Though she hadn't smoked in years, she marked the parallels in her current transformation. As she gathered with her new friends, another shift happened within her. The shadow self felt less like a weight and more like a flexible entity, untethered from her core. "I feel my heart opening," she confessed. It's strange, almost liberating. I used to think I had to protect it at all costs."

"Why protect something beautiful?" Clara asked, her brow raised in playful challenge.

Lucia shrugged, her heart lightening. It was easier to fight than to live openly. But now, I see—I don't need to hide. Letting go of those attachments, I can just... be. I can choose to live authentically."

The conversation shifted the atmosphere, grounding her in that moment. The warmth of connection spread through the group as they finalized their gratitude for their chance encounter. Unafraid, she embraced the power of choice—an open, loving self, no longer entangled in old habits.

***

They spent the evening watching the moon hover over the pyramids. The scene felt magical and deeply connective as an aura surrounded the glowing orb in the sky. After rich conversations and fresh insights with her new friends, Lucia felt lighter and different. When the time came to leave the temple, the triad invited her to join them for a late dinner in a nearby town. Accepting with eagerness, Lucia trusted them completely. They had quickly forged a bond, and Lucia knew she could trust them with her life.

Chapter Six

SYNCHRONICITY

When you stop existing and start truly living, each moment of the day comes alive with wonder and synchronicity.

~ Steve Maraboli

Lucia had embarked on many voyages in her life, taking solo road trips and even a journey to Prague without companions. And each adventure left her with a wealth of experiences. She learned that to continue gathering stories, she needed to keep moving, but it was essential to pause and reflect in order to truly integrate them. In those moments of stillness, she meditated, relaxed, and opened herself to the insights that emerged from her surroundings and her inner self.

Seeking a moment of quiet, Lucia found a modest room in the dusty little town near the temple, planning to meditate before the late dinner. The hotel's mistress warned her that soon, the city would come alive with festivities. Grateful for the current stillness, Lucia lit a candle wrapped in a silk scarf she had brought for such occasions. She closed the shades, slipped in her earbuds, and let the soothing notes of traditional flute music fill her ears.

With her eyes shut, her mind drifted through the day's experiences, allowing them to float by without attachment. Yet, she found herself grasping tightly to the memory of the captivating conversation earlier. Clara had shared her struggle with an existential crisis of the heart within their triad relationship. Clara explained she felt an overpowering belief that she should only commit to one partner, and it drove her to withdraw from both Max and Stewart. Despite her deep love for them, everything felt "off" to her.

Clara communicated that she had believed her intuition whispered that something was wrong or unhealthy. She finally voiced her feelings to her partners. They urged her to meditate and perform a clarification spell. Neither wanted to lose her, but they prioritized her peace of heart. That opportunity led Clara to her ultimate realization: her monogamous conditioning and religious upbringing had burrowed so deeply into her psyche that they distorted her perception of reality. Finally, Clara found that the absence of pressure deepened her love for them, and within that love, she discovered freedom from her social conditioning.

In her hazy hotel room, Lucia felt Clara's struggle as if Clara's heart had been yanked away from her mind. Lucia curled around her midsection. As she began to unravel Clara's journey, her body slowly loosened and expanded.

Lucia thought about what Clara had told her: she had left both partners for over a month to immerse herself in a retreat center, meditating, cleansing, and engaging in a therapy called Somatic Experiencing, or SE. Clara shared with Lucia that SE integrated physical, emotional, and mental responses, a process allowing her to unlock her nervous system's reactions to conditioning. Intrigued, Lucia resolved to look it up later.

Clara revealed that her understanding of ethical relationships stemmed from deep-rooted beliefs that had nothing to do with right or wrong. Her relationships didn't feel bad at all; instead, they had been clouded by the notion that polyamory was unhealthy or socially unacceptable or that loving multiple people was impossible. She recognized that her fear was rooted in social constructs unrelated to her own situation.

Inspired by Clara's introspection, Lucia admired her, applauding the complex work she undertook to unravel the ideas that had constricted her.

Lucia realized she had grown attached to this conversation during her meditation, feeling hopeful and inspired. She chose to let it go, recognizing that while the attachment was positive, it was essential not to grasp it too tightly. Clearing her mind, she allowed her body to fill with white light and took deep, intentional breaths.

A new kind of love washed over her with a flood of luminescent energy, one unlike anything she had experienced before. It felt familiar, reminiscent of the affection she had offered children after they stumbled and fell, a natural response. In that vibrancy, she sensed a nurturing presence, the feeling she imagined reversed from what a child felt when their mother soothed them with a kiss to mend a scraped knee.

Supported and secure in this love, Lucia's heart burst open as she envisioned a radiant white light shooting throughout the room. The tingling energy she'd felt at the pyramid now enveloped her entire being.

The colorless illumination transformed into a vibrant emerald green. In that moment, Lucia felt as though she dissolved into the Universe, feeling a profound connection with everything and everyone around her.

Tears streamed down her cheeks, jolting Lucia out of her meditation. Suddenly, Lucia caught the moonlight filtering through the curtains and checked the time, realizing she needed to hurry to the restaurant.

After quickly freshening up, she dashed out the door, heading toward the place that would change her life forever.

***

The new friends waited for Lucia at a table inside the restaurant, welcoming her with broad smiles and warm hugs that made it clear they liked her as much as she liked them. This simple openness nourished her spirit. Not long ago, she had battled the belief that people weren't interested in her, and this connection began to heal the wound of feeling misunderstood. Lucia cherished the chance to converse about her rich inner life during this transformative stage, able to express herself authentically without fearing she was "too much" for anyone.

Lucia had always been a personable soul, but the more she immersed herself in meditation and spirituality, the more introverted she felt. Once convinced she was an extrovert, she now found little desire for large gatherings. Since meeting Michael, Lucia became more social yet still avoided small talk. Instead, she craved deep, meaningful conversations. And the spark in her friends' eyes when her introspective tales inspired them fed her soul.

The evening deepened, and laughter strung their conversations late into the night. Lucia forged a strong bond with Clara, drawn together by their shared dedication to self-awareness and recognition of social conditioning. At the same time, she adored Max and Stewart for their vibrant energies and unconditional support of one another.

After one too many margaritas, they enthusiastically decided that Lucia would join them on a trip to the Yucatan Peninsula to visit the Black Pyramids in Xcambo. Eager to immerse herself in Mayan culture, Lucia had already planned to visit Cozumel for snorkeling, so this wasn't too far from her original intention.

She had long dreamed of snorkeling there ever since her friend returned from a vacation two decades ago, weaving tales of coral reefs and brightly colored fish. Her friend called it the most magical place she'd ever visited. It felt beautifully synchronistic that this adventure finally led her to Cozumel after all these years.

Lucia approached the bar when the server remained too busy to attend to them. She slipped beside a tall, handsome man with a warm, toothy smile, dressed in a relaxed button-up shirt and Bermuda shorts. Introducing herself with a warm smile, she hoped to spark up a light conversation as they waited together.

His name was Angel, which captured her attention—a unique name that hinted at his intriguing personality and potential contributions to her journey. Lucia was curious to learn more about this fascinating person and wondered what interesting stories or insights he might share during their moments together.

To her surprise, the conversation flowed with effortless clarity and insight. Lucia invited the charming man to join their group, and he accepted with an ecstatic grin and a soft chuckle. While she fetched the drinks, she noted how his smile held a secret, reminiscent of the Cheshire Cat in *Alice in Wonderland*.

As they talked, Lucia learned that Angel hailed from the area of Mexico City where she had recently stayed. This friendly stranger shared captivating stories with the group of desert adventurers, encounters with shamans, and his explorations of "certain mind-altering substances," as he humorously put it. Angel spoke of meeting animal guides and journeying through the Universe among cacti and dunes, each tale inviting them deeper into his world.

Angel shared tales of his oneness with all that exists, how he felt the Universe pulse through his cells. He claimed he recognized himself as part of everything and everything as part of him. He felt both tiny and insignificant yet vast and expansive. Angel explained how his teachers had shown him that everyone and everything is interconnected, illustrating a web of interactions, like a spider's silk, weaving through each life and choice. Yet, Angel revealed that he only completely understood this connection after losing his brother to cancer.

As he spoke of his brother, tears glistened in his eyes, and his voice carried a somber wisdom. He recounted the harrowing journey through the sudden onset of Acute Myeloid Leukemia and how the blood cancer swiftly consumed his brother's body and claimed his life within months. The group listened, captivated by every word tumbling from his lips.

"My brother Miquel's illness brought immense suffering to him and to all of us who stood by," Angel said, his heartache evident as he reflected on his brother's pain. "He didn't want to die. I tried to comfort him, painting the afterlife as a beautiful place. I helped him envision a warm light filled with love so strong, no one would want to leave it. I told him about the people waiting to welcome him home. For a moment, it eased his fear. But then the terror would return to his eyes, and I simply sat with him, watching him wrestle with death."

Lucia and the others sat in stunned silence, awestruck by Angel's honesty and vulnerability as he bared his soul in the bustling restaurant, surrounded by strangers. Clara blinked back tears, and Stewart wrapped his arm around her while Max held her hand, all of them visibly moved by Angel's story.

Lucia felt her heart break for Angel and his brother, the echoes of his pain resonating within her. Yet, she marveled at Angel's strength to engage in these difficult conversations with a brother he often clashed with. At the start, Angel had described Miquel as distant, struggling to grasp his spiritual journey. But all that changed when cancer made its brutal entrance. Right then, it was clear that Angel's sole focus was being present for his brother. He spoke of it as the most explicit purpose he had ever known, walking beside Miquel through his final days.

"When the cancer worsened, and my brother could no longer endure another round of chemo, we brought him home to die," Angel continued, his voice weighted with emotion. "Miquel often cried out how unfair it all was." That was the first time Angel mentioned his brother's name. "All I could do was agree. Each time he cried out to God for answers, pieces of my heart peeled away like layers of an onion. I held space for him, cried with him, shared in his anger. At times, he resembled a trapped animal, bewildered by his failing body. His fear was palpable, clinging to life like a mother tiger to her stillborn cub. With no escape in sight, the cage felt smaller and smaller."

By now, tears streamed down Angel's face, but he pressed on. "He lasted only four days in hospice. The day he passed, getting out of bed felt impossible to me; I had to cling to furniture just to stand. But I pushed forward; the thought of not being there with him was unbearable. He died peacefully that night after we eased his pain with morphine. When he left this world, I expected relief that he was free from suffering. Instead, I found myself wishing for just a bit more time. I wasn't ready to let him go, even knowing the weight of his agony."

Lucia listened, her own heart aching for Angel and the bond he shared with Miquel, a connection forged in struggle and unwavering love.

Angel looked at each of them and took Lucia's trembling hand. "This is the most interesting part, my dear," he began. "Through the pain and the tremendous grief I endured after losing my brother, I didn't let my heart harden. I kept it broken open."

Lucia let out a sharp cry, unable to contain it even with everyone surrounding them. The waiter glanced over but quickly turned away. She gripped Angel's hand tightly, almost too tightly to be comfortable. As the strange noise escaped her, she felt a wave of relief wash over her, and her body and grip loosened. She needed to hear this experience and connect with his story, but it was heart-wrenching. Angel's journey offered something she had always lacked: an open heart through suffering. He had a more expansive capacity than anyone she had ever encountered.

Angel excused himself. "Don't worry. When I return from a cigarette, I'll share some uplifting stories from my travels and maybe even about a few of my teachers. I always sandwich the hard stuff with the uplifting, as does life." With a loud scrape of his chair, he brushed back his hair and turned toward the door.

No one spoke for a long five minutes, sipping their drinks in silent reverence. Lucia couldn't tell if the others stayed quiet out of respect or wonder—perhaps both.

When Angel returned, he wore a giant grin, radiating the energy of an eager teenager despite being in his forties. He plopped down and exclaimed, "I just ran into one of the most fascinating women I know. She invited me onto her boat tomorrow! I asked if there was room for all of you, and she said absolutely! The only catch is she's headed to Cozumel and around the Yucatan Peninsula, and the trip will take at least a few weeks, maybe more. But she's got accommodations for all of us. Are you up for a little adventure?"

The friends exchanged glances, amazement lighting up their faces, and all at once responded, "YES!" Laughter erupted as the group shared they already had plans for the Yucatán.

Lucia, her heart racing at the thought of snorkeling, spoke up, "I've always wanted to go to Cozumel. It sounds like heaven." Angel nodded, his enthusiasm matching hers. The idea of mingling with fish in that underwater garden sent electric thrills across her skin.

Excusing himself again, Angel rushed off to fetch the woman. Moments later, he returned, accompanied by a captivating figure. They walked through the door together, laughter spilling effortlessly between them.

Lucia felt a rush of heat, goosebumps scattering across her arms as she locked eyes with this goddess striding toward them. In an instant, she was whisked back to the memories of her earlier meditation. This woman embodied love itself—at least, that's how it felt as the beautiful figure floated toward her.

This ethereal woman had long, flowing, ebony hair that swished with her every movement, following the curves of her body as if it were a supporting character in her movie. She wore sandals that laced up her calves, complementing her graceful, sun-kissed skin, and a white blouse that slipped off one shoulder, hinting at a casual elegance. Her patchwork skirt fell just below her knees, a riot of colors and patterns that danced around her legs, but Lucia couldn't distinguish the designs. Instead, she imagined each patch held a story woven from memories and experiences, and this woman was its keeper, a living tapestry of adventures just waiting to be unraveled. The air around her seemed to hum with quiet magic, and Lucia felt drawn to her as if she were meant to become part of the woman's enchanting world.

Lucia felt a surge of emotions wash over her as she became acutely aware that her mouth was hanging open. She had been locked in a gaze with the woman's dark, chocolatey eyes since the moment the deity of grace had entered the room. It struck her as strange how she absorbed every detail—the graceful line of the woman's profile, the way her presence seemed to command the space—yet all these observations collided in her mind in a single, vivid instant.

Snapping to attention as her thoughts raced, Lucia mumbled to herself, "Oh, shit, I think I might have had too many margaritas."

With that realization, she reached across the table for the woman's hand, captivated by her presence. The enchantress purred, "My name is Ixchel. I think I saw you at the pyramids. Who are you?"

Lucia struggled to find her words, stammering, "Lucia..." She inhaled deeply, trying to steady herself. "I saw you selling jewelry; why would you sell jewelry when you have a boat big enough to sleep so many?" The words tumbled out, a jumbled mix of curiosity and embarrassment.

Ixchel curled her glistening, luscious lips into a half-smile. "Never make assumptions, dear one," she replied, her tone sharp yet playful. The remark stung; Lucia suddenly understood how misguided her assumptions had been, equating a seller at the pyramids with poverty.

"Please forgive my assumption," Lucia said, her voice softening. "I'm ashamed to admit I thought I was above such misjudgments." Her humility hung in the air between them, a fragile bridge toward understanding.

Ixchel offered a sweet, deep chuckle, winking as she squeezed Lucia's hand. "Dearest Lucia, there will never be shame around me again. I don't believe in it. But I won't hesitate to point out your mistakes." Another chuckle followed, accompanied by a squeeze that sent a jolt through Lucia. Intimidated and enthralled, she found herself entirely captivated by Ixchel.

In that moment, Lucia melted into oblivion; no world existed beyond the two of them. Somehow, they drifted to the restaurant's dance floor, their bodies moving together as if drawn by an invisible force. They exchanged no words about the electric energy between them, yet the warmth of their connection lingered in the air like a melody. Each subtle touch felt like an unspoken promise; a truth shared without the need for details or discussion about the future. It simply was.

As the evening began to draw to a close, Ixchel informed the group that she would wait for them at the dock in Heroica Veracruz, where her boat awaited their arrival. The journey to the docks would take time, and she couldn't accompany them; family matters required her attention before her departure.

Ixchel had spent the day selling jewelry for her sister, who needed a break from her responsibilities. While in Mexico City, she explained that she had visited her sister, nieces, nephews, Mother, and Father while also tending to some work at her old school. Angel mentioned that Ixchel was once an accomplished architect and had built a comfortable life for herself, which allowed her to purchase a charming boat where she loved to host gatherings.

She shared that a spiritual teacher guided her on the path to self-discovery. This teacher had introduced her to Angel, and they both studied the Toltec Way under the same shaman. Despite her curiosity, Lucia sensed it would be inappropriate to delve deeper into their spiritual journey that night. The questions tugged at her, but Lucia chose to keep them to herself, captivated by the mysteries lingering in the air.

After seeing the visions of people scattering into the forests while touching the stones of the pyramid, Lucia yearned to explore the ancient ways of carrying the secret lineage. She believed that there would be ample time on the water to ask questions.

The thought of not seeing Ixchel again brought a heaviness to her chest, unable to imagine a world where they weren't connected. Each synchronicity resonated deeply within Lucia, hinting at it being necessary in a way she didn't yet grasp but could feel in her very bones.

That night, sleep enveloped her like a soft blanket, cradling her in warmth and potential. For the first time, she felt a core peace that seemed unshakable. In her dreams, she rode the sensations of Ixchel's skin against hers, a tender touch that mingled with the vibrant colors of coral reefs as they swam among the shimmering fish. The water swirled around them, alive with possibility, echoing the unspoken bond they shared.

***

Lucia tidied her affairs and checked out of her room. The mistress of the hotel asked, "Will you be returning, ma'am?"

Lucia paused, considering the question before replying, "We shall see. I doubt it, but there's always a chance." She hugged the kind mistress of the tiny hotel, pressing a kiss on her cheek before turning away toward her next adventure.

Outside, children played in the street, their laughter ringing with joyful abandon. Lucia lingered for a moment, captivated by their carefree voices and the palpable joy in their hearts. She cherished this beautiful start to her journey but reminded herself of the challenges that had brought her to this point.

How could she possibly explain to anyone that this journey with five strangers was a clever idea? Perhaps she didn't need to describe it. Trusting the Universe, she prepared for the trip while staying smart about her choices. Still, doubt crept in—was it wise to share a boat with individuals she had only just met? Yet, an undeniable urge drove her to leap. At this juncture, the risks seemed manageable. She told herself that she sacrificed nothing but time if things went awry, and Lucia had safeguards in place should she need to escape the boat.

Deep within her, a certainty resided: this boat trip was exactly what she needed. Telling anyone else about her decision, however, felt unwise. They would likely scold her, citing the dangers of trusting strangers. With a deep, all-consuming sigh, she muttered, "Oh well," as she stepped beyond her comfort zone.

Giving herself a pep talk, she asserted, "I have to do this! I can feel it in my bones!" With renewed determination, she walked to the bus stop to meet the others. Clara, Stewart, and Max were running late because they returned their rental car, panting as they approached. Angel strolled up last, appearing calm despite a sheen of sweat, squeezing into the bus between a frail old lady and a young man with earbuds who barely budged. The obliviousness of the man, who looked American, irked Lucia. Embarrassment washed over her; she hated sharing a country with someone so unaware of others in his space.

She scanned the tattered bus, studying the faces around her; each line and crease telling stories of joy and sorrow. What experiences had shaped them? Did they carry losses like Angel's, the pain of his brother echoing in his life? "Probably," she speculated. With each passing year, she understood that everyone faced hardship and loss. The people she admired—the ones who continued to grow and show kindness—held a quiet strength that inspired her.

The ride dragged on, yet a spark ignited when someone began to sing. By the journey's end, strangers had transformed into friends. It always amazed her how one inspired voice could break through the dullness, bridging gaps in a stinky, dusty bus rattling over dirt roads and highways.

As the singing filled the air, laughter bubbled up, and smiles bloomed across faces. They merged into a single entity, their intertwined differences dissolving in the pursuit of one simple pleasure: play. Even the guy with earbuds let the music seep into his world. Lucia swore that as the group sang, the bus felt lighter, the jarring bumps softened, as if the wheels glided above a layer of cotton, sharing a collective moment of joy and connection.

When they stepped off the bus, they embraced like a family reuniting—beautiful yet tinged with sadness. Each face glowed with a smile, and those they encountered throughout the day couldn't help but catch that joy. When asked about the source of their happiness, they simply smiled wider, leaving others to wonder. No one could quite articulate the magic that unfolded on the bus that day.

The walk to the docks stretched longer than anyone had anticipated, but they paid little attention. They danced through the streets like the children Lucia had watched playing earlier: carefree and playful, teasing one another as they went.

When they finally reached the dock, they spotted Ixchel preparing her boat with a few sturdy men and women—her dedicated crew. The larger fishing boat proved its worth as the team learned to find fruitful spots. Only one crew member would join them on this trip, but Ixchel promised to assist alongside Angel, who possessed a knack for navigation and seamanship. Their adventure felt like a promise, infusing an air of excitement into the salty breeze.

They launched an hour before sunset, coasting smoothly over the water as splashes of oranges and magenta spread across the horizon. It felt as though the ocean welcomed them with a stunning natural light show, a preview of the beauty that awaited as day transitioned into night. Jesus, the captain, promised Ixchel a moment of peace to watch the sky transform into a magnificent canvas of burnt oranges and purples. The colors shifted effortlessly, watercolors bleeding into one another, merging from one shade to the next, creating an ethereal display that seemed almost too beautiful to be real.

As they drifted along, the gentle sounds of the waves complemented the breathtaking view, inviting a sense of calm and wonder.

After what seemed like a year packed into twenty minutes, Ixchel announced dinner as the sun finally dipped below the horizon. The crew had caught more fish than they could sell that day, ensuring a feast. Unbeknownst to them, Angel had been cooking throughout the sunset, his attention devoted to the meal while they absorbed the beauty around them. He served freshly grilled fish paired with local vegetables and a lovely white wine. The flavors danced on their tongues as they savored Angel's culinary creations.

Clara leaned back, her eyes wide with delight. "This is the best meal I've ever had!" she exclaimed, laughter bubbling up as she realized how loudly she had declared it.

Angel's face lit up. He explained he had brought herbs from his mother's garden that very day, which was why he was late to the bus. Those herbs had traveled with him unnoticed throughout the journey. "Only my mother grows the herbs that create the 'best meal ever!'" he proclaimed, pride evident in his voice. They all shared a laugh as the boat began to glide forward again, the night air alive with camaraderie and the lingering scents of their feast.

Ixchel reassured them that they would sail through the night until the captain grew tired. At that point, they would anchor, allowing him to rest. When Ixchel awoke, she would move them again, ensuring the captain had enough time to sleep before they reached his favorite deep-sea fishing spot at the optimal hour.

Everyone settled in for the night except for Ixchel and Lucia. Together, they perched on the deck, fingers intertwined, gazing at the vastness of the starry sky. Ixchel spun tales of the astrological animals, her stories alive with detail and vibrancy, diverging from the dry facts Lucia had absorbed in college. Each word flowed like poetry, wrapping around Lucia's heart and filling it with warmth. She reveled in the silky rhythms of Ixchel's voice, reminiscent of old blues songs that soothed even the most restless spirits.

Suddenly, Ixchel paused, her gaze piercing as she searched Lucia's eyes. "Who do you want to be, my dearest?" she asked, her voice a gentle current amidst the cool night air.

Lucia, caught off guard by the question, took what felt like hours to respond, though only minutes passed. Finally, she spoke with a direct tone, "I want to be the best version of myself. I want to be authentically me. I believe that when I embrace my true self, I align with the flow of the Universe. When I shed all my distractions and doubts, I tap into a powerful Universal force." A half-smile creased the side of Ixchel's cheek, and a twinkle sparkled in her eye.

Ixchel grasped Lucia's hand, leading her beneath the deck to her cabin. Lucia trailed behind a quiet acceptance in her steps. The air thickened with the scent of salt and wood, wrapping around them as they descended into the cool, dim space of the cabin, where secrets waited to be shared. In a flash, Ixchel peeled every strip of clothing from her flesh as Lucia watched in amazement. However, she used more tenderness and care to dismantle Lucia's clothing. Finally, they stood facing each other, their gazes locked. Lucia recognized that shame had no place here, nor did anything else, except for their two naked bodies, exposed and unguarded. In that moment, the world around them faded, leaving only the electric connection between them raw and undeniable.

They melted into one another, their soft mouths meshing as one entity, pulsing, and writhing to bring themselves into one breath. The lines between them blurred, their movements synchronized, erasing any distinction between their cells. In that shared space, they became a single entity, pulsating with a rhythm that defied separation. Each gesture flowed seamlessly into the next, their connection deepening with every breath. In this intimacy, the world outside faded away, leaving only the heat of their proximity and the unspoken understanding that bound them.

As Lucia slid into Ixchel's vulva, she felt a surge of magic wash over her. A vibrant spectrum of colors spread across the Universe, each hue pulsating with life and energy. Ixchel tightened, and within seconds, they started to writhe together, the vibration surging from the tips of their toes, coursing up their legs and hips, settling deep in their bellies, and finally reaching their hearts.

The electricity crackled, weaving an unspoken bond between them that charged the air. Lucia immersed herself in the vibrant swirl of colors surrounding them, each hue palpitating with life and energy, pulling her deeper into the moment. Lucia felt a guttural howl coming from deep in her groin, pushing through her body and echoing from her vocal cords. They lost all control as they orgasmed together, their bodies writhing and spasming somehow in unison.

They collapsed, embracing, touching as much of one another's bodies as they possibly could. Lucia couldn't speak or move. They lay there still and naked, panting. At last, they drifted into sleep, merging into a warm, flesh-and-bone puddle on the bed.

Clara pounded on the door, shaking them awake. "You two want to join the party? Jesus left a note to wake you so we could get moving. It's time to fly, butterflies!" Her laughter echoed like a jackal, teasing them without acknowledging their moans from just hours before. The urgency in her voice cut through the haze of sleep, pulling them from their lovely dreams and into the chaos of the day.

It would take them around six days to reach Cozumel, allowing time for anchoring, resting, and fishing. Ixchel, who called Xcambo her sacred root, had navigated this route countless times; she preferred not to rush. The journey would be far more enjoyable if they spent time relaxing and savoring the sunsets.

No one mentioned the obvious connection between Ixchel and Lucia. Their mutual attraction simmered just beneath the surface, evident in the way they gravitated toward each other, rarely straying far from the other's side, except when Ixchel took the helm. It was a tension that sparked in stolen glances and lingering touches, a silent language they both seemed to understand.

Even in the group, their eyes would find each other, a subtle acknowledgment of the bond they shared. When Stewart, Max, and Clara relished their time learning to fish with Jesus, who exuded warmth and kindness. They practiced their Spanish while he worked on his English, exchanging playful banter as they teased one another about their novice fishing skills, each trying to master the local slang with a laugh. The atmosphere buzzed with camaraderie, illuminating the shared experience beneath the vast sky.

The vibe on the boat radiated calm and peace. Lucia realized she could no longer remember the grip of anxiety. Instead, they floated on the skirts of the Universe, witnessing the waves and currents weaving the threads of time and space. In stillness, they found tranquility, a delicate balance enveloping them. It was the most harmonious she had ever felt.

Her passion for Ixchel unfolded naturally, devoid of drama. Genuine sweetness blossomed between them, leaving Lucia's heart open and steady, free from the shadows of doubt or indignation. Often, she sat for hours at the stern with Ixchel, mesmerized by the waves, tracing their movements with her mind. It felt like a waking meditation, where she imagined the vibrant life swimming and thriving beneath them, a world teeming with possibility.

Slipping into a trance felt effortless in this sunlit space. One afternoon, as warmth kissed Lucia's face and a gentle breeze grazed her skin, Lucia envisioned herself as seaweed swaying beneath the waves. There was a surrender to the rhythm of the tides, her rhythm moving back and forth against the rocky shore. In that moment, she became the seaweed, flowing with the ocean's essence.

The sharpness of the rocks could not break her; instead, she felt their presence, a reminder of strength and resilience. In this role, she experienced a beautiful synchronicity between the reef and the water, a profound oneness with the vibrant life teeming in the currents.

The boat rocked gently beneath her, lulling her deeper into the imagery for nearly an hour. As she slowly emerged from her trance, she reflected on the soothing sensation of being at one with the Universe. Nothing could disrupt that harmony; it enveloped her in a serene embrace. She longed to carry this peacefulness throughout her life.

Then, Angel's tale about his brother resurfaced in her mind, where he spoke of the necessity of suffering for an open heart. She pondered how these contrasting truths might intertwine. Could she embody the seaweed and endure that kind of heartbreak? A sense of determination sparked within her as she resolved to share her thoughts with Ixchel.

After sharing her visions, Lucia asked Ixchel, "How does one feel like seaweed crashing against the rocks, unharmed, when facing a tragedy like what Angel endured?"

Ixchel's deep, rich eyes sparkled, revealing golden flecks that flickered like earthy fire. How had Lucia missed that magical quality? As memories of gazing into her lover's eyes filled her mind, her question slipped away. Only now did she genuinely appreciate the golden flames within them.

Ixchel's laughter drew Lucia back into the moment. "You are so easily distracted, love... are you ready for me to whack some philosophy on you?"

Lucia sputtered, nearly spraying sweet mango juice. "You mean wax?" she managed through peals of laughter.

"No, I mean whack!" Ixchel said, playfully smacking Lucia on the side of her leg. "Do you want me to answer or not?"

"Yes, I do. I'm just teasing, honey." Lucia grinned, warmth spreading between them.

Ixchel winked and continued, "You can embody seaweed during trauma, but it's not what you think. It's about releasing the need to control your feelings.

"One must fully experience suffering, death, and tragedy. Allowing oneself to be raw and tender is essential. It's easy to distract ourselves from that discomfort, especially when we grapple with repeated heartache.

"We tend to seek quick relief from pain. While this seems more effortless in the short term, the trauma lingers, stretching the agony longer.

"When we permit ourselves to experience grief completely—crying, screaming, resting when needed—the suffering moves through us instead of boring deep into our souls. From this movement, we find opportunities to grow rather than fester.

"This is how we become like seaweed; it's not that we cultivate such non-attachment out of indifference. We don't rise above our feelings because we claim to be spiritual.

"It's about facing trauma with open hearts, allowing ourselves to break repeatedly, trusting that this journey will lead to expansiveness beyond our imagination. It requires faith in the process and a commitment to remain present. None of us escapes hardship, pain, and grief."

Angel stood behind them, quietly absorbing their conversation. Finally, he spoke up, startling Lucia while Ixchel wasn't unfazed." "I agree with you, sister; your words carry wisdom. Yet, I'd like to gently remind us that suffering—both ours and other people's—does not serve a purpose for our growth. There's no mystical reason behind our pain. No one chooses to suffer, even from their highest, most ethereal selves." His voice resonated, echoing "into the vast sky. "Suffering itself holds no intrinsic meaning. What matters is how we respond, how we reshape pain into a chance to become more of ourselves."

Lucia felt a lump form in her throat. When she tried to speak, only a faint squeak emerged. She took a long sip of air, then stood, embracing Angel tightly. "Thank you for your insight and your open heart." She turned to Ixchel, kissing her softly. "I can't find the words to express what your wisdom means to me."

Ixchel took her hand and squeezed it firmly. "Some of us have learned these lessons the hard way. You've navigated many challenges, just not this one yet. Perhaps our experiences will help you stay grounded when grief inevitably comes knocking."

They all sighed, and Lucia offered to make dinner if Angel cleaned the fish from that day's catch. Nothing could compare to that first day's meal, but she would do her best. Cooking felt like an act of love, each movement pouring passion into the pan. Something had shifted with that day's conversation; the world shimmered with new clarity, as if a veil had lifted.

Angel strummed his guitar, and Stewart's voice soared while Max and Clara banged on empty buckets, keeping the rhythm alive. Ixchel and Lucia danced, their movements intertwining, though Lucia often stepped on Ixchel's feet. Eventually, they found their footing, anchoring in the magic of the sunset. They sipped the fancy tequila Jesus had brought, laughter spilling from them like music, freeing them from all cares.

As the sun sank into the horizon, two dolphins arched gracefully from the water. Just as the sun took its last breath, a fleeting green flash ignited the sky. Jesus grinned, and Angel explained how rare this phenomenon was. They embraced it as an omen, a sign that they were precisely where they needed to be. They decided to anchor through the night so they could reach Cozumel by the following evening, eager to continue their celebration with Jesus by their side. When he pulled out his harmonica, they welcomed him into their joyful ensemble. With spirits lifted, it felt as though an enchantment had freed them from long carried burdens, leaving only lightness and joy in its wake.

Chapter Seven
FINDING BALANCE

Dance with the waves, move with the sea, let the rhythm of the water set your soul free.

- Christy Ann Martine

Cozumel felt like a dream, with the sweet scent of flowers greeting Lucia at every turn. The vibrant colors of the market danced around her as stalls brimmed with handcrafted goods and fresh produce. The laughter of vendors mingled with the chatter of locals, creating an intoxicating atmosphere that wrapped around her in a lovely embrace. The sounds of lively music floated through the air, adding to the enchantment of the scene, and Lucia couldn't help but smile as she soaked in the energy of this paradise. Each moment felt like a celebration of life, pulling her deeper into the heart of the island's charm.

As she wandered away from the bustling crowd, she found herself strolling along a rough dirt path, lost in the moment and fully immersed in the experience. While her thoughts drifted, a giant red hibiscus suddenly brushed against her face, startling her. She chuckled softly, recalling her father's familiar words: "Be smart, not scared." Questioning whether she was being clever right then.

Though fear didn't grip her, a wave of uncertainty washed over her as she continued along the dusty, isolated road, flanked by towering palm trees and the distant sound of waves lapping at the shore. The solitude offered a sense of freedom, yet a small voice in the back of her mind whispered doubts, reminding her to stay vigilant amid the beauty surrounding her.

In an instant, a teenage boy emerged from behind a parked car. His movements were sharp and threatening. Wild hair framed his face, giving the impression that he hadn't bathed in days or weeks. Desperation glinted in his eyes; he squinted at her, sizing her up. Lucia's heart thundered in her chest. He seemed to expect fear; a reaction he didn't get from her.

Taking a steadying breath, she held his gaze. She noticed the dark, wet stain on his torn pants, uncertain if it was blood or something else entirely. As he fidgeted, she recalled the importance of flowing with him. She gently stepped to match his unpredictable rhythm, keeping her body in sync with his. A smile broke across her face as she reached out and touched his shoulder.

Surprise flickered in his eyes; he jumped back, confusion painted on his features. Her calmness disarmed him. "¿Cómo te llamas?" she asked softly in Spanish. His response was mumbled, almost inaudible. Without another word, he turned and sprinted down the alleyway, leaving her wondering about the shadows he carried within.

She stood there, reeling at what had just happened, realizing the potential for a much darker outcome. Gathering herself, she scanned her surroundings, reflecting on the many places she had wandered alone since her trip to Mexico. She had trusted the Universe for care, yet her father's words echoed starkly in her mind. Random suffering felt inevitable, but she believed that remaining authentic, aware, mature, and true to her integrity is essential for an extraordinary life. Recognizing that facing suffering is inevitable, she would strive to be her best self in the midst of it.

Trusting her place in the Universal flow, Lucia knew she had to be pragmatic. Balancing ideals with the chaos of pain and hardship proved crucial. As she reached the dock, she sank into a seat at a bustling café. The high from her journey made it challenging to stay grounded, leaving her in a mild state of dissociation. She felt like a balloon, floating above it all, the week spent on the boat having lulled her into a cocooned bliss. Still shaking, the nervous system buzzed after the encounter with the boy.

As Lucia approached the dock, Clara's voice rang out, "Are you ready, gorgeous?"

Lucia shook off her thoughts and recalled their afternoon plans to venture out on the boat to one of the best local snorkeling spots. "Yes, love! I'm coming!"

***

The water sparkled like tiny diamonds, whispering in Morse code to the ocean's spirits. They circled the island toward a secluded spot Ixchel had visited countless times. Lucia felt a deep connection with the world beneath the boat, sharing with friends that it felt like home.

As they pulled the boat into the magical cove, palm trees lined the shore, standing tall against a rippled blanket of soft tan sand. Not a soul lingered nearby; fortunately, this was not tourist season. While the risk of rough weather loomed, gentle breezes caressed their cheeks, cooling the sun's relentless heat. The water calmed alongside them, swaying barely enough to rock the boat. Vivid colors of the sea and shore enveloped them as Jesus broke bread, preparing them for the hours spent in the dimension below.

Finally, Lucia and Ixchel jumped in together, their masks and flippers snug against their bodies. Lucia followed Ixchel, who glided through the water like a mermaid. In her imagination, Ixchel transformed into a siren, singing with open-hearted love and profound wisdom. They passed colossal pieces of vibrant coral jutting from the rocky reef. Fish of every imaginable color swam around them, unafraid and curious.

Lucia almost lost Ixchel, captivated by the mesmerizing seascape. After what felt like ten minutes of swimming, Ixchel slowed. They found themselves surrounded by bright yellow and orange coral, almost glowing in the sunlight filtering through the water. The depths had grown shallower. An eel poked its monstrous head from a crevice in the rocks below, startling them. Lucia hovered a few feet back, mesmerized by the gaping mouth that opened and closed, waiting for a meal.

A swarm of silverfish enveloped them, a shimmering wall of movement. Ixchel gently guided her hands through the fish, and they flowed as if responding to an invisible conductor. "A conductor and her orchestra," Lucia thought, watching the graceful dance unfold beneath the waves.

The magnificent scene went on for what must have been minutes until a giant grandmother turtle interrupted the scene, separating the sheet of shimmering gills with her ancient fins. The ancient creature's flippers sliced through the water as she floated toward them with gentle determination in her eyes. Positioning herself between them, she munched on something Lucia couldn't quite see. The audible crunches suggested coral, and they hovered just above her massive body. The turtle's shell was a majestic mosaic of deep greens and earthy browns, each color shimmering in the sunlight that filtered through the water. The surface was rough and textured, resembling weathered wood, with intricate patterns etched like ancient runes telling stories of the sea. Wisps of algae clung to its edges, adding bursts of vibrant green that contrasted beautifully with the shell's natural brilliance. As the turtle glided gracefully, the shell arched upward, displaying its powerful, rounded shape reminiscent of a fortress that had withstood the test of time. Below, the colors deepened, revealing hints of azure and golden hues, like reflections of the ocean's embrace. Each movement sent ripples cascading around her, emphasizing not only her strength but also the serene grace with which she inhabited her underwater realm. Temptation tugged at Lucia to reach out and touch her, but she recalled the importance of not disturbing sea life and stopped herself.

An array of marine creatures approached, drawn to the edible discovery. It was likely few had ever encountered a human before. Long, pointed needlefish darted past, while a giant neon parrot fish lingered nearby, its substantial lips poised to chew on its own chunk of coral. The grandmother turtle remained with them, drawing in a host of splendid companions with her centered focus. The yellow and black-striped fish captivated Lucia; with their flowing fins, they appeared both delicate and powerful. Friendliest of the bunch, they swam so close to her that they nearly tickled her.

This magnificent kingdom welcomed the humans with open arms, as if it recognized them as its own, weaving them into the fabric of its vibrant life. The water shimmered with magic, and every creature seemed to embrace their presence. Then, as gently as she had arrived, the grandmother turtle glided away, leaving a ripple of calm in her wake. As the turtle disappeared into the deep blue backdrop, Lucia felt a profound shift within her—a transfer of ancient wisdom coursed through her being. It was as if the knowledge accumulated over lifetimes in this enchanting realm flowed into her, filling her with insights and stories that transcended time itself.

Suddenly, the two women found themselves eerily alone, surrounded only by a few fish. They grabbed each other's hands and swam, fast and free. First, they glided through the water, moving their fins as if they were part of their beings. Synchronistic, they flipped and flowed in unison with the ocean's current. As the lovers slowed, the sun shimmered on the surface in front of them. Lucia thought, "My heart overflows. It is so full it may explode...I could die right now and already be in heaven." Everything felt perfect.

Hours had passed in the water while others lounged on board, sipping margaritas in the sunshine. Jesus had made fresh guacamole, which awaited to be devoured with homemade corn chips from Cozumel.

Ixchel ascended the ladder first, the golden-brown skin glistening in the sunlight. Lucia could swear Ixchel glowed from within. Long black hair cascaded down her back as she untied it and slipped off her mask. This beauty, a personal goddess to adore, filled Lucia with awe. Waves of blessings pulsed through her, tinged with joy and excitement; Lucia's heart nearly burst with the moment's intensity.

This love differed from any other Lucia had experienced. It felt sacred and infinite, free from pettiness or the usual relationship struggles. It was as if they had remained in their higher selves since meeting. What once seemed important faded; Lucia's ego had disintegrated and rebuilt into something solid, something real. The foundation of her experience of the world shifted, aligning seamlessly with her soul.

As thoughts of romantic attachment flitted through her mind, Lucia checked in with herself, reminding herself that this was only temporary, like all things. Everything changes, evolves, waxes, wanes, ebbs, and flows. Happiness, like sorrow, shifts over time. This truth stood out clearly—everything would change. And for the first time, it felt genuinely okay.

After drying off, they finished the second bowl of guacamole and planned several days of snorkeling around Cozumel, exploring ruins as they neared them. Collectively, they decided that when they felt ready, they would journey to Xcambo to see the black pyramid.

Each day in Cozumel sparkled with enchantment, but the most meaningful moments emerged from deep conversations about life, love, death, the afterlife, and all the rich nuances in between. One evening, as they enjoyed an enticing dinner at a local restaurant, Lucia asked Ixchel for specific details about her life.

"How did you find your spiritual path, mi amor? I'm curious about how you arrived at this point," Lucia asked, her tone inviting.

Ixchel replied, "I grew up in a small town outside Mexico City, anointed as a child to be a holy person. Yet, I resisted that path, eager to carve my way. I pursued a degree in architecture, landed a job, and soon secured a significant project in Mexico City, earning quite a bit of money along the way—which allowed me to buy my boat.

But beneath my success, something felt amiss. One day, at a sacred site, the very one where I first encountered you, mi amor, I prayed for guidance from the goddess of the waxing moon, seeking clarity and inspiration for the journey ahead. The next day, I leaped—I chose to step away from my career to delve deeper into the mysteries of the Universe.

This decision felt exhilarating and a bit surreal; it struck me as amusing that at the peak of my career, when so many would cling to their successes, I dared to forge my path instead of simply shaping the world around me. It was a moment of self-discovery, a willingness to embrace uncertainty in pursuit of something greater.

"Before that break, daily prayer and meditation formed part of my routine, alongside visits to sacred sites and engaging with local thinkers over cocktails. So, embarking on the spiritual path wasn't entirely new; it had subtly woven itself through my life already. I hadn't completely escaped my path as a holy person; I simply did not prioritize it.

"I had mislaid my focus. The pleasures of achievement, while exciting, always led back to a familiar melancholy. Upon dedicating my life to self-awareness and connecting with the divine, I discovered something far more profound and expansive than any fleeting success.

"Thankfully, my sound investments during my financial success allowed me to buy my boat, where I began to travel, seeking answers, living on my boat when at sea, and staying with friends on land in exchange for its use. For two years, I sought a teacher, asking everyone about the holy people, shamans, brujas, and healers of each area. Then, in my third year of searching, I surrendered. That's when I entered my dark night of the soul. Have you heard of it?"

"Yes, I have. I have encountered something like it, myself," mentioned Lucia without intent to go further at that time. "It's a time when someone, intentionally or not, confronts their blockages and shadows. It feels like a spiritual crisis. But it serves a purpose, right?" Lucia replied, her confidence wavering.

"You're right, love. However, I would expand to say that this period involves deconstructing one's spiritual identity and way of being. By that point, I had transformed much of my life and felt little attachment, yet the absence of a teacher plunged me into a spiritual depression. I had to navigate through it to uncover who I truly was.

"That time was terrifying and dangerous to my psyche. I barely made it through that year and a half of darkness. I engaged in immense shadow work, exploring the deepest corners of my patterns and essence, yet I didn't feel lighter. Instead, I carried a heavy weight, as if every feeling accumulated within me. It took remarkable effort to free myself from that burden.

"Ultimately, the process was so profound that I withdrew from others. I stopped laughing and playing, realizing that I needed to consciously choose joy by not taking myself so seriously.

"One afternoon, at a birthday party for a friend's child on the Yucatan Peninsula, I played with the children and experienced joy unlike any I had known before. At that moment, I understood I was on the brink of discovering what I sought—teacher or no teacher. I finally released my obsession.

"As I left the party, an older man in a fedora approached me, offering a tattered piece of paper with an address and time scribbled on it. He said, 'See you tomorrow.' I felt rattled and bewildered, but sensed I had to be there.

"The next day, I went to the cafe at the address, arriving when he indicated. He wasn't there. After sipping coffee for over two hours, frustration mounted, and I spun tales of his antics at my expense. Just as I prepared to leave, he walked in. He took a seat while I stood across from him and said, 'Patience and trust in the web of interactions will definitely come into play here.'

"I settled back down, and three years later, I met Angel as a fellow apprentice of our Toltec teacher."

Ixchel paused, her attention drifting to the server approaching with a friendly inquiry about their needs. With a gentle, warm smile, Ixchel replied, "No, thank you, my dearest. You were wonderfully attentive and knew just when to stay away. I appreciate you."

The sweet young woman returned to the bar with a bright smile. Lucia reflected on the power of a few kind words.

Grateful, she thanked Ixchel for sharing her story. Max, Stewart, and Clara looked a bit baffled, but they showed their support. Angel, however, beamed with delight. "She was my sister long before we met. Our journeys intertwine in many ways," he said.

Ixchel reached for Angel's hand. "I love you, brother," she declared.

Their smiles lingered, a shared moment of understanding. Angel continued, "Someday, we'll share some stories from our Toltec training."

Laughter filled the air as the group shifted to lighter topics, curiosity igniting their conversation.

***

The day finally arrived for the much-anticipated trip to Xcambo, and the group was buzzing with excitement as they divided up tasks. Lucia took charge of communication with the car rental company, feeling a sense of responsibility to keep everything running smoothly. However, at every turn, something went wrong, disrupting her vibe. The journey so far had unfolded in such synchrony—each step seemingly falling into place—that she had begun to expect the same harmony everywhere they went.

Yet, as Lucia spoke with the customer service representative, it became increasingly evident that congruity would not be the case. The representative's accent was heavy, and the technical jargon used was impossible to understand, causing frustration to bubble within Lucia. She could feel her voice rising, an unsettling heat spreading from her chest that she struggled to contain. After a moment of grappling with the rising tension, she stepped outside the shop to catch her breath, hoping the fresh air would help clear her mind and restore her composure.

Behind the building, a striking mural caught Lucia's eye—a giant blue flower blooming against the urban backdrop. Blue, the color of communication, radiated tranquility that resonated with her thoughts. Deep breaths filled her lungs as she envisioned wrapping herself in a soothing blue light. Lucia inhaled, her mind beginning to clear and her spirit calming. The fog of confusion lifted, unveiling a truth she had neglected to articulate. Instead of expressing what truly mattered, she had shared only what seemed important to her, overlooking the essentials her heart yearned to convey. In that moment, the vibrant blue of the mural reminded her to pursue clarity and authenticity in communication.

With a smile, Lucia stepped into the car rental shop. Approaching the manager, she articulated precisely what kind of car they needed, for how long, and that it required a return to the exact location. Specificity replaced ambiguity, and to her astonishment, they handed over the keys and took the credit card. Finally, she had secured what she wanted. It amused her that the phrasing remained essentially unchanged; the shift lay in her directness and intent.

In that moment, Lucia recognized how the reactions had stemmed from her own conditions, failing to consider the circumstances of those she sought assistance from. A grin broke across her face as she walked toward the vehicle she had procured.

Soon enough, Lucia found herself on the road, picking up the others in the SUV. Pride swelled within her, a feeling of conquest. Giddy, she drove up, beaming like a cat that had just eaten a canary.

A few hours later, as they drove off, Lucia shared what had happened. Angel chimed in, "Oh, that was one of my biggest lessons, right, Ixchel?"

She nodded in agreement as he continued, "I struggled with expressing my intent, especially when it came to speaking my truth. It wasn't about sharing my opinions—I had no problem with that," he chuckled, aware of his tendency toward mansplaining. "This was deeper. I had to distinguish between my true self and the urge to be right or any of the other issues I carried."

Clara's curiosity sparked. "What do you mean by your issues?"

"Conditioning, traumas, all of that—the way I engaged with the world. I thought I was being honest, but I wasn't really revealing myself. I had to peel back so many layers…" Angel sighed, shaking his head.

Clara pondered, "How do you separate truth from issues? I struggle with that."

"Ah, the golden question. First, recognize what feels right and what feels off. Now, envision something that resonates entirely with you—something uniquely yours. Pay attention to the sensations in your body when you reflect on these things. Those physical feelings are indicators of your truth. Your body reacts differently to a moment from your past where you may have acted in a way that doesn't align with who you want to be.

"For instance, think back to a time when you fought with a friend or lover and said something cruel in anger. How did that feel in your body during and after that? Did they deserve that reaction, or did it stem from past trauma? The sensations are how you tell the difference between truth and issues. Your body serves as the compass.

"When you feel open-hearted and expanded, you are in your truth. The key is to observe your physical sensations. Does your body tighten or loosen? Do you feel relaxed or constricted? Is there a tingle of excitement, or does fear or regret weigh heavily on you?

"Look for those subtle nuances as you decide your path. It's essential to pay attention to all aspects of yourself, but this provides a solid starting point. As you learn what is true, you build trust in yourself. When you trust yourself, you can trust the Universe."

Tears glistened in Clara's eyes as she listened, struggling to recall even a few moments when she'd connected with her truth. After a long pause, she nodded to Angel, remaining quiet for the rest of the afternoon, lost in contemplation.

The car ride flew by faster than any of them expected. They engaged in philosophical musings—not whacked this time, Ixchel joked, explaining the difference between times for whacking and times for waxing. Occasionally, they would pause to admire the landscape, breaking the silence with playful teasing that danced through the air.

As they pulled into Progresso, the group decided to find some food before heading to the sacred site of Xcambo, a place shrouded in mystery and history. Lucia marveled at the proximity of this magical place to civilization, only uncovered a decade prior. It amazed her that people had lived in the surrounding areas for so long without any knowledge of its existence, the ancient ruins hidden beneath layers of dense jungle growth as if nature had intentionally concealed them.

While exploring the town, they spoke to an older local woman who had lived there her entire life, completely unaware of the site's existence. She shared stories of how she, along with her mother and grandmother, often felt a unique energy in the air—a power that seemed to resonate from the Earth itself—even though they had never seen its physical form.

It was as if the ruins, steeped in history and spirituality, had remained wrapped in an invisibility cloak concealed by the lush greenery. This profound connection to history they couldn't see left

Lucia and her companions in awe, stirring a sense of anticipation for what lay ahead.

In the small town, Lucia couldn't help but notice the blue that seemed to saturate the surroundings. Roofs shimmered in ocean steel hues; the sky mirrored the electric cobalt of the painted doorways; even the royal blue of a young man's uniform struck her. A beetle crossing the dirt road caught her attention, glinting with an intensity amplified by the vibrant atmosphere. All day, something vibrated in Lucia's throat—a mix of oddness, heightened awareness, and surreal excitement. She longed to see the Mayan salt mines and the newly uncovered pyramid.

Yet, something scratched at Lucia's insides, a curiosity mixed with discomfort that she couldn't quite pinpoint. It gnawed at her sense of peace, reminiscent of the feelings she had experienced when meeting her friends. Controlling much beyond her ability to pay attention remained a challenge, but managing the discomfort had become slightly more manageable.

Like her previous visit to the pyramids outside Mexico City, this feeling lingered, yet the weight had lessened, allowing her to relax into it. The anticipation of something significant was the similarity that struck her about the timing of this feeling. Before, it had led to meeting Ixchel and her remarkable friends. Further, this time, a fear of destruction didn't overshadow her thoughts.

***

After a round of delicious fish tacos, Ixchel and Lucia received kind greetings from everyone along their route. Lucia asked how Ixchel knew so many locals here.

"I spent a lot of time in this area after beginning my teachings," Ixchel replied, her eyes glimmering in the sun. "I was drawn here, not quite understanding why, but the mysticism is always tangible here. Additionally, arriving alone in the tiny town of Progresso, I found my voice."

Ixchel's words carried weight. "I befriended a young woman in that little shop we just passed. She introduced me to her grandmother, her mother, and her three aunts. They invited me to stay and participate in rituals with them. These women, powerful matriarchs, showed me a strength unlike anything I had encountered. They are brujas, dedicating their spare time to healing the wounds inflicted by patriarchy. They have taught many women how to embrace their true selves, use their voices, and share the power of the feminine with the world. I feel honored that they chose to impart their wisdom to me."

Lucia struggled to find a response. Choking on her words, she asked for more details about what they taught her. Suddenly, a tremor ran through Lucia's throat, her heartbeat echoing in her ears. This moment frightened her slightly, but she took it as a sign to listen more intently.

Ixchel responded to Lucia's reaction with gentleness, placing a hand over Lucia's throat. A chill enveloped her body as if an imaginary ice pack pressed around her neck. The sensation felt incredible, but confusion stirred within Lucia's mind.

Ixchel explained, "This land represents an energy vortex— chosen by the Mayans for its potent, embodied feminine energy. Women here have always felt this force more intensely than men. They harness this energy to empower one another, focusing less than most cultures on men and children. The men work hard, relying on women for decisions and sharing equally in housework and childrearing. While women also contribute to labor and caregiving, they have the space to pursue their growth and connections because the men share every responsibility. The community support among them is remarkable.

"This place will stir your authentic feminine connection, whether you acknowledge it or not. For many assigned female at birth, the voice often remains suppressed, as if it holds no value. Countless women carry this blockage, conditioned to silence themselves.

"These people and this place give rise to that voice. Blockages manifest in the throat, just as you experienced a moment ago. I could barely speak upon arrival despite having held a whole conversation just hours before. I had to go inward to reclaim myself—every instance when I felt limited by being a woman, every time men talked over me, even while I led the discussion. I reflected on the moments I dimmed my light to keep others comfortable and the times I judged other women for the very choices I made.

I confronted memories of my mother, who avoided speaking her mind after my father repeatedly silenced her with disdain for any opinion she expressed. I had to dig into my feelings of powerlessness around when I was raped, and I couldn't scream for help. I had to open all these parts within myself and dismantle them. You and Clara will feel this here, too. It's up to you to decide whether to engage in the work or remain silent until we leave this place.

"I'll be here if you need extra energy to help you through the process. What I did for you, Lucia, was help you cool the heat of restriction in your voice. I can't do the work for you, but I'm here to support, not to take it on."

Lucia and Clara nodded. The men sat in silence, honoring the feminine strength surrounding them. Angel, Max, and Stewart forged an unspoken pact, pledging to lift the women as they discovered their voices. They recognized it wasn't their show, stepping back from their socialized urge to dominate.

Arriving at Xcambo, silence shrouded the group. Ixchel nodded and mumbled a prayer as she recognized the guardians of the sacred site, immediately dissipating tourists and opening the way for them. They wandered through ruins scattered with palm trees, surrounded by an emerald jungle. The energy quaked around them, so intensely that they felt the vibrations dance through the air.

They discussed splitting up to experience the place individually, agreeing to reconvene whenever a strong pull drew them back together. Lucia headed toward the pyramid immediately, eager to reach its summit and scope out the surroundings. Excitement bubbled within her as she anticipated the sensations waiting for her up there.

The heat weighed heavily, but a refreshing breeze made it bearable, cooling sweat that beaded and trickled down her sun-kissed skin. Just as exhaustion threatened to halt her ascent, the soothing air wrapped around her like a gentle embrace. At the top, she paused, absorbing the expansive panorama, reminiscent of her visit to the temple of the moon.

Lucia spotted a nearby resort rising above the treetops, surrounded by rich foliage and the salt flats near the ocean. The view exuded majesty. She swam in the energy of the people who once toiled the land, aware of a darker history beneath her feet. In her mind's eye, families lived and worked here, and she felt the intense power of the feminine in that space, though it's meaning continued to elude her. A wildness lingered just beyond her grasp, a stark contrast to the other pyramid she had encountered, one that had morphed into something power-hungry.

Lying on the warm stone, far from the entry point, Lucia gazed up at the powder-blue, cloud-swept sky and drifted into memories of childhood. Her mother had never embodied strength; instead, emotions often clouded her decisions, leaving Lucia and her sisters to navigate life after their parents' divorce. Lucia's mother swam in trauma by her sister's death. The tragedy that occurred when Lucia was twelve darkened their lives, prompting years of avoidant behaviors that fractured their bond.

A lack of understanding around her mother's grief brought judgment. Lucia had struggled to find a role model of solid femininity during those formative years. As a result, feeling connected to the feminine as a source of power proved elusive. An image of a young woman arose, one who distrusted other women, over-masculinizing herself to claim strength amidst sensitivity. Control had become Lucia's armor against a world that threatened to push her around.

In a single breath, realization struck—she had unwittingly played into the patriarchal narrative that portrayed women as weak, femininity as unstable, and overly emotional. This internal battle with other women stemmed from a misunderstanding of true femininity, one distorted by a false model forced upon them all. It was time to reclaim what had always belonged to women: sovereignty.

Lucia had become more self-actualized throughout her life, grappling with her feelings about being a woman. But in that moment, she sensed a more profound power in her femininity that she had never touched on before. Images of Maya Angelou filled her mind, illustrating the strength that women embodied. Resilience and a capacity to feel fully flowed through her art, a manifestation of the divine feminine—circular, in flow, unlike the patriarchal linearity that dominated so much of the world.

Though Lucia had wielded her femininity as power, it hadn't stemmed from her innate essence. Instead, it drew from the behaviors of the men surrounding her. Now, an awakening unfolded: empowering herself and other women marked an essential evolution to embrace. In the past, Lucia treated herself and other women as the system dictated, not as they truly were.

Wisdom of the feminine surged within as she recognized that power need not be demanded or taken from others. It could flow easily accessible, not finite. The lesson that only a few seats at the table were available for women had clouded her vision, instilling a belief that uplifting others meant sacrificing her place. That notion echoed throughout American culture, where limited female representation in power positions taught women to fight for their rights rather than share them with other women, especially women of color. The patriarchal structure stifled multiple female voices in a world that allowed only a handful of representatives, all while women constituted half the population. "This has to change!" Lucia screamed in her mind.

Images of getting raped when she was fourteen surfaced. Drunk and disoriented, Lucia found herself at a party, flanked by her boyfriend and a stranger inviting her to his apartment. When her boyfriend stepped away to make a phone call, unease tightened in her chest.

As soon as she was left alone with the guy, the room felt smaller, and shadows crept in as the remnants of laughter faded into the distance. The man she was left with raped her, and when her boyfriend returned, he heard her muffled cries through the door. He looked through the keyhole to see his girlfriend having what he thought was consensual sex. Lucia's boyfriend had assumed she was willing and left her there.

Awakening early, she found the cushion beneath her wet, her bottom half cold and sore, without underwear. Exiting the apartment, she dialed her boyfriend's number from a payphone in the building's hallway. His anger erupted, and as she struggled to explain her fragmented memories, the blame pressed down. Eventually, he arrived to pick her up; his only request was never to speak of it again.

Nothing happened; no conversations occurred, and immense shame consumed Lucia, planting the thought that perhaps she must have somehow enjoyed it. To everyone else, the incident vanished as if it never existed. The experience infected her, festering in silence. Her voice was silenced, her pain minimized and forgotten, shaping the way she approached relationships for decades.

A tear traced down Lucia's cheek as a lump rose in her throat, rendering swallowing impossible. An urge swelled within: "I was hurt. No one let me talk about it, and no one cared. I lost my voice." Lucia felt every ounce of pain. As it processed through her, somehow, her power started to return, although this time, the power was different; it came from a true strength.

She said to herself, "I will speak, taking care of myself and letting my sisters support me, allowing myself to be heard!" Tears streamed down her face, and the lump in her throat finally released. She swallowed hard and inhaled deeply, each sob cleansing the burden she carried.

Lucia recalled every time laughter erupted from men when her emotions swelled within her, each moment women in her life lost control of their feelings, wrapped in their own turmoil, seemingly oblivious to the needs of others. Memories shifted to her father's declarations that she could achieve anything she desired, that her worth held no bounds, muted by gender.

Thoughts turned to her mother's journey—a battle fought against despair, culminating in a hard-won peace. Strength emerged from the depths, revealing a woman whose emotions had once tangled into toxicity, born from a lack of tools to navigate her grief. Lucia recognized the resilience that had allowed her mother to push through the loss of her sister, ultimately rediscovering joy after losing everything.

This long-held perspective transformed inside Lucia. No longer weighed down by her mother's struggles, she finally saw her as a beacon of determination and hope. This deep understanding of a shared wound seeped into Lucia's very being, altering her essence. Awareness settled into her, reshuffling her epigenetics in ways she had never imagined.

Lucia also recalled how many times she had stood up for herself and risen, even when others doubted her. She realized that her voice mattered in the world; expression, example, and empowerment emerged from the metamorphosis swirling inside her.

Opening her eyes, Lucia surveyed her surroundings, feeling the heated megalith against her skin. The air was alive with the sounds of birds chirping in the vibrant jungle trees, while a gentle breeze caressed her cheeks, bringing with it the fresh scent of damp Earth and blooming flora. Stretching her arms overhead, Lucia smiled as if awakening from a long, restorative nap, feeling a sense of rejuvenation wash over her.

Taking a moment to collect herself, she closed her eyes again briefly, soaking in every sound, smell, and sight with heightened clarity. The rustling of leaves whispered secrets of the forest, while rays of sunlight filtered through the canopy above, casting playful patterns on the ground. A sense of adventure bubbled within her, urging her to explore the wonders that lay just beyond her immediate view.

An urge to howl or growl surged within, awakening a primal instinct. A deep vibration pulsed through Lucia's core, a pure sensation coursing through every part of her being.

Then, a resounding wave of cries from billions of women worldwide struck, knocking the breath from her lungs. Each cry resonated a collective call that intertwined with her own, echoing the depths of shared strength and yearning.

Vivid visions surged through her: a mother cradling her dying child, tears streaming down her cheeks, yearning to scream at God but stifling it to show strength for the community. Men struck women hard across the face for daring to speak their minds; some women lost their tongues for talking too loudly.

For certain women, the experience proved far more harrowing. Each moment echoed with the weight of their struggles, a relentless tide that threatened to pull them under. Shadows of fear and doubt loomed large, encompassing their lives in an oppressive darkness.

The pain was not just theirs; it resonated through their families, friends, and communities, creating a chorus of silent suffering. Some fought valiantly against the tide, while others found themselves adrift, longing for the shore of understanding and solace. Many were beaten bloody, bones broken, all because they attempted to speak truth in the presence of men, sometimes for no reason at all except that there was a desire to exude power over women.

Lucia imagined the women who had their clitorises circumcised so they would never cheat on their husbands, preventing them from ever finding pleasure from their genitals, and as a way to eliminate the temptation of sexuality. Hidden and abused, women faced strict limits on their behavior, expected to act like ladies—dutifully playing the roles of adult children who were merely there to be seen, not heard.

Lucia envisioned the women glancing over their shoulders as they hesitantly walked down the street. Women are facing accusations that their clothing invited assault, silencing their voices with shame. Many harbored their secrets, convinced no one would believe them or, worse, that indifference would drown their cries. Too many had learned that speaking out felt like a second violation, just as brutal as the assault itself. Each reluctant step echoed the weight of their stories, a burden too heavy for silence yet too daunting to share.

Seeing board meetings where professional women faced a barrage of interruptions, Lucia's head echoed with their voices barely rising above the chatter of men speaking over them. Media narratives streamed messages insisting that to find happiness, love, and success, women and girls must conform to conventional beauty standards. Little girls heard constant praise for their looks but rarely received acknowledgment of their intelligence or talent.

Suddenly, it was apparent that many women toiled harder than their male counterparts, pouring their efforts into studies and careers, only to earn less and receive patronizing advice to smile more. Daughters endured discouraging words from fathers who deemed their aspirations futile, planting seeds of doubt about their potential for greatness. Millions of women and girls feel trapped, believing their path demands a facade of thinness, sweetness, and gentleness to make any progress in the world.

Lucia envisioned women forced to mimic their male colleagues to secure influential positions, balancing the demands of careers with raising children and preparing dinner. They exerted tremendous effort to grasp control, striving to succeed and thrive while sensing an invisible barrier that limited their ascent. A quiet resolve lingered, a whisper that true potential remained tantalizingly out of reach, hidden behind expectations and societal norms.

Women's bodies had been bought, sold, and traded throughout history, then told they should embrace healthy sexuality now that credit cards bore their names. With the power to own homes or choose their partners, they faced the impossible task of navigating mixed messages of sexual expression and cultural suppression, hearing that they were too much and not enough in the same breath.

As visions swirled, Lucia's guts churned. Tears streamed down her sun-kissed cheeks, and atop this ancient pyramid, a vow crystallized: to speak the truth, regardless of consequences in this patriarchal world. Lucia's commitment to herself and women around the world ignited a new sense of purpose within her.

She decided to stand up for those still searching for strength and for those who had risked everything to make their voices heard. She aimed to change the tide for those who felt they had no choice but to go along with it.

A role model emerged within Lucia for little girls who needed to see that they could pursue their dreams, knowing the risks but understanding that persistence could spark change. Lucia internally declared, "Nobody should dictate how girls dress, whether they wear makeup or what their body size should be." She committed to illuminating their unique beauty and perfection just as they were.

Lucia recognized her privilege; the chances of self-expression leading to death were slim. In many places, women risked their lives and livelihoods by rising up. With this awareness, she could leverage her status as a white American to advocate for those without the same advantages—women and marginalized individuals who needed support to approach a similar level of opportunity. A deep, full-body sigh escaped as she absorbed the weight of this realization.

Finally, climbing down the pyramid, Lucia felt as if a truck had run over her. Pain radiated through her body, yet her thoughts drifted to the countless other women who endured even worse fates. When Lucia reached the temple's base, grief enveloped her, and she collapsed under its heaviness. Heart-wrenching sobs escaped as she mourned the lost power of the divine feminine, yet her newfound passion accompanied the mourning with an ignited hope.

At once, Lucia's friends gathered. Surrounded by her people, Lucia felt their unconditional love wrap around her. Gradually, she found her breath again and stepped into the world, grounded in her identity as a woman.

Chapter Eight

AWAKENINGS

The problem with gender is that it prescribes how we should be rather than recognizing who we are.

~ Chimamanda Ngozi Adichie

That evening, Ixchel led Lucia into the jungle surrounding Xcambo, revealing a sacred space known only to women who understood their kind's collective suffering. They waded through thick vines that tangled the path. At the same time, Ixchel wielded a machete, slicing through the creeper plants that resisted their passage. The air felt heavy with neglect; it seemed no one had ventured here in months.

Lucia murmured this observation, and Ixchel responded, "The jungle grows swiftly. Someone could have stumbled through just a week ago, and already it's overrun."

"Listen to your intuition," Ixchel reminded Lucia as they navigated the dense foliage. "Do not forget that the Universe guides us in places like this. If we cling to ego or fear, the jungle will swallow us whole, never to be seen again."

The weight of these words settled on Lucia, drawing a startled expression across her face. Her lips curled downward, and her brow furrowed as her eyes widened with the thought of foreboding danger.

Ixchel laughed, resonating a deep and comforting sound. She reached out, placing a hand over Lucia's heart. "Don't worry, love. I've got you. If you forget, I will remember." Warmth radiated from Ixchel's touch, and Lucia felt her tension ease. Her shoulders dropped as she inhaled deeply, a smile breaking through her apprehension.

They held hands momentarily, their connection strengthening as they navigated through the thick underbrush. The foliage rustled softly around them, the sound merging with their synchronized breaths. Suddenly, the dense greenery parted, revealing a clearing dominated by an ancient and weathered large stone altar. Lanterns hung low from gnarled branches, waiting to be lit, their presence hinting at the rituals of old, casting flickering shadows that danced in the encroaching twilight.

The air was thick with the earthy scent of moss, ever-growing grass, and yellow jasmine, though the origin of the sweet scent seemed almost impossible to find in this untamed wilderness. A sense of reverence fell over them as they approached, feeling the weight of history enveloping the space as if the very ground beneath their feet held countless secrets waiting to be uncovered.

Magic permeated the clearing, and as Lucia stepped into the circle, a rush of goosebumps danced along her skin. A high-frequency hum enveloped them, a whisper only perceptible to those who listened closely.

Lucia felt light, as if she were a child again, racing through the woods behind her house, untouched by the harsh realities of the world. It was the sensation of freedom before the realization of judgment before the trauma and alienation that society imposed on her. Here, at this moment, she reclaimed a piece of herself, buried beneath layers of pain and adaptation in a destructively disheartening world.

Ixchel began her tale, drawing Lucia into the depths of womankind's transformation. "We stand on the brink of a new age. The elders in this town understand this shift. Gender, as we know it, is fading from relevance, and soon, it will mean little to the rising generations. But first, we must heal the wounds of marginalization before we can genuinely advance without festering anger.

"Each day, society grows more accepting of female-bodied individuals who choose to become male and male-bodied individuals who embrace femininity. In fact, for many, claiming a gender at all feels unnecessary. It's vital to support the efforts of these gender pioneers. Transgender individuals have always existed, yet only recently have their voices begun to emerge in various parts of the world.

"Understand me; countless gender non-conforming people still face violence for expressing their identity. We find ourselves at the dawn of a cultural transformation, and this progress provokes backlash. Ignorance often breeds fear, especially regarding change. Those who challenge the rigid boundaries of gender not only enrich their own lives but also uplift people born female who identify as women, or what is termed cisgender. They dismantle outdated paradigms and pave the way for a new understanding of gender.

"Transgender individuals navigate a unique set of challenges, and we must stand firmly beside them in their journeys. They often struggle to find their voices and to feel safe in our world. Meanwhile, cis women carry their burdens stemming from societal expectations. The visions you experienced earlier merely scratch the surface of the myriad of issues facing those socialized as females across the globe. Our history is marked by ownership of our bodies, silencing of our voices, and confinement of our agency within social constraints.

"Throughout history, a few brave women have risen to challenge these norms. These rebels serve as our role models, illuminating the path forward. By acknowledging the suffering endured by women throughout history, we begin to mend the damage within ourselves and our lineage, ensuring a better future for the daughters and sons we bring into the world. We must confront the discord that accompanies being a woman, for only then can we truly transform the world around us.

"What you felt today captured just a glimpse of the pain women everywhere endure. Every human faces suffering, yet women bear their own distinctive burdens, often feeling objectified and undervalued. Tonight, we arrive in this sacred place to heal— together and collectively—for all women. Let us emerge strong enough to bear the weight of the world upon our shoulders."

Lucia nodded, recognizing this experience as essential to her life. Without these adjustments, discord would linger among other women and within her own identity. She often felt she was fighting against others, herself, and the heaviness of the patriarchy. This socialization ran deep within her psyche, as it did for every woman raised in a patriarchal society. Lucia began to understand that many women remained silent because of the internalized misogyny embedded in them, how they assimilated the belief that women held value only as mothers or in their utility to others.

Lucia reflected on how society had warped female sexuality into a performance for others rather than an authentic experience. Women often prioritized the needs of others, stifling their sense of self for their lovers. She realized that the hard-fought attainment of rights layered on new responsibilities because men refused to share the burden at home. The significance of this insight felt immense and overwhelming, yet somehow, a glimmer of hope emerged within her. For the first time, she grasped these truths with startling clarity.

"I will hold this container for you, my love, and I want you to remember all you witnessed today." Ixchel spoke in a steady tone. "Let your tears cleanse your heart and mind. Wail, cry out, be angry, scream, stomp, and yell; no one can hear you. Listen closely to your body and its desires to expel the pain in your DNA. It's acceptable in this space to contemplate your experiences and those of others. This is for your healing; it resonates with all the women who cannot find their voices."

"What if I can't summon these feelings?" Lucia asked, her voice trembling slightly.

"Don't worry; they will come," Ixchel replied, her tone solid.

In a flash, she placed her hand over the front of Lucia's neck. The familiar warmth surged back to her heart, but then, unexpectedly, a lump once again formed in her throat. Vivid images swirled in Lucia's mind: women judging one another, their spite and anger serving as weapons given to them by men who wanted them wounded. She saw white women directing their frustrations at women of color and other marginalized individuals. A wave of sadness crashed over her as memories flooded in, tightening around her heart—each pang a reminder of how she had judged others and been judged, in turn, how hard it was for her to trust women.

Tremendous guilt welled within her for the pain she had inflicted on her fellow women. Sensing her turmoil, Ixchel placed a comforting hand on Lucia's back, gently thumping in rhythm with her heartbeat, grounding her as she let the tears fall.

More memories surged forth, and she plunged deeper into the feelings stirred by her earlier experience atop the pyramid. Each recollection pulled her further into the tangled emotions of her life, weaving together the joy, sorrow, and wonder she had felt in that moment. Lucia started choking violently as the urge arose to scream out. A shrill noise began deep in her groin, creeping up to her belly and spilling from her mouth. The sound curled her stomach, a tight coil of tension that echoed in the air around her. Her voice reflected the cry of an eagle piercing the thickened air, resonating within her, sending shivers through her entire being. A primal urge surged through her, compelling her to stomp her feet and pound her chest, echoing the fierce energy of a Māori war dance. She surrendered to the rhythm of her body and voice, letting instinct guide her movements and sounds. Intense and rhythmic, she moved with the earth beneath her, pounding her chest ferociously. Each stomp resonated, sending vibrations through the ground, a powerful connection to her ancestors. The wild energy coursed through her veins, urging her to embrace the raw essence of life, to dance fiercely in the moment.

The images of all the women in the world consumed her thoughts. She wept and howled like a grieving mother, her anguish unending. Each cry resonated in her womb, a heavy echo of loss as if she mourned her own child. Their pain intertwined with hers, an unbearable weight that pushed her deeper into despair. She embraced all the losses of every woman, feeling an ache in her vulva while tapping into those who had been raped. Accessing those who had been mutilated, those who had been forced to marry, and all the women's bodies who were being used by those they never wanted.

Lucia screamed for all those born female, stripped of ownership over their bodies. Those stolen, sold, and traded to men who drained their spirits and forced them into servitude. She roared against the societies that labored tirelessly to keep women under men's control, to weaken them, to ensure their dependence. Her voice became a weapon, fierce and unwavering, challenging the very foundations that sought to suppress every marginalized person. Through her cries, she summoned the strength of those silenced, eager to ignite a fire in every heart that dared to listen.

Lucia suddenly felt livid, like a bull who saw a red cape after spears had been plunged deep into its leathery skin, simply for entertainment. Lucia wanted to meet the gaze of every man capable of inflicting such harm on women. She sought to understand the darkness that resided behind their eyes; to measure the extent of their cruelty and the indifference they often wore like armor. These thoughts stirred a mixture of resolve and dread within her, propelling her deeper into a world where accountability felt painfully distant. A rough growl vibrated her bones until it came out of her mouth. She chomped and growled like a rabid wolf who had had her pups stolen. Stomping and beating her chest, growling, screaming, and yelling at Father Sky. Finally, releasing all of the anger and pain into Mother Earth, to be transformed.

Ixchel hit Lucia swiftly with a flattened palm between her shoulder blades, and the growl turned into a whimper. She became a scared rabbit, glancing around, her heart racing at every sound in the jungle. Wrapping her arms around her legs, she cradled her weakened body, echoing the posture of countless women who had endured violence and been forced into lives not of their choosing. Fear gripped her, a tight knot in her chest, as memories of pain and loss surged through her mind. The jungle, once a vibrant world, now felt like a prison of shadows and whispers, with every rustle a reminder of her vulnerability.

Ixchel cradled Lucia in her arms, rocking her gently as she whispered words of love, strength, and safety. Under Ixchel's soothing presence, Lucia began to feel her strength resonate within her. Her muscles tightened and pulsed, awakening to a newfound power. As she listened intently, the sounds of creatures emerged around her—voices that promised guidance and connection rather than control. In that heartbeat, Lucia understood that she was not merely a victim; she was part of something larger, something alive and waiting to teach her.

As she looked up, her vision sharpened, revealing the moon hanging carelessly above her, its beams pouring down like a gentle embrace. The moon was her friend, guiding her cycles and urging her to nurture herself. She recognized its power and luminescence, feeling its love for her in return. Her heart swelled with immense affection for the celestial body.

She perceived her own crimson flow as a wellspring of divinity, a powerful connection to the earth and her essence. Her breasts symbolized nourishment and comfort, grounding her in her femininity. As her womb caught the moon's light, she felt her creative energy radiate from within. It became clear to her that motherhood was not a prerequisite for recognizing this capacity; she could birth anything from that sacred space. Whatever she envisioned, she had the power to manifest it in the world.

Ixchel pressed her finger gently against Lucia's forehead, and in an instant, the wisdom of the feminine current surged within her. A profound certainty blossomed in her mind: she held the key to everything in the Universe, a power bestowed upon all people. Yet, she understood that those assigned female at birth possess a unique gift, unveiling this ability with astonishing ease if given the space to do so. All they needed was to shed their constraints and attune to the Universal force to access their innate intuition. As Lucia's forehead pulsated, a rush of violet light flooded her senses, calming her overactive nerves and lulling her into a state of unfathomable tranquility.

Ixchel caressed Lucia's hair, and a frisson of sensations swept through her entire head. The world around her vanished, becoming both nothing and everything simultaneously. It felt as if they floated in a vast, soft cloud. Her body mirrored the same ethereal density as the air enveloping them. No longer did she sense any separation between herself, Ixchel, or the vibrant jungle that hummed with life around them. In that moment, the boundaries of individuality melted away, and interconnected-ness reigned supreme.

After an eternity of simply being, Lucia took a deep breath, gradually reconnecting with her physical body. She looked up at Ixchel's angelic face and grinned. Ixchel kissed her deeply, guiding her to the stone altar. Lucia found herself lying atop it, her clothing gently peeling away from her softened form, baring her to the world around her. The air shimmered with an otherworldly energy, heightening her senses as she surrendered to the moment.

Ixchel moved Lucia's core, aligning it in succinct motion with her own. Their nakedness glowed in the moonlight, a sight only the great mother observed. Their decadent lips consumed one another, merging into a single entity. Their bodies unified into a vibrant mass of love that flowed through the jungle, germinating in the hearts of animals and humans for miles around. The lover's bodies shimmered in the moonlight as they awakened a deep resonance of pleasure in every woman across the globe.

The perfect bodies moved in harmony, creating a song for the goddess herself. Ixchel stirred something deep within Lucia, heightening her senses to an intensity she had never known. Overwhelmed by the flood of sensations, Lucia paused, needing to ground herself in reality for a moment. As she took a breath, the world around her sharpened, allowing her to regain her balance amidst the vibrant energy that pulsed through the air. This fleeting thought vanished, and she felt herself enveloped in a nebular blanket of universal force and flesh, their breaths merging into one. There was no separation; it was the most natural sensation in the world. The essence of connection wrapped around them, soothing yet invigorating, as if the Universe itself had conspired to erase the boundaries between them.

In those moments, Lucia felt her heart brimming with love for Ixchel, but even more, for all women. She recognized her place in the world as a strong, independent woman, free from the chains that bound others. Never before had she experienced such an outpouring of love and compassion. Lucia felt an intense bond with every person who had been treated as an object, used, and discarded. Embracing her worth and pain simultaneously, she realized she had never fully understood her own truth, let alone extend that understanding to others. In this moment of clarity, sympathy blossomed within her, deeply rooted and profoundly transformative.

A different sensation, one Lucia had never experienced, built in her groin, and slithered through her belly, embedding itself in her spine. She felt a profound openness and surrender as it coiled upward, a force she couldn't control or resist. In those moments, Lucia experienced her whole existence; memories and emotions surged through her mind. Then, without warning, her senses slipped away, and the person she had known her entire life unraveled, dissolving like wax in a flame. Her body abruptly stiffened, flushing fluid out of her vulva. Suddenly, a blinding light projected from the top of her head, illuminating the space around her. At this time, she felt a pure presence entwined with all that is. Then, she collapsed, motionless, her breath ragged as tears streamed down her cheeks.

Ixchel gazed at her radiant form, kneeling beside her and whispering in a language not of this world. Ixchel's words sounded ancient and divine; a melody filled with unearthly resonance. As Lucia watched, Ixchel's face transformed into a kaleidoscope of expressions, each one emanating an over-whelming love.

Above them, stars cascaded from the sky, wishes unfurling like delicate petals, calling for every woman on the planet to unearth her purpose and embrace the magic of the feminine current.

The next few hours held them, the forest singing affirmations with the soft air's caress, the moon shining down happily at the power their souls had created—the shifts that they would now carry into the world. They remained silent until they donned their clothing and began their journey through the forest toward the vehicle.

Gliding through the shadows, Lucia turned to Ixchel. "Do all the women who come here experience this?"

Ixchel laughed, "Not quite, love. Each experience is unique."

Lucia felt a heat rise to her cheeks, embarrassed by her question. She couldn't help but laugh at herself, her amusement bubbling over into an almost hysterical giggle.

She suddenly realized how seriously she had taken herself. Amusement and joy washed over her, dissolving the serious-ness that had anchored her for so long. Lucia discovered that she could embrace the sacred rage of all women, transforming it into a higher way of being—a force that nurtured the world rather than tearing it apart. But she didn't want to live as a perpetually angry person, realizing that rage can coexist with joy. In that interval, Ixchel vowed to guide Lucia in integrating these feelings, helping her channel this understanding into something productive instead of destructive.

Lucia wondered why it had taken her so long to lighten up. She recalled the years spent with her ex-husband, burdened by worry and concern for her son, consumed by the fear that her life would crumble if she didn't keep it all together—the phrase, "What if...?" echoed in her mind more times than she could count. There are so many "what ifs," yet not enough giggles. How could she let her joy become so dampened amidst the beauty of life? It struck her as both sad and absurd, utterly ridiculous, actually. What if her life had fallen apart? What if her son made a wrong choice? Who had convinced her that she alone bore the weight of responsibility for everyone?

With a chuckle, she entertained the image of slapping her-self across the face with a wet noodle. The absurdity of it; she'd never escape the noodle's vengeance! Laughter erupted as she conjured more silly scenarios, reveling in her newfound lightness.

Ixchel laughed, recognizing the spark of realization in Lucia's eyes. She expressed that she had felt that same awakening long ago, well before the thrill of newfound desire had colored her perceptions. The understanding bubbled between them, grounding their bond in shared experiences and unspoken bliss. Her experience had been far more innocent, lingering in the realm of PG-13. The women of the town had escorted her, alongside other initiates, to this place, a threshold marked by expectation and unspoken rules. They had shed their clothes and consumed hallucinogenic plants, seeking deeper awareness. As the methods varied, the result remained unchanged. Ixchel clearly found her orgasmic method much more direct. She grinned while explaining this to Lucia.

***

Lucia woke up talking, her energy rivaling that of the ingestion of a gallon of coffee. Clear and active, her mind raced with thoughts of the night before. She had poured her heart out to Ixchel, recounting the journey that had brought her to this moment.

She reflected on her struggle to share her true self, a self she hadn't even known existed. For years, she had believed she was self-aware, but now she recognized the fog of social conditioning that had clouded her vision. Those fleeting glimpses of truth that she had caught over the years tugged at her like a distant heartbeat, never quite resonating with the fierce rhythm pounding in her chest now.

As she spoke, the clarity of her newfound understanding enveloped her. Each word felt like a step further into her own emerging self, a self that had been waiting silently beneath layers of expectation and fear.

Lucia felt a rush of excitement and emotion, struggling to articulate her thoughts to Ixchel. Words tumbled from her in fragments, disjointed and raw. There was so much... so much awareness, so much understanding. Everything clicked into place, but the intensity of it all left her feeling overwhelmed.

Ixchel listened with patience, her eyes wide with empathy, mirroring Lucia's fervor. Each nod and smile ignited a spark of recognition within her, reminiscent of her awakening. Finally, as Lucia paused to catch her breath, she sought confirmation from her beloved partner.

Ixchel's calm, gentle voice broke the silence. "My love, I recall vividly the moments you describe. The joy and wonder in your eyes echo my own past experiences. I understand what you're feeling right now," she said, her smile radiant.

"I hardly slept more than a few hours each night for at least a week after my experience at the sacred altar. I spent my nights writing, painting, and gazing at the stars through my newly awakened eyes. A part of me had healed—a part I had long ought to fill my entire life—and another part shattered open. It felt like magic, and at times, it overwhelmed my human mind.

"After a few weeks, I plunged into a sadness more intense than I had ever known. This wasn't the familiar ache of grief or loss; it was a deep, personal melancholia. It centered solely on me, an existential angst that took me months to unravel. You see, love, when you open yourself completely, you invite both the ecstatic and the shadow within. I want to help you navigate this experience far more than I understood how to when I faced it alone. After leaving the support of the women here, I found myself enveloped in those feelings on my own. But you will not walk this path alone—at least, not until you are ready."

Lucia's eyes remained wide, untouched by Ixchel's warning. She croaked as she tried to speak, clearing her throat before continuing, "I trust you will guide me, but I now understand that I am the microcosm of the macrocosm of the Divine. Your words don't concern me as they once would have; I've known this truth in the depths of my being since before I was born. I can now face the darkest parts of myself and the world without it altering my conviction. I do want your help—absolutely. You've brought me to this point, and I know you will lead me further. But once we return to the boat, I need to kiss you and make love to you. It feels as if holding back might make me explode."

After a brief drive through the jungle, they reached the boat. The air buzzed with the scent of damp earth and vibrant foliage, the sounds of the ocean enveloping them. Lucia felt her pulse quicken with anticipation; she could not wait to devour her lover. The boat bobbed gently on the water's surface, ready to carry them into the heart of passion. Lucia felt as if she would swallow her lover whole. Within seconds of breaching the quiet bow, her body found every inch of Ixchel's skin. No part of them neglected to touch the other; Lucia felt as if they had merged into one entity.

Lucia watched, spellbound, as her Latin goddess transformed before her eyes. With each shared breath, Ixchel's golden eyes morphed into a deep sea of emerald and cobalt, sharp with energy. Even her lashes softened, turning a delicate shade of blond. The air thickened with their connection, wrapping around them like a warm embrace, and Lucia felt the pulse of their unity resonate deep within her.

The new person Ixchel embodied looked at Lucia with pure love and adoration. Lucia studied them with a mix of curiosity and wonder, her thoughts swirling like the colors of a sunset. She felt a pull, an invitation to discover the depths of this connection, and her heart quickened as she searched the depths of those eyes shimmering with warmth and sincerity. There was no resistance to opening her moistened legs to this lover. She felt like she had longed for this person for centuries. As she widened her hips, she felt Ixchel move into her and could viscerally feel flesh move in and out of her open yoni.

Ixchel was there. Lucia knew this by the scent of her skin lingering in the air, yet she had shifted into an entirely different form. Lucia felt the emergence of lightning within as Ixchel moved what felt like flesh faster and harder inside her. Ixchel bit Lucia's neck as she took her over and over again. They were lost in one another, entwined, wet, and furious. Ixchel's eyes transitioned from the water to the precious earth. The erection that Lucia felt penetrating her couldn't indeed be an organ, yet it felt like flesh; it felt like it was Ixchel's own body that held a phallus. She fucked Lucia for hours until she started to quiver in such an extreme manner that Lucia finally collapsed.

They fell into each other, and when Lucia reached for her lover's appendage, she found Ixchel's wet and swollen lips and nothing more. There was no cock to be found. Lucia squeaked, "We should find your strap-on before it gets lost and forgotten." Ixchel shot her a playful glance and replied, "That was all me, my love, and trust me, I felt everything."

Ixchel's transformed image addressed Lucia as though she had always inhabited a male body. With a blush, Ixchel explained that she believed it was one of her past life personalities making an appearance or that their energy had intertwined in that moment. "I've never felt this before," she admitted, "and it must be because we shared a past life."

Lucia erupted into laughter, a deep, hearty sound that bubbled up from her core. Ixchel joined her, their laughter spiraling into a joyful cackle that left them both gasping and clutching their stomachs, overwhelmed by the thrill of their shared experience with gender fluidity.

***

They settled in Progresso, but within a week, Lucia felt the melancholy creeping in. For over a month, Ixchel guided Lucia through the tumult of emotions that surfaced with this newfound awareness. Their explorations had become sacred, a space where Lucia could explore her feelings openly and without judgment. However, the time came when Ixchel had to return home to support her brother, who had been diagnosed with mesothelioma. This devastating cancer casts a long shadow over their lives. Watching her lover confront such a harsh and bewildering reality filled Lucia with a heavy heart, a mix of sorrow and empathy welling up inside her. Yet, amid the pain, she couldn't help but admire the way Ixchel faced the news with quiet strength and resilience, embodying a grace that inspired Lucia to find her courage in the face of the unknown.

When Lucia shared her worries about Ixchel's emotional state during this tumultuous time, Ixchel met her gaze, her eyes warm and knowing, as if they held the secrets of the Universe. "My sweet love," she said, her voice steady. "I understand that this will be a powerful storm for my family to navigate. Yet, I will remind myself that this storm is simply a part of life. To embrace the joy of living, I must also endure hardship.

"It will be devastating to watch my brother suffer. We will face each day as it comes, and I will do everything I can to support him as he navigates this challenging experience. Hardship is an inevitable part of life, and my family and I are not insulated from cancer's relentless grip. Many endured this pain, and now it is our turn. Please don't worry about me, my dear. I understand that this is part of the Universe's design. I will remain present and love him with all my heart. Although I regret breaking my promise to guide you through your transitions."

Ixchel's powerful presence took Lucia's breath away. She admired how, even amid crisis, Ixchel remained balanced and steady. Her heart drummed deep and rhythmic, swelling with immense love for this woman's humanity and spirituality.

Suddenly, energy radiated from Lucia's chest, flowing through her ribs, bones, and beyond her flesh. She embraced love for all beings—love for loss, pain, kindness, and community. In that instant, she became one with the world's heartache and joy, realizing she couldn't control any of it. It all belonged to life. Yet, insecurity gnawed at her. Would she ever be that strong? Could she stay present in the eye of the storm like Ixchel? Full of admiration, Lucia grappled with the fear that she might never integrate her spiritual knowledge with the harsh realities around her.

Ixchel observed Lucia with a curious gaze, noticing the vibrant intensity emanating from her synchronized field. In that instant, Ixchel explained that she understood that Lucia was experiencing a profound wholeness. Yet, she sensed that challenges would soon emerge, testing Lucia's resolve and self-awareness.

Lucia held on to the understanding that she had discovered a connection to every soul, a bond that would shield her from the isolation pain often brings. The memory of this moment would linger in her heart, a flickering flame that banished loneliness. However, she would need to continuously remind herself of the lessons etched into her being, practicing a new way of living with each challenge life threw her way. Only through facing these trials would she genuinely learn the depths of her experience.

As Lucia absorbed this knowledge, she recognized Ixchel's choice to remain silent. Ixchel had been clear that she understood the importance of this moment, knowing that no explanation could capture its essence without pulling Lucia from her experience. Lucia felt gratitude for Ixchel's wisdom, an unspoken support that would guide her through the complexities ahead.

Lucia realized that thriving required more than a spiritual connection; it demanded the integration of that connection into every facet of her humanity, including the messy, tragic, and painful moments. She understood that being present in every aspect of herself transformed life into something sacred.

The clan dispersed quietly, their shared laughter and songs from the previous night echoing in the air. Hugs and expressions of gratitude flowed freely but tears and promises to reconnect remained absent. They had enjoyed more time together than they could have hoped for, and an unspoken understanding lingered: it was time to embark on new adventures.

Though distance lay ahead, they held onto the certainty of their connections. They had the means to stay in touch, and deep down, they knew their paths would intertwine again when the moment was right.

Ixchel took Lucia back to Mexico City. They shared a passionate goodbye filled with deep kisses that lingered like a sweet memory. No promises bound them; no vows to reunite hung in the air. They accepted that if fate brought them together again, it would be a blessing. If not, it simply meant they had moved on to other lessons alongside different souls, and their time together had reached its natural conclusion.

The beauty of their experience lay in its fleeting nature. Lucia stood still, watching Ixchel walk away, her long black hair swaying, gracefully framing her hourglass figure. Bittersweet pangs threaded through Lucia's heart, underscoring the weight of this farewell. Lucia embraced the essence of what they shared, knowing it had transformed her in ways language could scarcely capture. It was the mother tongue of the heart.

Chapter Nine

BECOMING ONESELF

No one can heal you. You must learn to be your own company, your own cure.
You cannot retreat into someone else for fulfillment.

- Janet Mock

Lucia struggled to say goodbye to Ixchel. Their connection ran deep, and she couldn't imagine a world where Ixchel was entirely absent from her life. Even now, she felt Ixchel's essence intertwined with her own, and somehow that presence sufficed.

Lucia chose to fly back to the US, where she would rent a car for a solo road trip that diverged from her original plan. She set her sights on Santa Fe, New Mexico, where she could meander toward home at her own pace. After months away, time felt both fleeting and expansive, like the blink of an eye alongside an entire lifetime.

Lucia sensed the need for solitude to process the whirlwind of her experiences. There was a deep longing to settle into herself before applying everything she had learned in Mexico, and how it wove into her experiences before she left Seattle. There remained a nagging sense that something indistinguishable awaited her on the horizon. Because she did not yet feel complete with what that could be, she decided to embrace that uncertainty and allow whatever came next to unfold in its own time.

In Mexico, Lucia immersed herself in deep personal work, but her focus on Ixchel limited the spaciousness essential for proper integration. She needed to rest, to allow everything to settle within her. Eventually, her awareness would braid it all together, but for now, fatigue weighed on her.

It became clear that Ixchel didn't require Lucia's caretaking, which felt disconcerting; remnants of her past still drove her to nurture those she loved. Yet, Ixchel had provided Lucia with the room to explore new dynamics in their relationship, inviting her to recognize when old patterns needed to unravel.

Lucia recognized the urge to lose herself in another, aware it could lead her to neglect the vital task of becoming genuinely comfortable within herself. She understood that remaining vigilant was crucial; this journey was hers alone—a chance to untangle the narratives imposed by others and those she had spun for herself. Deep down, she harbored that knowledge, allowing it to guide her as she navigated the paths of self-discovery.

In the past, Lucia had allowed her life and relationships to drown her in the other person's needs. Now that her head emerged above water, she embraced the freedom to be her most authentic self in the world. Lucia could not afford to slip under again for anyone or anything. Even as the strings of desire strummed old tunes of sacrifice and nurturing, she chose herself.

This choice didn't mean she disregarded others or failed to prioritize them in her life; it meant she refused to lose herself in their demands or the swimming concern for people's suffering. She knew the muscle of self-preservation required constant exercise, growing stronger with each act of defiance against its erosion. It needed to become so thoroughly integrated into her soul that prioritizing her own well-being felt natural, devoid of internal conflict.

As Lucia stepped through the airport's doorway, waves of heat that nearly stole her breath gave way to the cool, recycled air, unable to decide which sensation was more welcome. Lucia longed for a middle ground, a space where she could inhale the sweetness of grass and flowers while the warm breeze danced around her skirts as she walked barefoot through summer moss. Yet, it was necessary to venture toward the dry expanse of the desert. Somehow, she sensed this stark landscape held the answers she sought, although uncertainty flickered in her mind about what awaited her in the barren land.

The lush green earth of the Pacific Northwest had soothed her soul countless times before, but now it was different. Lucia needed to find solace within the red earth. For some reason, she believed this task unfolded best amid the stark landscapes of layered rock and hardy plants that thrived on minimal water. A literal drying out after months steeped in emotional and physical saturation was necessary. A sly grin crossed her face as she recognized the truth in that thought—it was both dirty and liberating.

She had lingered on the boat far longer than expected, but the time had soaked her in passion, salt water, and wise support. Meeting Ixchel had empowered her, not only in her understanding of desire and her heart but also in her connection to divine femininity. Sitting alone in the desert felt like a new chapter, one where she could embrace the arid quiet and reflect on her journey. It was a profound contrast, this serene solitude, yet somehow, it promised the same richness her spirit had found in Mexico. Here, in the unobstructed vastness, she would peel away further layers of herself and confront the essence of who she had become.

The ocean, the jungle, and the sense of freedom she had discovered filled her in ways she never imagined. That nurturance wouldn't vanish through leaving her haven in Mexico, but she wondered how it would unfold on this new planet she chose to enter. Lucia felt a deep connection to the elements of fire and earth, envisioning the women before her, completely interwoven into the natural rhythm and cycles of life, death, creation, and destruction—the magical presence residing within all of it. Goosebumps rose along her limbs as she pondered this connection.

As she stood in line at the airport's security checkpoint, she allowed the warmth of possibility to envelop her heart. Unexpectedly, the people around her appeared more distinct, as if she had slipped on glasses with the perfect prescription. She observed them entirely, each individual a tapestry of stories, emotions, and experiences. Lucia soaked in every moment of this opportunity to witness their lives, reveling in the shared human experience that pulsed around her.

In one of the bustling lines, a curious child peppered her mother with questions about the machines. The mother skillfully loaded the conveyor belt with their items, explaining each device the child pointed out. It was impressive to watch her balance the demands of the moment; each explanation delivered with patience amid the chaos.

Directly in front of Lucia stood an older man who paused to assist a young woman whose phone had slipped from her grasp while her hands were full. He offered her a warm smile as she thanked him, then hurried off with a wave. Lucia noticed that the security professionals surrounding her each had their own unspoken stories.

One female-presenting security agent stood out; her gestures animated as she instructed the young male-presenting trainee by her side. When someone spoke over her, asking the trainee a question, the agent's expression tightened with irritation. Lucia recognized that look, a familiar frustration born from years spent in male-dominated fields—an all-too-common dismissal of expertise simply because of gender.

Each figure in this scene contributed to a rich tapestry of human experience, a reminder of the small acts of connection and resilience woven through everyday life.

Lucia took a deep breath and smiled, sharing a knowing look with the woman too far away for words. A powerful connection sparked between them as if they shared a lineage; it felt like family. Overwhelmed, she longed to stride up to the man talking over her and shout, "She's training him, you jackass!" Frustration bubbled within her over this absurd societal wrinkle, a glaring error in humanity's fabric.

As she scanned the room, strong women lined the walls, more patient than they should be, and weathered far more than they deserved. Lucia sensed their collective pain, a weight that reached back through mothers and grandmothers. She finally grasped how the system had twisted women and marginalized individuals into mere objects, cast aside and unrecognized. Social expectations stifled their nurturing spirits and undermined their health.

So few of these women had the freedom to shape their own lives; instead, they mirrored society's dictates about who they were meant to be. They wore patience like armor, protected until the tide turned. Then, someday, they could channel their anger, rise together, and reclaim their power. Perhaps they could care for themselves and their sisters, honoring the goddesses they truly embodied. Yet, women remained trapped in suffocating boxes created by society, from which they struggled to break free.

It had become clear to Lucia that false beliefs and fear of feminine chaos fortified the walls of every structure. It had become apparent that the patriarchy held disdain for the unknown and the powerful, creative force residing within every woman. As the pendulum swung in the other direction, Lucia sensed that self-control might slip away for a time, guiding them toward a long-overdue balance. This realization struck her as strange; women, in her experience, wielded more self-control than any man socialized into the rigid confines of masculinity. Individuals perceived as female by society adapted remarkably to survive and quietly pursued pathways to thrive.

At that point, Lucia grasped the truth: the disruption of masculine potency terrified men. The rage simmering deep within women could upend the status quo if only they could break free from their imagined cages. She recognized a heaviness in men's hearts surrounding this inevitability; it became clear why so many fought fiercely to keep women powerless. The fear of their potential unleashed created a cage not only for women but for men themselves, locking them in a cycle of dominance and denial.

Lucia thought that if women gained the freedoms they had long been denied, they might ignite a transformation that could reshape the world. The ancient wisdom that pulses within women—a divine intelligence and a profound connection to nature—had been forgotten. She knew that this innate understanding brings balance, even amid the chaos, when fires roar and pandemonium threatens to overtake what fragile structures society has built on fear and deception.

Lucia remembered something that Ixchel had said to her, "Divinity seeks balance, for it exists in the very fabric of being. As the initial rage subsides, fertility and genesis will flourish. This harmony resonates within all beings, regardless of gender, for we all sense it deep within our hearts. The denial of our true selves has kept us from realizing our potential, and society has perpetuated this denial for far too long."

Lucia felt an electric thrill surging through her neurons as she pondered these truths. Suddenly, everything illuminated with a clarity that made her heart race. A fire ignited in her belly, fueled by awareness and contemplation. She understood the plight of many men; they, too, suffered under the weight of patriarchy.

Society often denied them the richness of feeling, intimacy, and nurturing friendships. From early childhood, they learned to be strong and to dominate, tasked with ensuring their families' safety and security. It was no surprise that many turned to objectification and control, trapped in a cycle that robbed them of their vulnerability and depth.

In acknowledging this shared struggle, Lucia felt a surge of empathy and a fierce determination to foster change, not just for women but for all who longed for a world rooted in authenticity and connection.

Lucia had recently read a study showing that men died by suicide at a far greater rate than women, exploring the reasons behind this alarming trend. "That is so much pressure," she thought. She longed to embrace every man she encountered, to whisper that vulnerability and authenticity were their actual sources of strength. Yet a troubling realization settled in as this urge had been shaped by the exact societal expectations that convinced women they must bear the emotional weight of men. How could change ever unfold when everyone remained trapped by rigid ideas of how to be?

As she delved deeper into these thoughts, her throat tightened, a visceral sensation as if something lodged in her esophagus resisted release. The internal struggle made her feel like she was choking, and soon, coughs erupted, escaping her control.

The man next to her patted her on the back, his touch gentle, while the woman in front of her took her hand, speaking softly to calm her spiraling emotions. Their combined actions coaxed the lump downward into her heart, and suddenly, a warm sensation radiated between her breasts. Thick, intentional breaths filled her lungs as she absorbed the kindness and concern shining in the eyes around her.

In that moment, Lucia grasped a profound truth: people do want to help; they yearn to support one another. All it takes is a reminder to reconnect with the heart.

That balance served as a divine connection to the earth, guiding us back to the flow; it was the heart. Everything naturally resides in the heart; we only need to pay attention and focus on it. Through art and kindness, the desire to help others, nature, and the planet's rhythms, we can navigate the deviant story that ensnared us all.

Lucia suddenly felt trapped in a tunnel, her head spinning wildly. She took a deep breath into her belly, then another, and another. Gradually, the world opened up again. In an instant, sounds and movements rushed around her, and she found herself standing in the X-ray machine, arms raised above her head.

She moved slowly to a nearby bench to regain her bearings and put on her shoes. Moving to the following security check proved foggy, those forty minutes feeling like a dream. Clearing her throat, she stood and practically floated toward the following line.

She breezed through that checkpoint, finding her concourse and settling in to wait for her flight. It felt as if she was about to step into a portal where space and time would suspend while she soared through the sky. She donned her headphones and prepared for the show before her, readying herself for the next leg of her journey.

Then Kate Bush came on, and she heard "Waking the Witch" resonate through her mind, stirring her deep within. Lucia flashed back to the moment she heard that song in the bathtub, its crystalline notes marking the beginning of her adventure. An alchemy had begun, stirring magic into her soul. Each note resonated, awakening dormant dreams and infusing her with a vibrant energy that reshaped her existence. In that quiet moment, she felt both the whirlwind of the past and the exhilarating promise of what lay ahead.

**

The plane rolled down the tarmac, and Lucia positioned herself to find balance for takeoff. She reveled in the thrill of flight, that visceral sensation that transformed her. Each ascent from the earth felt like a shift deep within, a moment she never wanted to miss.

As the aircraft rose above the dusty landscape, Lucia observed the tapestry of life below—houses, cars, trees, and hills shrinking into insignificance yet holding immense meaning. As they climbed, she let the vibrant tapestry of civilization fade, the clouds enveloping her in their embrace.

A spark of synesthesia danced in her mind as she imagined reaching out to touch the softness surrounding the plane, almost tasting the sweetness of cotton candy as it pierced through the clouds. The fluffy formations became whimsical mounds of wonder, separating everyone aboard from the animation below. They had entered another realm, a sanctuary of the skies that felt forbidden yet tantalizingly accessible.

In her mind, she traced the blanket of texture that wrapped around her, immersed in the profound Zen she had only discovered in flight. Here, time lost its grip, and she surrendered to the vastness that was out of her control. This altitude brought serenity, a soft lullaby that cradled her equilibrium, guiding her into a tranquil abyss where beauty reigned, and worries vanished into the horizon.

Lucia eventually struck up a conversation with the woman sitting beside her. She was a Dominican woman who had settled in Mexico for a few years, working in marketing after a previous career as a therapist in the United States. Melinda appeared surprisingly youthful for such a significant career change, but her dark eyes sparkled with excitement as they spoke. Lucia found the energy her new friend carried captivating.

Their exchange meandered through Melinda's therapeutic approach and her upcoming move to Seattle to be closer to her sister while pursuing a promotion. "How succinct," Lucia thought as she eagerly shared recommendations for the best spots in Seattle to explore diverse cuisines and vibrant neighborhoods. They laughed at the irony of meeting in Mexico, both of them eventually heading toward the Pacific coast.

Melinda described her unique form of therapy, which revolved around identifying the values each individual holds dear. Together, they aimed to remove obstacles that hindered those values and goals. Intrigued, Lucia felt a pulse of recognition; she had once considered becoming a philosophical counselor, weaving together belief systems and existential themes in her practice. This new method struck a chord.

As Melinda elaborated, she emphasized the significance of writing down personal values. "Values serve as our guiding light," she said. "If we follow them, we find our path. I remind my clients that while values may shift with changing priorities, regularly revisiting what matters most makes decision-making clearer."

Lucia absorbed these insights, impressed by Melinda's approach. The idea of helping others align their actions with their values resonated deeply, leaving Lucia inspired to weave this practice into her psychological journey.

Melinda shared stories about visiting her mother, describing the challenges of growing up with her mother's borderline personality disorder. Seated next to one another on the plane, the fast friends mused over their tendency to reside in their heads, acknowledging how difficult it was to connect from the heart.

Their conversation shifted to polyamory and monogamy. Melinda intended to maintain a long-distance relationship with her boyfriend, and Lucia wondered if they had ever considered polyamory a path to success. Melinda hesitated, wrestling with the complexities of discussing the potential for other relationships. They both recognized how deeply ingrained the notion of monogamy was in societal expectations.

At one point, Lucia noticed their voices rising above the plane's noise and felt a twinge of awareness that their openness might draw curious glances from nearby passengers. She hoped their discussion could challenge some beliefs and spark connections among strangers.

They reflected on their successes and failures, recounting valuable lessons from their journeys. Amid laughter and shared vulnerability, they decided to nurture their friendship once they both settled in Seattle. It felt incredibly synchronistic that fate had placed them next to each other on this flight at this precise moment, forging a bond that promised to deepen in the days to come.

Lucia pondered what allowed this circumstance to surface in her life so often. She didn't believe she possessed any unique charm to attract the people she needed to meet. Curious, she asked Melinda why they seemed to encounter such fortune. Melinda replied, "I'm not sure it truly matters. We embraced the moment and didn't shy away from the chance to connect. Opportunities for connection surround us constantly; we need to notice them."

They exchanged smiles, warmth radiating not just from their faces but from the relaxed muscles throughout their bodies, harmonizing with the vibrant symphony of connection unfolding around them. In that quiet moment, they locked eyes and agreed it was time for a nap. One at a time, they surrendered to sleep, their conversation fading like the last notes of an unfinished melody.

As Lucia drifted into the dream state, she felt herself buoyed in a vast sea of intellect and intuition, reminiscent of the tranquil places the monks retreat to in films. Whispers of wisdom echoed around her, each thought like a gentle ripple on the surface of water. The air filled with a sense of calm as if she were enveloped in a celestial embrace that invited deep reflection and insight.

In this serene realm, the worries of the world faded away, leaving only the pure essence of thought and understanding to guide her. This experience departed from the deeply rooted embodiment she had encountered before. It bore no resemblance to the feelings stirred during her trip to Mexico with Ixchel, where she had explored her connection with the divine and anchored her feminine power within her physical form. In this dream, Lucia navigated an ethereal presence, inviting new revelations to unfold.

It was light and airy, composed of clouds and wind. This place offered no grounding. As a child, Lucia envisioned a life here, in this separated divine where nuns dwelled and shamans visited before returning to the earth. It felt effortless to her, and she understood that many longed for this existence, a realm where they could shed their bodies and transcend the self. It felt holy, yet something vital felt absent. Now, she recognized what that was.

Lucia realized that the divine could not exist in transcendence alone; it needed embodiment in the world. The sacred resided not only in the unknown or within the things cradled in God's hands, but it also dwelt within our very selves. Sex holds the same sanctity as this ethereal realm; grief carries equal weight, and our physical bodies mirror Divine essence. She became fully aware that as the macrocosm reflects the microcosm, we form an integral part of all that exists, and it lives within us. This truth stretches beyond explanation, encompassing everything within us and the world around us.

This light-filled, intangible place allowed Lucia to grasp what lay beyond her; it mattered only if she could weave it into her actual existence. As she awakened from this dream, a profound understanding of Universal truth washed over her, urging her to transmute these insights into her life. All the mysticism in the world held little weight if she couldn't engage with it in her relationship to physical existence.

Lucia recognized that integrating every part of herself, especially this newfound awareness, was essential for her wholeness. Discovering her power ranked alongside touching the divine, and both demanded her attention. She knew that opening her heart hinged on confronting her truths—her baggage, her conditioning, and the burdens she carried. The splendid vastness she had explored stood as a guide, not a distraction. It offered a glimpse of the ethereal, a taste of the mysteries that mystics had sought to articulate for eons.

Lucia understood this realm and whispered that more exists beyond sight, that purpose and intelligence permeate every encounter. Through that place, she has the potential to transform her difficulties and pain into steppingstones that lead toward a deeper connection with her true self.

She felt her body collapse, heavy and weighted, her head growing fuzzy. So much thought and revelation flooded her in such a brief time. She listened to her body, resting while staring out the window at the clouds and the sun peeking below them. The thrust of her development over the past hours—many months to years, really—had been overwhelming.

She knew she had to pause and surrender, to let the Universe take over, or her frail human body would surely reject all the added information crashing through her mind. With a sigh, she settled deeper into the moment, allowing the gentle rhythm of time to cradle her.

So, she rested.

***

The journey from the plane through the airport felt insignificant, almost to the point that Lucia couldn't recall the steps she had taken to navigate through it. Her mind had settled into a serene calm, making her feel like she was sleepwalking as she picked up the rental car and headed toward a hotel in Santa Fe. As Lucia drove, the vibrant Southwestern art and adobe buildings caught her eye. Passing a school for the blind, she realized how crucial it was for those who are blind to have spaces designed for them, places where they could thrive and connect. The thought struck her, "It must empower them to share their world with others without the need for constant explanation."

Santa Fe embraced her with its soft, welcoming aura. The hotel offered comfort, and the restaurant downstairs served mouthwatering meals. With a sense of contentment settling in, she decided to stay for a few days, perhaps even a week. Lucia slipped into a more penetrating rest than she had ever known. She spent over half her time there asleep, indulging in leisurely meals whenever she felt hunger tug at her. Free from any obligations, she reveled in the luxury of time, with no need to rush or push herself toward any destination.

Strangely, Lucia didn't talk to anyone. It wasn't intentional; she lacked the drive, and the Universe obliged by keeping those around her wrapped up in their own lives, unaware of her presence. Moving through the picturesque city, reminiscent of the Southwestern art seen in college, Lucia felt like a ghost. In those moments, she didn't crave connection. The days turned into a week, then into two, and she drifted through it all without purpose.

Lucia hadn't engaged with the philosophical or psychological reasons for her experiences over the past year—those blissful moments that tangled together in vivid patterns and confusing antipatterns. Instead, she floated through her days, existing in a kind of quiet detachment. The world bustled around her, yet she felt insulated from it as if she were an observer in her own life.

Finally, after nearly two weeks had passed, Lucia woke one morning and headed down for breakfast. She overheard a couple discussing their recent visit to Taos, praising the remarkable art scene. They described the galleries and spoke of a town alive with creativity. Their conversation drifted to a place called Chimayo, just over thirty minutes from Santa Fe, near Taos. Though she couldn't grasp all the details, the mention of "holy dirt" and the magic of the land intrigued her.

That conversation ignited Lucia's determination to leave Santa Fe. She decided to visit Chimayo first, eager to uncover the source of the couple's enthusiasm. Approaching the clerk, she inquired about the holy dirt. He directed her to a mural on the side of a building, hinting at an arrow leading her to the Catholic church. Grateful for any guidance, she set off, even if his instructions felt vague and the topic seemed steeped in secrecy.

Navigating the winding roads, she arrived at the curious grounds. A few buildings surrounded a stucco church with dark wooden beams. Entering the courtyard, she was drawn to a large memorial honoring all the lost babies from abortions. The church's attempt to control women's bodies repelled Lucia.

"Okay, keep an open mind," she reminded herself. "You can feel the energy here; don't let this deter you." The atmosphere pulsed with somber reverence as she decided to absorb the weight of history and grief lingering in the air, a testament to both loss and hope.

Lucia had never believed the church's motivations for opposing abortion. To her, it revealed another way the patriarchy pressed its boot on women's necks. She refused to let this symbol of oppression hinder her; she continued past the pulpit and approached a small door at the back. Inside, a room overflowed with crutches and thousands of photographs depicting those who had found healing or were under prayer. She wondered if this place had received official recognition as a miracle by the Catholic Church.

Navigating through the sea of devoted Catholics, Lucia noticed a dimly lit room off to the side, its small doorway barely visible amidst the gathered crowd. Curiosity pulled her closer. Within, she found a two-by-two-foot hole where visitors eagerly scooped dirt into little jars and baggies. She overheard someone mention that the dirt never depleted, an endless supply for the hundreds who visited each day to take home a piece of holy earth.

Lucia approached the story with skepticism but felt fortunate to have a small Ziplock bag tucked in her pocket. She settled onto the cool, packed earth, her fingers diving into the space where the holy dirt lay. A soft, comforting energy surged from the earth, flowing through her hands and arms, nurturing her chest, abdomen, and groin, then rising back up. It washed over her in a gentle, cleansing wave—pure and filled with a compassionate benevolence for all living things.

Suddenly, rain poured down in sheets, relentlessly drumming on the structure's roof. Lucia sensed that it was time to leave. She walked deliberately to the car; the holy dirt cradled beneath her shirt. The rain cascaded down her body, a powerful force that swept away any trace of sin or shame, leaving her invigorated and light.

Climbing into the car, she sat dripping yet renewed. As she glanced out the window, the rain ceased, and the sun broke through the clouds, casting a warm glow over everything. A vibrant rainbow arched across the sky, more brilliant than any she had seen before. A wave of grace enveloped her as if she had just emerged into the world—untouched, unblemished, free from the burdens of past mistakes or harm.

Her humanity had taught her to forgive herself for not being perfect, but this felt different. The burdens of her past lifted completely from her shoulders, and she embraced a profound sense of grace for herself.

Oddly, Lucia didn't honestly believe in sin or the kind of divine grace the Bible described. To her, this feeling completely transcended religion, but that framework offered a way to make sense of her experience. This blessing crystallized within her, and she resolved to remember the feeling, to acknowledge the possibility of such grace. She knew this euphoria wouldn't last; she had to etch it on her heart, ensuring it would never fade into oblivion.

Drenched in gratitude, she whispered her heartfelt thanks to the sacred place, recognizing its significance long before the Catholics arrived. It had likely held profound meaning for the natives who first tread upon this land, serving as a site of reverence and connection to their ancestors. With a quiet prayer of gratitude, she carefully gathered the handful of dirt, its texture a reminder of the history woven into the earth and placed it in the glove box. In this way, she carried a piece of the holy ground with her as she drove away, a tangible connection to the past that would stay with her, grounding her spirit wherever her journey led.

Chapter Ten

INTEGRATION

Wholeness is not achieved by cutting off a portion of one's being, but by integration of the contraries.

- Carl Jung

Taos was the next stop on Lucia's quest, and a sense of lightness surged through her. With every passing mile, she felt stronger, ready to face whatever challenges lay ahead. Wind and water churned within her; she was vibrant and full of life. As she cruised down the road with the windows down, dust swirling behind her, the steering wheel suddenly yanked to one side. The car began to bounce violently.

Pulling over to the shoulder, Lucia stepped out and stared in disbelief at the shredded tire, strands of rubber and wire draping over the rigid steel rim. A chuckle escaped her lips at her misfortune, and she reached into the trunk for the jack and spare. Under the blazing sun, the heat enveloped her, and the once-refreshing breeze vanished. As she wrestled with the wobbly jack, she sliced her hand. Frustration welled up when she struggled to loosen the lug nuts, and in a moment of exasperation, the jack tipped, causing the car to crash back down with a jolt. Angry at the stubborn tire, she kicked it, then paused, guilt for her impatience washing over her. Taking a deep breath, she steadied herself.

Glancing around, she spotted a decent-sized rock nearby. Positioned in a more stable spot beneath the car, she used the rock to tap the tire iron gently. With a satisfying twist, she felt the lug nuts begin to yield. Encouraged, she repeated the motion until they all came off.

The sun burned against her neck, and irritation threatened to seep back in. Exhaling slowly, she noticed the wide-brimmed sun hat that she had bought at the airport gift shop for her mother resting in the back seat. Slipping it on, she shielded herself from the sun and swiftly replaced the flat tire with the spare. Once satisfied with her work, she climbed back in the car, revived in spirit and ready to hit the road again.

Lucia, overwhelmed by the situation, recognized it certainly sucked. Yet, she managed to navigate through it. Although not as gracefully as she would have liked, a brief respite eased her mind. Accepting the struggle as part of the learning process brought her some comfort. As she crept down the road on the donut tire— cautious not to blow that one out too—pride welled within. At least she knew how to change a tire; not everyone possesses that skill these days.

Rolling into Taos just as the tire shop closed, she dropped off the busted tire and sought out a quaint B&B nestled in the heart of town. The couple who ran this charming Southwestern home-turned-hotel radiated warmth and eccentricity. Vibrant alien art adorned the earthen stucco estate, and the Delancey name decorated every corner—on the mailbox, the mantle, in the garden, and even in the kitchen.

Mrs. Delancey, clad in overalls, had wispy white hair cascading around her pointed nose, her genuine smile exuding intelligence and warmth. Mr. Delancey, with wild blond hair standing on end, wore a crooked smile on his round, reddened face. He spoke in metaphors and stories as if carrying the secret knowledge of a universal joke, chuckling to himself. Attentive and caring, he ensured everything needed for comfort was at hand.

Her room tucked down a Southwestern-style hall bursting with vibrant turquoise and burnt orange, welcomed her in. The moment she crossed the threshold, relaxation washed over her.

Lucia strolled through the charming downtown, seeking a restaurant for dinner. After thanking the Delancey's, she set off to explore. Her eye caught a quaint cafe wine bar, choosing a spot outside to sip a Pinot Grigio while enjoying some tapas. A few couples walked arm in arm, but the number of single women outnumbered men, a detail she noted for later curiosity. People seemed carefree as they ambled down the street, their laughter mingling in the air.

Nearby, two women, old friends, animatedly shared jokes and laughter, their camaraderie radiating genuine warmth that seemed to brighten the entire patio. The infectious joy of their conversation echoed down the street, creating a lively atmosphere. They noticed Lucia watching with a smile on her face and nodded to her, still chuckling.

Lucia took the opportunity to learn more about them. "You act like sisters," she remarked, prompting another round of hearty laughter from the duo.

"We've only known each other for a week," one replied with a playful grin, her eyes sparkling with the thrill of their newfound friendship. "But you are right; it feels like we've known each other forever!" the other chimed in, agreeing enthusiastically. Their connection was undeniable, and Lucia couldn't help but feel a twinge of envy at their instant bond.

They explained their meeting as artists, bonded over shared experiences, and embraced their authenticity. As older women in Taos, they felt a responsibility to set an example for younger women, embodying the idea of living free from the weight of others' expectations. Their laughter echoed, sparkling with the joy of self-acceptance.

"We are too old to care," they declared. "Younger women need to learn this sooner." They explained that true happiness came from being genuine and adapting to life's challenges. Reflecting on their past struggles, they found solace in their current authenticity.

Maggie, the more eccentric-looking woman, was wild-haired and adorned with ample, chunky jewelry, chimed in, "Darlin', we waste so much time trying to fit into other people's expectations. To truly live, you must let go and be yourself!"

Her cackle rang out as Judy, her companion, draped in vibrant scarves, added, "The sooner you discover who you are, the better. I spent 25 years married to a man who never actually saw me. One day, I woke up and realized I had abandoned myself in my twenties to become someone I never wanted to be.

"That day, I packed my things, told him I wanted a divorce, and moved to Taos to pursue art. Struggling at first, I eventually found someone who recognized my work, someone who believed in my truth. Now, my art sells worldwide. Once I embraced my identity, everything fell into place. When you live as your true self, failure becomes impossible."

The vibrant ladies bestowed a blessing upon Lucia before returning to their lively conversation. Their candidness enchanted her, igniting a desire to embrace that same freedom one day. She sought a state of reckless abandonment, free from societal expectations. While invested in discovering her true self, these women revealed a comfort within her that she needed to access. Ingrained conditioning had long kept Lucia from fully accepting socially unacceptable aspects of her identity, regardless of circumstances.

At sunrise the next day, Lucia woke to a breathtaking display of oranges, pinks, and reds spreading across the sky like a painter's masterpiece. It was a rare experience, and the scene felt magnificent, almost otherworldly. The early colors wrapped everything in warmth, glowing through a rose-colored lens that made the world seem softer and more forgiving.

In that sliver of time, she sensed the hues held all the answers—quiet truths that needed no words. The vibrant tones ignited a spark of hope within her, whispering promises of new beginnings and endless possibilities that awaited just beyond the horizon. Finally, she began to embrace the unspoken parts of herself, releasing the pressure to confine them. Cradling that feeling as she sipped her coffee, she gazed out the window, humming an unfamiliar tune while watching the world awaken.

Today, she planned to visit the galleries mentioned by the women at the café. Picking up her tire weighed on her mind, and the cost nagged at her. Recent realizations about her dwindling savings were concerning because she was fueled by a desire to take her time and reluctant to rush back.

Lucia meandered through Taos, stepping into galleries that drew her in. One space captivated her with its soaring ceilings, where natural light poured through expansive skylights, creating a warm and inviting atmosphere. The illumination highlighted oval tables adorned with vibrant colors and intricate stones, each resembling miniature solar systems, sparkling as if they held galaxies within them. The overall effect was mesmerizing, drawing her in and inspiring a sense of wonder and creativity.

Suddenly, a persistent pressure pushed against her forehead, nearly knocking her off balance. Nothing physically caused it, yet the force felt robust and undeniable. A leathered woman in the corner raised an eyebrow, and Lucia felt the urge to reassure her with conversation.

The woman introduced herself as Kaya of the Hopi people, gently taking Lucia's hand. "My sweet girl don't feel the need to make small talk with this old woman. I've seen many souls and am seldom surprised. But being old now, I have little time for pleasantries; that merely fills space, and we have far more engaging matters to discuss."

Visions of sparks in shimmering shades of purple swirled gracefully around Kaya, illuminating the air like ethereal fireflies dancing in the twilight. Each flicker cast a soft, warm glow, wrapping Lucia in a comforting embrace that ignited a profound sense of safety within her.

As she stood across from this ancient being, the vibrant bursts of color only served to highlight her own youth and inexperience, a stark contrast to the deep wisdom and timeless presence of Kaya. It was abundantly clear that Kaya had long inhabited this land, her very essence intertwined with the earth, flowing through its rivers and whispering in its winds, history, and knowledge far beyond Lucia's grasp.

Kaya spoke candidly. "You need to learn how to integrate your gifts into your life. This realization comes with the understanding that everything is accessible to you and anyone open to it."

Confusion clouded Lucia's thoughts. "But I am practicing openness. I've worked hard at it for years," she replied, disappointment creeping in at the lack of acknowledgment for her efforts.

With a soothing tone, Kaya eased Lucia's defensiveness. "I sense you've shifted into a space of authenticity and attunement with the essence of women in the world. You've done important work here; I feel your growth in my bones. And yet... there's more ahead. You lack a connection in your movements. Embrace what you've learned, but never assume the journey ends here. I intend to nudge you toward an awareness that remains unfamiliar."

Lucia felt disoriented but embraced the surreal conversation. Kaya pressed on. "There exists a profound space between what we see and what we feel—a delicate zone that holds the tension between our internal selves and the expressions we project into the world and share with others. Picture this space as an intricate spider's web, intricately woven through every interaction in our reality and those realms we may not fully comprehend. Each strand of this web represents a thought as it precipitates action, a shimmering filament connecting our intentions to our behaviors.

"Every nuance that exists between subjects—between one individual and another, or between our desires and our reality— shapes a relational dynamic that is both complex and dynamic. This web is not merely a passive structure; it vibrates with the energy of our emotions, the weight of our experiences, and the myriad thoughts swirling within us. In this intricate interplay, we find ourselves navigating the subtleties of connection, understanding how each thread influences the whole, reflecting the fragility and strength of our human experience.

"What we learn about reality teaches us that we are subjects, while everything around us exists as objects to observe and interact with. This perspective complicates our grasp of oneness and our connection to nature and the vast systems of the Universe.

"We often separate ourselves from other beings, whether they are people, birds, mountains, the ocean, fish, cacti, or scorpions. Yet, the truth is that a vast web of interactions connects us all. If we view others as subjects with whom we share relationships, rather than as mere objects to engage with, we cultivate a genuine sense of honor and respect for all that exists."

Lucia must have looked thoroughly confused. Kaya paused, took a deep breath, and then locked her gaze onto Lucia's eyes. It was as though Kaya reached into the depths of Lucia's mind, tethering her to what seemed like another dimension.

Another push against Lucia's forehead sent her head tipping back; again, no touch accompanied the force. Suddenly, her consciousness shifted, revealing a white smoke-like web connecting her to Kaya. It flowed between them. Kaya smiled and snapped her fingers. Instantly, the web stretched beyond the door to Seattle, where Michael sat at his computer, his focus sharp. Lucia felt his unwavering motivation to change the world and uplift marginalized communities. Somehow, she understood he was devising a workshop for this purpose, even though they had never discussed it.

Kaya snapped her fingers again, and Lucia glimpsed Ixchel inside a small cathedral in Mexico City. Ixchel spoke with a priest, discussing her family's wishes for him to be present should her brother's last rites be needed. Lucia absorbed Ixchel's anguish and grief, as well as her presence in that moment. Yet, what surprised Lucia was the dismay residing in Ixchel's heart. The whirlwind of family obligations and sadness had momentarily swallowed her whole.

As Lucia's consciousness stepped back into the room, she turned to Kaya and asked, "What just happened? I saw the web, but then—I was transported to two people I love. I felt as if I experienced their moments in real time, sensing their inner feelings in a way that seemed impossible to access. Was I filling in the gaps with my assumptions? Was I imagining what they might be doing?"

Kaya regarded her with warmth and patience. "No, you weren't imagining anything. You connected with them, with their spirits, through the web that binds us all. Lucia, the Universe holds all knowledge; we each have access if we recognize the relational threads among everything. We are part of all things, and they are part of us; we are undeniably connected.

"What you experienced was an example of tapping into energy at any moment. Your dedication to your path has prepared you for this step. Often, our fears of division stop us; we objectify one another, limiting our access to the infinite. By maintaining self-awareness of the constrictions within our psychology, we begin to open. The more we open, the greater our capacity to recognize this web among everything, which is the active facet of divinity.

"The passive facet of divinity mirrors what Buddhists have discovered in silence— a space of stillness. It's crucial to understand that many aspects of divinity exist, each influenced by the perceiver, just as the witness adapts to it. This interplay explains how mystics often convey accurate perceptions of the Universe despite their seemingly contradictory experiences, each taps into a unique facet of the same diamond of truth.

"Every mystic carries their own cultural conditioning, upbringing, personality, and authentic essence. Each experience filters and reshapes the knowledge they share with the world. Everything adapts to the beholder, and divinity follows this rule. There isn't a single absolute truth; instead, many fluid truths reflect the divine. Each spiritual tradition emerges from mystics who explored different complexities of that divinity.

"Now, it is true that some people are mystics yet still practice division, and that works for them. Perhaps they need to focus on one area in this lifetime. Their souls will eventually align with full divinity while remaining human and engaging with the world. Finally, my dear one, you must remember that the ultimate spiritual expression comes through our human form, not by transcending it."

Lucia fell silent, grappling with Kaya's wisdom. It rang true but felt foreign, like a distant truth she had only brushed against until now. She had touched on these concepts before, but fully internalizing the possibility of such knowledge remained elusive. Something within her recognized Kaya's words as genuine; they felt infallible, sparking a profound awareness.

"What do I do with this information? How do I walk with it, Kaya?" Lucia's voice trembled with urgency.

"You may sit with it for a while, consider it, and pay attention to what stirs within you," Kaya replied gently.

Discombobulated, Lucia sought something to anchor her thoughts. Just then, a family entered the gallery, drawing Kaya's attention to their questions about her art. Their presence offered some grounding. Deciding to retreat for the day, Lucia slipped out, intent on returning tomorrow.

After that mind-blowing experience in the gallery, Lucia craved a connection to the earth. She drove into the mountains toward Lobo Peak, less than half an hour away, longing to be cradled by nature.

Overwhelmed, her heart racing, and her breath shallow, she struggled to find calm.

Deep breaths threatened her consciousness. Instead, Lucia's focus sharpened on the tangible—the road ahead, the yellow lines offering patterns of guidance and solidity. Wiggling toes and flexing fingers became her rhythm for the drive. Music filled the car, each lyric drawing attention and grounding her—every effort aimed to cultivate presence in her body.

At last, a turn-off appeared for a viewpoint and trail. Pulling over, Lucia parked and took to the path. As she walked, the air filled with the crisp scent of pine, a refreshing contrast to the lingering warmth of the sun. She soon reached a clearing, mesmerized by the breathtaking view. Towering mountains jutted toward the sky, their rugged peaks dusted with the remnants of snow, glistening like diamonds in the sunlight.

Little purple flowers blanketed the land, a shock of color that unfolded like a vibrant violet carpet beneath her feet. Their delicate petals danced gently in the soft breeze, creating a stunning visual symphony against the backdrop of deep green grass and rocky outcrops. The sounds of birds chirping filled the air while a distant waterfall murmured, completing this serene oasis in nature.

Lucia wandered toward a rock in the clearing and settled on top of it. Air filled her lungs as the pounding in her chest slowed. The tension in her body was released, and her focus sharpened. Caressing the rock's surface, she fell into its sturdy embrace, whispering a silent thank you for its support. At that moment, a stark black bird glided overhead, letting out a raspy caw. It soared gracefully, commanding the currents of the sky. Lucia had never witnessed a raven in its natural habitat before. Those seen in zoos or on animal cards had never prepared her for the sheer size and powerful presence this one possessed.

The raven circled above, repeatedly, before suddenly disappearing. Moments later, it returned with its partner, and both hovered above. Lucia noticed the smoky white thread weaving them together, connecting them to her—a delicate bond that felt almost tangible.

Lucia transformed from an observer into a participant. A sense of familiarity enveloped her as these birds seemed like family she had known forever. The ancient wisdom they embodied provoked a deep understanding of nature's teachings that surrounded them. Laying back, she watched their dance in the sky, feeling their essence blend with the wind, earth, and her own being.

Insight began to unravel, revealing the truths Kaya had whispered about: nothing exists in isolation, yet each energy carries its uniqueness. The movements of the ravens lulled her into a sacred rhythm, a timeless dance with the Universe itself.

Lucia wove through the air, blending with the meadow and stone, merging with nature's embrace. Then the presence faded, and the clouds drifted by, singing a timeless song—a melody woven by original peoples across the ages. It was the song of the dreaming; a tune etched deep in the collective memory.

Driving down the mountain, Lucia felt fully immersed in the moment. The sun began its descent behind the majestic peaks, casting a radiant purple hue across the sky that danced playfully with the dazzling light of the lunar bulb, illuminating the landscape with an other worldly glow. As she navigated the narrow, winding curves of the road, one eye remained fixed on the ethereal glow above, taking in the way it enveloped the surroundings in a soft, silvery light, while the other focused intently on the path ahead, each twist and turn demanding her full concentration. The cool mountain breeze swirled around her, carrying with it the scent of pine and the faint whispers of the quiet evening, enhancing the beauty of the moment.

The haunting sound of Native American flutes and rhythmic drumming vibrated deep within Lucia, awakening ancient tunes in her heart. Just as she prepared to exit the canyon, a white wolf leaped across her path, chasing a small rodent. She slammed on the brakes, the wolf pausing to lock eyes with her in the headlights, an intense blue reflected.

Taking a moment to breathe, Lucia witnessed the creature slip into the underbrush. A sudden jolt coursed through her as if Mother Nature herself had spoken: "PAY ATTENTION!" The words echoed within her, a clear call to remain present in the world around her. And she did.

***

After a fabulous meal of creamy wild mushroom risotto, Lucia wandered the town, guided by starlight and shadows dancing before the almost full moon illuminating the horizon. Sweet notes floated through the air from a guitar down the street, drawing her toward a glowing archway.

A middle-aged man sat there strumming his acoustic guitar, vibrant twinkles in his eyes shining through his shadowed silhouette. She paused to listen, captivated by the way his hands stroked the metal strings as if they were flowing from his very being. A small crowd gathered, mesmerized and silent, as the wind carried his music into the hearts of many.

Looking around, Lucia noticed a white radiance surrounding everyone, including herself. This musician united them, sharing a light that drew them closer. Did he realize the effect he had, or was it simply a natural gift? As she stood immersed in the moment, she began to see the web of white smoke connecting them, too. Each person affected the others; the music touched every soul present.

After what felt like hours of enchantment, the man thanked the crowd and started packing up his things. As the audience gradually dispersed into the night, Lucia approached the guitarist. He grinned as she introduced herself, revealing his name was David. They exchanged pleasantries, and Lucia asked if she could buy him a drink or a snack. David replied that he didn't drink alcohol but would gladly accept a cup of tea from a nearby late-night coffee house.

They sat in a quiet corner booth, sipping herbal health teas that warmed them against the cool desert night. Lucia turned to David, eager to learn about his background and what had drawn him to Taos.

As he spoke, a light filled the space around him. "I was born and raised in Florida—don't hold it against me," he chuckled, a grin spreading across his face. "I grew up in the bible belt of central Florida near the Kennedy Space Center. My childhood was tough; I learned to navigate life mostly on my own. I immersed myself in the church, trying hard to fit in."

He continued, "I knew I was David, but I was born Sarah. In my community, LGBT felt so foreign, almost like an alien concept. All I understood was WWJD—what would Jesus do? It was hard navigating those feelings in an environment that didn't seem to accept them. Socially, I presented as female, adhering to the role I was assigned at birth. Yet, inside, I always felt distinctly masculine." David paused for a moment, taking a deep breath as he gauged Lucia's reaction. She offered a warm, encouraging smile and a slight nod, signaling her support, and understanding, which provided him with a sense of comfort and courage to continue sharing his truth.

Reflecting on the challenges of those formative years, he shared, "I wore dresses to church and dedicated myself to my faith, but something always felt off. I began changing my name at four, desperately trying to join the boys' lines in gym class. I passed as a tomboy for years, but every time someone called me Sarah or insisted on how little girls should behave, I cringed.

"As I approached adulthood, I found comfort in a supportive lesbian community. My professional life in finance allowed me to embrace a more masculine identity without much questioning. Although coming out as a lesbian meant losing my place in the church, I soon discovered a spiritual path that fully accepted me, including my sexuality."

With increasing confidence, David explained, "After years of success in my career and a number of failed relationships, I started reading about people who were coming out as trans men. When I ran across it, I was enthralled. I read and watched everything I could find about people who were not gender-conforming.

"Something shifted in me, and I decided that I needed to start a new life as the person I feel I truly am. I moved to Taos because I had always been attracted to the art here, and I felt like I could express myself in a town full of creative types.

"Turns out, many people move to Taos to start over. The desert has a way of burning away the past. I started testosterone and have lived as David ever since."

He paused, thinking, then continued, "It's been about ten years now. Nobody even remembers what I looked like when I arrived; I was so different. I play music a few evenings a week and work as a caregiver for a wonderful older native woman who lives with her sister. They treat me well, and I feel privileged to be a part of their lives. Kaya needs me only during the days with Aponi."

Lucia's eyes widened, and she interrupted David, excitement bubbling over. "I met Kaya at her gallery just today!" She realized her outburst was a bit loud for such a small town, where connections seemed inevitable.

"Yes, she's an amazing crone who has supported me since I first stepped into this town. Kaya helped me acclimate and made me feel at home when I struggled to find my place. I'm glad you met her! She's my favorite person," David said, mirroring Lucia's enthusiasm.

Lucia refocused on David. "How do you feel now? As a trans person navigating the world, as a spiritual individual, in yourself?"

Continuing with his story, David explained, "I am generally at ease in my body now. Dysphoria—the feeling that my body doesn't align with my true self—is gone. I feel comfortable in my skin.

"When I first came out, discussing my journey, this openly felt impossible. I would never have shared my birth name with you back then. For years, I worried about how to look and act. But Kaya helped me relax and not take myself so seriously. She gave me the freedom to just 'be' without the weight of social expectations, judgments, or criticisms.

"When I had that space to be my authentic self, I stopped conforming to what I thought society expected of a man. It was profound and kinder to my spirit. Kaya taught me that being true to myself matters most on this journey and that authenticity is the clearest expression of God. My faith transformed into a journey of self-care rather than a destination to achieve."

Lucia was deeply moved by his sincere affirmations of his life and worth. She felt grateful for his openness and honored that he trusted her with his story. He mentioned that many didn't know his background because he passed so well, but with Lucia, an unexplainable connection blossomed.

David asked about her journey, but she responded briefly, eager to listen to him. "I'm unraveling my authenticity and desires. Thank you for asking, but I've been too focused on myself lately. I'd love to hear more about your hopes and dreams." She smiled and signaled to the server for more tea.

For hours, David shared stories about Aponi and her dementia, how she had illuminated his life, and what he had learned about being present with her. He recounted hiking trails in the mountains and strumming tunes on porches as tourists wandered by.

He spoke about music's ability to transform and how it anchored people in the moment—playing an instrument felt like gifting others a moment of peace in a chaotic world. David viewed his talent not as a personal joy but as a privilege to share with those who gathered to listen.

Lucia appreciated David's unclouded energy. He exuded clarity, free from overwhelming thoughts or existential questions. His unabashed authenticity sparked admiration in Lucia; she thought that if more people embraced their true selves, the world would shift toward simplicity, kindness, and joy. Suddenly, it struck her— Ixchel had spoken of gender revolutionaries, and David clearly represented one of them.

As they said goodnight, Lucia considered inviting David back to her B&B. The attraction was undeniable, and the chemistry sparked between them hinted at mutual interest. Yet, this didn't feel like the right moment for intimacy. Something magical had unfolded that evening, and it felt essential to preserve that moment. The night had unfolded perfectly, leaving her completely satisfied.

They exchanged contact information, promising to reconnect in a few days, both aware that something significant had begun.

* * *

Lucia rose with the sunrise once more; the cool, arid air filled her with vitality. A sense of peace enveloped her as the moon lingered on the horizon, casting a dreamy backdrop of stillness. The scene, utterly calm one moment, transformed the next. The sky shifted so subtly that she missed the changes, only noticing once they had occurred. Light, she mused, worked that way—constantly transfiguring through shifting perspectives. The intensity and direction of light altered how one perceived the world, creating a metamorphosis of imagery that redefined interaction with reality.

She chose to have breakfast at the same café visited with David the night before. As Lucia ambled down the drowsy street, a melody hummed from her lips—unfamiliar yet comforting.

The door chimed as she entered, greeting her with a lively atmosphere. Patrons swarmed the space, glasses clinking, and cooks shouting orders. A sweet, perky blonde welcomed her, guiding her to a seat by the window.

Lucia marveled at the number of early risers in this artsy town at 7:30 in the morning. Typically, mornings would find her lingering in bed until nine or ten, but here, laughter and conversation filled the air as locals savored farm-fresh eggs and gourmet coffee. The bright, spirited crowd exuded a warmth that reminded Lucia of her travels in Mexico.

Nowhere felt more inviting than this cafe, where a lively group of people exchanged playful banter. Each person engaged in conversation effortlessly, adding warmth to the atmosphere. The server glided from table to table, her smile radiant, balancing plates effortlessly along her arms. With grace, the woman in her fifties delivered food, making every guest feel like a VIP.

After savoring coffee and whole-grain toast topped with goat cheese, berries, and a drizzle of honey, Lucia noticed the cafe was beginning to slow down. The hostess wiped down tables and gathered condiment bottles, creating an organized display on the table in the back where Lucia and David had shared stories the night before. By nine a.m., only a handful of patrons lingered, sipping their coffee while deep in conversation.

A jovial, wrinkled man flirted with the barista; his voice gentle as he recounted the tearful moment he first met his newborn granddaughter. Lucia felt a stirring of surprise at his emotional openness. His words painted a poignant picture of life's bittersweet nature, revealing how joy often acts as a guiding light through sorrow.

He described gazing into the faces of his family as he expressed how that small child embodied hope and promised teachings yet to come. As he spoke, it became clear that this precious girl would hold an unshakeable place in his heart until his last breath.

***

Lucia left the café after hardly speaking to a soul, yet she felt as if she'd completed a course on humanity that morning. Gratitude exuded from her as she entered the light-filled gallery, eager to share her experience with Kaya—recollecting the tea with David and the synchronicity of it all. Scanning the gallery for Kaya's sweet face, she spotted a short, stocky woman rustling papers in the back.

"Do you know when Kaya will be back?" Lucia asked, her voice hopeful. The puffy-faced woman turned abruptly, tears streaming down her cheeks. "Kaya is... was my aunty," she stammered, struggling to find her voice.

Lucia's heart sank. "What do you mean? I just saw her here yesterday. What do you mean... was?" The weight of the room shifted as the reality settled in.

"She passed on last night. David found her this morning when he went to care for Aponi. She peacefully died in her bed. Are you Lucia? I am Lillian."

"Yes, did David mention me?" Lucia asked.

"No, honey, there was a note on the bedside table with your name. She must have known she was leaving last night. I have it here; David gave it to me when he came to tell me this morning." Lillian handed Lucia the envelope, her hand resting gently on Lucia's shoulder. "You should go outside and read it."

With tears brimming in her eyes, Lucia stepped outside and opened the letter.

Lucia,

Never forget that the dynamic force is within you, outside of you, and in everything. So, keep noticing, and do not limit yourself to what you think you know. A long journey ahead will bring you closer to harmony of spirit.

The most important lesson is that you are never above anyone or anything; you are a part of it. Therefore, as you learn extraordinary things, do not use it as an excuse to distance yourself from the world. Every experience is sacred, every interaction is unique, and you will miss them if you lose your reverence for every living thing.

You are soon entering an even more exciting adventure that will take you all over the world to hold space for people who experience facets of the divine. You will be the bridge to them, lending your wisdom to the world. It is a big and beautiful life that you will live. Be true to yourself, and you will always do your best in this life.

Finally, I may have left this earth, but I have not stopped teaching you. So, keep your mind's eye open, and I will be with you, guiding you. I know it feels like we only got an instant together, but you have been in my awareness for years.

Many Blessings, my Sweet Child. It was a pleasure to have met you in person.

Kaya

Lucia stepped back into the gallery. "May I keep this?" she asked gingerly, trying to hold back tears. Losing Kaya felt like losing her own grandmother.

Lillian, matter-of-fact yet gently, replied, "Yes, of course. She wrote it for you. A year ago, she described you to me, saying she'd seen you in a dream. Kaya believed she was meant to guide you, to remind you of something important. She knew you'd show up eventually, and now here you are, meeting her on the day she passed. Her magic never ceases to surprise me, though I should expect it. That woman was a powerhouse of wisdom, bridging worlds as if it were second nature. Did you know she was ninety-eight?"

"No! I thought maybe she was in her late seventies!" Lucia exclaimed.

"She has always been an elder, teaching and walking the line between dimensions. Known across many tribes for her insight, the fact that you entered her awareness is incredibly special. Don't take it lightly." Lillian's tone held an urgent sincerity.

"I won't, I promise," Lucia replied, speaking from the depths of her heart.

"If you'd like, choose a small piece of art to take home. Kaya would want you to have something," Lillian offered, her voice trembling with grief.

Lucia felt grateful as she selected a small, round necklace adorned with an infinity symbol, which captured the essence of eternal connection.

After stepping outside, she realized she hadn't hugged Lillian. Turning back, she retraced her steps only to find the doors locked, the lights off, and a sign that read, "CLOSED UNTIL FURTHER NOTICE." A sense of finality washed over her, as if the weight of the world had settled on her shoulders. She paused for a moment, taking in her surroundings, acutely aware that this was it, a finality she hadn't expected.

She thought about how she was in that little cafe, and life was bustling while David, Kaya's family, and friends were grieving. As people suffer, others thrive. Both exist side by side. That's why the man in the café spoke the truth: we must embrace joy whenever we can. Fully present, we can appreciate every facet of our experience.

With a loud sigh, Lucia noticed the startled glances of passersby. A shy wave and nod acknowledged them as she strolled down the street toward the park. Long strides carried her forward, her gaze landing on children laughing and playing on the playground. She meandered toward a patch of flowers, inhaling their sweet aroma, drawing their essence deep into her being.

An image of Kaya appeared in her mind, a radiant smile lighting the memory. Suddenly, a gentle thump against her forehead jolted her attention. Before her, a translucent form floated between the blooms. The familiar energy emanating from this presence mirrored the connection she had felt with Kaya just the day before. A strange comfort enveloped her that decimated her resistance. Kaya wasn't gone; she remained, hovering between worlds, free of form yet vividly present.

Lucia sensed that this bond would continue to guide her, though she couldn't articulate how it would manifest along her journey.

***

Lucia called David to express her sorrow for his loss and to talk about Kaya. David wept as he shared how much he would miss her but acknowledged the blessing of having known the wise sage. With gentle clarity, David indicated that it would be best to reach out when the weight of grief lightened. Lucia understood that this would take longer than he anticipated. She explained that she would be leaving Taos but welcomed his contact, whether it came in a day, a week, or even years.

After graciously checking out of the B&B, Lucia remembered David mentioning the scenic highway between Flagstaff and Sedona, Oak Creek Canyon. That became her destination.

A strange emptiness settled in her gut, compelling her to sit with the feeling rather than rush to fill it. Embracing this void, she drove, letting the road be her only focus. With each mile, she remained present in her emotions, allowing the experience of moving forward to unfold naturally. As the profound small town receded in her rearview mirror, she continued to navigate the landscape of a world filled with pain and joy simultaneously.

Chapter Eleven

TRANSFORMATION IS THE HARDEST PART

The true beauty of a woman is reflected in her soul.

-Audrey Hepburn

Kaya's death felt surreal, unlike the other losses in her life. Lucia's thoughts drifted back to years prior when her ex-boyfriend and friend, Gabriel, had died. Having been in Hawaii when it happened, there was difficulty feeling supported in her grief. With his curly blonde hair and cobalt eyes that seemed illuminated from within, Gabriel opened new worlds for Lucia that she never anticipated. He introduced her to a labyrinth that led her through corridors of philosophy, where ideas danced and debated, igniting a spark of curiosity that kindled a thirst for knowledge within her. Alongside this intellectual awakening, he introduced her to the intricate realm of kink. This curious mix thrived in the intimate spaces of her mind, urging her to explore the boundaries of trust and vulnerability.

Each interaction with Gabriel felt like peeling back layers of herself, revealing desires and thoughts she hadn't yet acknowledged. The way he spoke about ethics and morality, intertwined with discussions about pleasure and consent, made her realize the depth and variety of human experience. Lucia's experience with her unconventional lover was her first glimpse at the diversity of her desires, a sensory awakening that was both intoxicating and terrifying, even if she didn't fully grasp what it meant for her at the time.

Lucia often imagined Gabriel as a reincarnation of Socrates, a philosopher who traversed life as if he inhabited multiple realms. His profound and elusive thoughts frequently left others struggling to keep pace. She loved him deeply, though never in a conventional romantic way.

Their bond danced between friendship and romance, perfectly balanced across the hour of distance that separated them. They dated other people freely during their time together, and Lucia cherished that sense of freedom. She hesitated to label it polyamory, as she had not taken any of the people she dated too seriously during that time.

They had wavered in and out of each other's lives for nearly ten years. When Lucia met Andy, she felt the urge to deepen that connection and made the difficult decision to end things with Gabriel. She knew it shattered his heart, but right then, she could love and commit to only one person. They hadn't repaired that damage when Gabriel died. The loss of their relationship as her lover weighed heavily on her heart, yet she remained hopeful that their paths would cross again.

A month before his death, she reached out to him, and he urged her to find him on a dated social media platform that she had never used. Motivated, she finally logged onto the site he had suggested. But when she arrived, she discovered the heartbreaking news: Gabriel had died just twenty-four hours before she found his profile.

Lucia was devastated and struggled to accept that he was truly gone. She found herself on a rocky cliff overlooking the ocean, clutching a single burgundy calla lily. In a quiet moment, Lucia spoke to his spirit in the only way possible: by performing a little ritual to say goodbye.

With stones in her chest, she tossed the flower into the waves, a simple yet poignant farewell. At that time, intellectualizing her grief was her only way of processing it, romanticizing death as an ethereal connection between them. She held onto the hope that somehow Gabriel would reach out to her from the other side.

Despite her sense of loss, she hadn't fully internalized that he was lost to her forever. She clung to the belief that he would send messages about what lay beyond. For years, that hope softened her heartache, leading her to think that if he could communicate with anyone, it would be her. Yet time passed, and silence filled the void he left behind.

As the years wore on, Lucia grappled with the harsh reality of absence, feeling the deep ache of a loved one lost. She found herself questioning her significance in his life. Did s? Had she broken his heart too profoundly for him to reach out? Perhaps he had moved on to another life, one where communication was impossible.

A twinge of irritation crept into her heart; why hadn't he pushed through the veil for her? Though she recognized this frustration as selfish and petty, it remained a thorn in her side, one she allowed herself to carry as a reminder of the love they once shared.

Lucia focused her thoughts on Kaya. Kaya had made Lucia feel valued; she truly saw her, striking a chord deep within Lucia's isolated heart. The connection they shared—before and after death—felt like an extravagant gift, one that Lucia had never imagined receiving. Kaya's ability to make Lucia feel important was both strange and exhilarating.

For as long as she could remember, Lucia sensed a hidden knowledge inside herself, a thread that connected her to the universe's mysteries. Yet, the outside world had never confirmed this as truth until Kaya. That feeling of being misunderstood widened the chasm between her and the rest of humanity, making it nearly impossible for her to forge attachments.

While she had discovered a genuine connection with Michael and Ixchel, they did not affirm Lucia in the same way Kaya did. Lucia had always secretly hoped that a psychic or a healer might recognize her unacknowledged gift, but no one ever did. Once, years ago, while dreaming of owning a coffee shop where people gathered to share ideas, an energy worker had told her that her vision was limited—that she was destined for much greater things, but that was the extent of affirmation in Lucia's life.

Kaya, ancient and wise, had chosen to bond with Lucia, igniting a spark of wonder within her. This bond felt surreal, yet Lucia found herself replaying it, reading the letter Kaya had written each time she made a rest stop on the road. It was actually quite tricky for Lucia to accept what had happened between them.

Her heart swirled with gratitude and grief. One moment, Lucia felt thankful; the next, an overwhelming sadness washed over her at the thought of Kaya leaving the physical world. Memories from the past filled her mind, spinning and bouncing like a rubber ball, making it impossible to grasp what was real.

"What is happening to me?" she thought, frustration bubbling beneath her surface.

Drawing a deep breath, she drove into the painted desert, the barren landscape sprawling before her. Pulling into a lookout point, Lucia stepped out of the dusty car, the heat enveloping her like a suffocating blanket. She climbed a large hill, her mind racing, oblivious to the path beneath her feet. The air felt thick and hot in her lungs, short and breathy, while her heart raced, heavy within her chest.

As she continued up the incline, a leaden weight settled in her legs, pain creeping into her hips with every step. She halted, grounding herself with a deep, intentional breath. A sharp awareness dawned on her: her body mirrored the chaos of her mind. It responded to the frenzy, dense buzzing coursing through her skin, burrowing deep into her muscles, and aching all the way to her bones. Her marrow throbbed with a profound fatigue, demanding release.

Lucia recalled a session with a healer named Isabel from years past. The woman had endeavored to teach Lucia about the profound interplay between emotions and the mind in shaping the body. Isabel had always emphasized the holistic necessity of treating the self as a unified mechanism.

Lucia vividly remembered Isabel's words, "The body, mind, emotions, environment, and social self-function as one," Isabel explained. "At times, you may focus on one aspect more than another, but they are all interconnected. Think of it like a complex machine: when a specific part wears out, the entire mechanism might seem intact yet neglecting that single piece leads to a cascade of problems, ultimately causing the whole to break down. Our bodies work the same way; consider it emotionally—one facet influences the others.

"Personal well-being arises only when you address the entirety of yourself. You're fractured, viewing each part as a mere sliver to compartmentalize. This approach serves no better than a band-aid on a deep cut. Picture how we must clean a wound to eliminate bacteria; that process is critical. It doesn't stop there; we also need to ensure the wound stays clean. The way antibodies and blood collaborate to fend off infection is equally vital."

These words resonated within Lucia, a reminder that true healing required more than superficial fixes. She could almost hear Isabel's voice urging her to embrace the entirety of her being rather than dismiss the interconnectedness of her experience.

"Everything in your body collaborates to heal wounds, but if you neglect to tend to them, your body falters. The environment can either harm or nurture our emotional health, while our mental well-being similarly influences our physical state. This dynamic opens us to the spiritual realm, which in turn supports or stunts our emotional growth, affecting our mental clarity and, ultimately, our bodies.

"We cannot learn to manage stress and pursue overall wellness without engaging with the emotional body and the nervous system. Likewise, we can't address the nervous system without untangling our thoughts about it. These cycles weave together endlessly. The vital truth is that everything connects, and every aspect is significant."

As Lucia recalled the healer's words, she recognized how they had eluded her understanding then. Although she had grasped intellectually that her body and mind were intertwined, she had failed to appreciate the depth of that connection until now.

She felt a subtle shift within her, a realization illuminated by her past experiences. The intimacy of her sexual encounters had drawn her closer to her body, revealing how pleasure and freedom transformed her sense of self. Yet, the stark effect her emotional and mental states had on her overall system struck her as more profound. She sensed the wholeness of her being—every interaction changed her fundamentally, including the way her muscles responded and the heaviness that now accompanied her. This newfound awareness flooded her with understanding, a tapestry woven from the threads of her body, mind, and spirit.

As she absorbed the weight of it all, Lucia glanced at the dry Earth on the hill, spotting a lizard perched on a rock, its gaze fixed on her. She met the ancient creature's watchful eyes and attuned herself to its steady breathing. She noticed how its scaled belly rose and fell in sync with the heartbeat of the Earth. With one eye on her and the other focused on a bug dancing in the air, the lizard flicked out its tongue, effortlessly capturing its prey while remaining perfectly still.

Inspired, Lucia yearned to mimic the lizard's grace. It moved in harmony with its surroundings, centered and mindful even as it fulfilled its needs. She reflected on the times she had spiraled into anxiety, feeling as though she was spinning her wheels in the mud, getting nowhere.

Determined to live more consciously, she recognized the importance of facing life's challenges rather than skirting around them. The answers didn't lie in relentless positivity; they thrived in the grit of honest struggle, where she could awaken to her emotions and allow them to pass through her. She understood that these feelings did not have to become rigid and stagnant within her body and heart; instead, they could serve as gateways to insight rather than barriers.

Taking a deep breath, Lucia thanked the lizard for its unspoken lessons, offering quiet gratitude to the healer who had imparted this wisdom. She regretted that it had taken her so long to understand. Suddenly, a wave of energy surged through her, urging her to move, and she began to shake her body free, embracing the rhythm of the moment.

She glanced around to ensure no tourists lingered nearby, then wiggled as she walked down the path. Her arms shook, her hips and back swayed, and her body moved freely with each step. She must have looked ridiculous, but she couldn't help it; laughter bubbled up from her belly, filling the air with snorts and guffaws. By the time she reached the top of the hill, her cheeks ached from grinning so wide. Grateful that no one had witnessed her foolishness, she twisted and stretched, wringing out the heaviness in her bones, letting the ground absorb it.

Approaching the lookout, Lucia paused with an overwhelming sense of awe. Before her lay a watercolor landscape pulsing with ancient magic, a tapestry of hues woven with the threads of time. Lime greens bled seamlessly into soft coral pinks, merging into sun-soaked golden flecks that sparkled like lost treasures hidden within the Earth's embrace. A shadow swept across Nature's canvas, a fleeting specter that ignited the mountains of stagnant rock with a sudden, fierce intensity. For a brief, breathless moment, the colors deepened, rich and dark, as though the Earth itself held its breath. Then, as the cloud drifted on, everything erupted back into light, brighter and more vibrant than before, as if the very essence of life had been rekindled.

The painted desert before Lucia undulated, alive with the sun's dance, each brushstroke of color vibrating with a heartbeat of its own; it was very much alive. She felt an irresistible pull as if she could tumble headlong into that vivid world, surrendering herself to the thick, intoxicating power that threatened to engulf her like a wet acrylic mess, lush and limitless.

She stood gazing out for what felt like days, though it was probably less than an hour, becoming lost in the vast flow of brilliantly composed pigments. Lucia felt a deep sense of wonder as she contemplated the ways humans can disrespect Nature as if they exist apart from it. She was reminded of the conversation about how we objectify what surrounds us. A swell of gratitude rose within her for the immense blessing of living in this world and being able to witness the beauty of this living entity in front of her.

As people began to flood into the lookout, she gathered her thoughts and descended the hill, feeling lighter with each step. Once inside the car, she revisited her realizations around the heaviness and overwhelm that had clouded her earlier.

At that point in time, a deep-seated ache reflected in Lucia's heart—a feeling of never being seen as the person she truly was. Longing for others to notice her, understand her, and appreciate her unique gifts had shaped much of her life. A vivid memory surged forth, a snapshot of her as a child—no more than four—when she stood before her parents, her voice ripe with desperation, insisting, "Why don't you believe me?" She could hear the words repeating in her mind, each utterance echoing her frustration.

In that childhood moment, she tried to convey a vision, an authentic glimpse into her reality. Yet, in response, her parents dismissed her, arguing it couldn't be real because they didn't perceive it. That dismissal stung, planting seeds of doubt and making her feel unimportant, as if she had to prove that her insights were genuine. Lucia recognized now that her parents, though oblivious to her truth, viewed her as an imaginative child. They failed to grasp the depth of her experience, the reality she occupied while they remained blind to it.

As she recalled her younger self, a wave of sadness washed over her for that little girl who felt overlooked and unvalued. In that realization, Lucia understood the root of her lifelong struggle: the unrelenting urge to prove herself and seek validation in a world that too often felt indifferent.

Lucia had felt an urgent need to convince everyone she wasn't fabricating her reality. Having learned to adapt to her surroundings, to sidestep the label of "crazy." The sense of being misunderstood clung to her through her teenage years, far into adulthood. Remembering the many times she envisioned herself perched on the edge of a fishbowl, dipping her feet in while the other fish swam and interacted just out of reach.

Then she met Michael, and everything began to shift. He offered her a space where openness felt safe; she didn't need to prove her worthiness for his care and attention. Preemptively, Alex had bolstered her sense of acceptance and openness. But on a deeper level, Lucia experienced a profound acceptance of her gifts with Ixchel, touching her soul on a spiritual plane. Despite this, she still felt like a student of Ixchel's lessons.

Lucia understood that she would always be a student of life, yet something distinctly different stirred within her in Kaya's presence. It was as if Kaya had passed her a torch—not merely as a student, but as someone destined to carry on her work. Kaya recognized the person Lucia had always aspired to be. She saw the potential in Lucia's highest self, and though it left her feeling overwhelmed and sent her nervous system into a whirlwind, her soul felt honored.

Kaya's belief in Lucia, though daunting, ignited a fierce motivation within her. Lucia had often realized that she responded better to encouragement than to criticism. When Kaya expanded her vision to encompass Lucia's potential rather than her shortcomings, Lucia found herself eager to rise to the occasion. She was determined to meet those expectations. After just one encounter, Kaya recognized Lucia's capabilities clearly enough that she handed over the keys to her metaphorical castle. Now, it was Lucia's time to embrace the challenge of someone finally believing in her.

But Kaya had died. That strange twist gnawed at Lucia: even though Kaya had passed shortly after their meeting, she felt present with every step. When Lucia sensed the pressure on her forehead, it was apparent that Kaya lingered with her still, a guide she would never lose again.

As Lucia returned to the road, clarity washed over her. She processed the trauma that had cast shadows over every relationship, including those with her family. She recognized how she had sabotaged herself in her pursuit of approval and love.

The thought of living authentically filled her with quiet joy. Lucia understood now that the more genuine her life became, the more success would follow. It seemed accurate for everyone. "If only we could all sift through the burdens we carry," she mused, recalling Kaya's wisdom and Daniel's insights, "then we could uncover our true selves. There's no way anyone would fail."

As Lucia drove through the parched land, tinged with sharp and stinging life, she stopped to let snakes and armadillos cross the road. This land felt sacred, and she honored its wildlife, feeling a connection that whispered secrets to her soul.

***

Lucia drove into Flagstaff, meeting the sunset; the sky blazed, casting fiery hues that seemed to burn off the universe's impurities. The desert heat echoed the colors above, and in that instant, she recognized a yearning deep within her. The passion the fire had for the sky mirrored the fervor desired for her own life. If she surrendered to that flame, she could transform into something attuned to her own potential, finally stepping into the person she was meant to be.

She approached a rundown, single-level hotel, its facade glowing in the evening light as if it harbored a secret code visible only at that precise hour. Lucia clutched her night bag, pausing to drink in the last moments of the magical illumination, allowing the vibrant colors to wash over her. In the stillness of the parking lot, she tilted her head back, immersing herself in the beauty of the dusk, when a car's horn pierced the air, jerked her out of her trance, and brought her back to reality.

Stumbling through the squeaky office doors, Lucia stepped into a cool, musty room. An older man with long white hair stood behind an intricately carved oak desk. Beautiful paintings of landscapes adorned the dirty brick walls, depicting red rock canyons streaked with greenery and ancient ruins. One canvas featured a river flowing through a sunlit gorge.

Clearing her parched throat, she asked if he had a room for the night. "Sure, a queen, okay?" he replied. She nodded, then hesitated before asking about the paintings. His face lit up. "I'm the artist!" He reached across the desk to shake her hand.

"I am Blaze, nice to meet you. I paint the vortex zones in Oak Creek Canyon. It's one of the most powerful places in the world." As he spoke, Lucia studied the paintings, captivated by their vibrant colors and evocative imagery. Blaze talked with enthusiasm about the magical land, sharing tales of the natives who once thrived in that rugged terrain. "The Anasazi people," he said, his eyes gleaming with passion. "The Navajo called them 'the ancient ones who weren't us.'"

He explained how the Sinagua Tribe followed, learning to construct pueblos in the canyon from the Anasazi. "They were the Indigenous people of the land without water," he added, his hands gesturing animatedly. Blaze described how the land's energy had drawn these ancient cultures to these sacred places.

"I can't imagine anyone driving through that canyon and not feeling the land's enchantment," he declared. "The vortexes make me feel as if I'm walking in another dimension. Be sure to get your footing before you step into that ancient place; it'll throw you for a loop, I guarantee!"

Lucia smiled, agreeing to be cautious while expressing her appreciation for his art and knowledge. Blaze chuckled. "I don't have any wisdom, young lady, just a heap of information I get to share with people like you." He handed her a key, directing her gaze to the far corner of the hotel.

Grateful, Lucia turned toward the door and asked if he would be available later to discuss the space between Flagstaff and Sedona. "Yes," he replied. She promised to stop by after dinner, eager to delve deeper into the stories woven into the land.

Lucia felt a curious pull toward the vortexes, intrigued by the notion of energy points hidden in the canyon. Memories of her time in the lush Mexican jungle with Ixchel surfaced vividly in her mind. Leaving her wondering if she truly experienced that power or if Ixchel had amplified it for her. She hoped to tap into the same energy on her own in this stark desert landscape. Because she'd always considered herself a woman of water and green forests, the allure of the arid surroundings struck her as peculiar.

She strolled past the rugged wooden doors of the hotel nestled against layered cliffs, finally reaching her room, number thirty-three. A smile tugged at her lips, for she had always felt an affinity with the number three. The door stuck, causing her to force it open, loudly revealing a modest, tidy room lined with wood paneling—a space barely large enough to navigate around the bed. An old TV occupied half the dresser, its presence a reminder of simpler times.

She collapsed onto the bed, releasing a deep sigh. The prospect of food lingered in her mind, but fatigue threatened to pull her into sleep's embrace. All this self-reflection exhausted her.

Reluctantly, Lucia rose, not solely for the sake of dinner but also because she had promised Blaze she would return. She craved more knowledge about the hiking trails in the canyon. After a short walk, a small café on the corner appeared, providing a quick and straightforward meal. Sitting quietly, she savored her tomato soup paired with a grilled cheese sandwich on sourdough. Laughter filled the air as the server playfully coaxed guests into ordering pie, and many left with slices tucked under their arms. Lucia found comfort in the simple joys of ordinary life, a soothing balm for her weary spirit.

Not lingering beyond her meal, she made her way back to the hotel office. Peeking through the door, she spotted Blaze, his grin brightening the space. His smile radiated warmth, energizing her as she stepped inside.

He shared tales of the Paleo Indians, each rich with detail and evoking her imagination. Though she sensed he shaped these narratives through his hopeful lens, her curiosity deepened. Blaze provided directions to several trails leading to ancient ruins, then, recognizing someone had entered the office, bid her goodnight, and turned his attention to the new guest.

She left and sank into a heavy sleep, dreaming vividly. In one dream, drumbeats echoed behind her as she walked into a river. Suddenly, she found herself submerged in icy water, breathing in the liquid as if it were air. Someone in white grabbed her shoulders and pulled her back up, shouting, "You are saved!" Startled, Lucia woke up, a twinge of sadness lingering; in the dream, this experience had stripped away something essential—her sense of freedom.

She vaguely remembered seeing herself as a native in that dream, an unsettling realization. The Christians had arrived and were baptizing the Indigenous Americans. This dream reminded her of privilege as shame washed over her for being born white. The imagery ignited memories of the stories she had heard about the Christian settlers and the atrocities they committed against the Indigenous people. She had never felt proud of her ancestors' actions nor of the ongoing injustices perpetrated by many in her community against Indigenous, Black, and marginalized individuals.

Her privilege felt like a heavy halo, a mark of pain, turmoil, and destruction wrought by her people to so many. Lucia took a deep breath, praying for ways to repair the damage her ancestors had inflicted. She longed to use her privilege to uplift those that society had undermined, striving to do so in ways that honored their voices and needs. She refused to impose her "right" answers or further colonize their experiences, understanding that genuine support required listening and understanding, not simply imposing her will or white guilt.

Eventually, she drifted back to sleep after a couple of restless turns. This time, she entered a dream where she cared for an infant. It wasn't hers, yet she felt the weight of responsibility. She knew she had to nourish the tiny being before her. As she cradled the child, it transformed into a blinding white light that spilled into the room, then flooded the building, and finally enveloped the world. When Lucia woke, dazed, and disoriented, the sun had risen, signaling it was time to pull herself together for a hike to the ruins.

After a quick stop at a quaint coffee hut for a warm, flaky croissant and a steaming latte, she drove onto the narrow highway cradling Oak Creek Canyon. As she entered the surreal chasm, breathtaking beauty unfolded in every direction, leaving her stunned. The rust-colored rock, worn and weathered by time, jutted majestically from the Earth, glimmering in the sunlight with flecks of deep orange and red. Tiny jade-colored bushes clung precariously to the rocky outcroppings, their vibrant green contrasting sharply with the canyon's warm hues.

Layers of land rose and intertwined like Blaze's canvas, each stroke revealing mesmerizing textures ranging from smooth stone to rugged cliffs lined with ancient trees. She understood why she felt an irresistible pull to this sacred place; it was an invitation to explore the untouched beauty of Nature. As the shaman's drumming thrummed in her brain, the imagined sound began to resonate a deep rhythm that sought to replace her heartbeat, guiding her deeper into the canyon's embrace.

An ancient energy buzzed through her, filling her with electrical waves of vitality and wisdom that brushed over her through the whispers of the wind against the rocks. Power pulsated in the air, urging her forward, beckoning her to uncover the secrets hidden within the wild heart of this enchanting landscape.

Stopping at the first trail Blaze had recommended, Lucia pushed through the bushes and rocks, her hike promising to unveil a stark landscape. Yet, life buzzed all around her—bugs skittered over the soil, snakes slithered through the sharp grass, rabbits darted among the underbrush, and lizards basked on sun-warmed stones. Above, birds and dragonflies danced playfully in the air, their presence a welcome company. She continued down the dirt path, absorbing the striking contrasts of rusty reds and vibrant greens. The land pulsed with power, compelling her to pause for deep breaths every few hundred yards.

Suddenly, a snake crossed her path, halting to meet her gaze briefly as if imparting wisdom about change and growth. The steady pounding of its tiny heart echoed within her. For a fleeting moment, she envisioned the serpent entwined with an old shaman, dancing beside him as he summoned transformative lessons for his people. This vivid image vanished as quickly as it appeared, leaving Lucia enveloped in a profound sense of oneness with her surroundings.

Just as Kaya had taught her, Lucia understood she was not merely an observer; everything around her held its own essence and narrative. They interacted, weaving a tapestry of existence together rather than separating themselves into a mere subject and object. She felt a twinge of sadness thinking about how people had distanced themselves from Nature, treating it as something to dominate and control. "If humans could recognize their interconnectedness with nature," she mused, "they might become harmonious participants in the greater whole."

She realized that it was their responsibility to collaborate with Nature, not fight against it. She understood that all the answers to life's riddles—health, death, synchronicity, and social bonds—echoed within the natural world, waiting for those willing to tend the Earth and heed its lessons.

Lucia felt an ache in her heart for the dissonance that had plagued her for so long, a rift between herself, Nature, and the universe. The importance of her relationship with all things loomed large in her mind. Lucia considered how some mystics proclaimed this separation was an illusion, a mirage rather than the essence of life. Yet, it was not the unity preached by many, either. It embodied the dynamic force that flowed between all subjects. Each piece of life resembled a cell in the intricate body of the divine and the universe. The connection, the relationships, formed the critical core of existence.

She pondered lessons gleaned from Buddhism. "Many in body, one in mind" resonated with her. It merely represented another facet of the whole, a sparkling diamond that captured the essence of life. Buddhism illuminated the importance of releasing attachments that stifled growth and opened pathways to peace amidst the tumult of existence. She understood the Buddha's path called for recognizing the sacredness in the world while fostering balance within us, ultimately allowing clarity to emerge.

Paganism and witchcraft drifted into Lucia's thoughts, another facet of the grand tapestry. The harmony of masculine and feminine life forces vibrated throughout Nature and manifested in the practice of magic. Here lies the power of will, revealing humanity's capacity to engage with Nature, animals, and each other. Spells unfolded as a conscious manipulation of the web of interconnections, an awareness of one's ability to create, destroy, flow, or resist. This connection allowed her to attune herself to the divine pulse that threaded through all of creation.

Her mind also wandered to her college classes on Hinduism. One professor had shared insight about the Gods and Goddesses, who represented aspects of the human psyche. They stood like beacons, guiding and guarding the spirit through the darkness. Each deity illuminates the drives and desires that shape our journey, helping us navigate the hills and valleys of existence.

Lucia pondered the myriad of spiritual philosophies that guide us through the complexities of the self, each seeking to explain our place within the vastness of existence and considering how the depth of the mind and heart mirrors our mental capacity. As humans, we instinctively embrace aspects that feel beyond our grasp; acceptance becomes our path.

Pondering the complexities of spirituality while weaving in her recent lessons, Lucia formulated solid thoughts on the subject, "Many have felt the call of the active and participatory divine, yet this invitation carries the weight of responsibility for one's life—a burden most shy away from. Instead, they seek rigid rules and regulations to follow, avoiding the discomfort of questioning. Too commonly, people accept keys handed to them by others, relinquishing the quest for truth in their own hands. While these keys may unlock certain truths, they reveal only facets of the whole, often leading to neglect of deeper self-exploration.

"In our journey, we splinter from our total beingness, a process that gives rise to confusion and discontent. We lose sight of our essence when we cease to examine our engagement with our unique selves and how it benefits the world. As we blossom into our true identities, the divine radiates through our existence, urging us to understand our role within the larger tapestry of life. This realization highlights the imperative of self-awareness."

As this wave of intense thoughts passed through Lucia, her awareness sharpened to her surroundings. The bushes and cacti stood out vividly, revealing their intricate details as though the Earth itself opened to her. She moved gracefully, gliding toward the clay bricks that formed the canyon wall. Alone in this serene landscape, she felt liberated. No one scrutinized her as she approached the ancient native ruins, and she reveled in the freedom to engage with them intimately. Sitting cross-legged in the red dirt inside the three-foot-tall walls, remnants of shelter from the past, she began to hum softly, connecting with the history that surrounded her.

She didn't know why she felt the urge to hum, but she refused to ignore it. Months into her journey, she had learned to heed the bubbling instincts within her, even when they seemed absurd. Sitting there, she began to hum, a deep resonance rising from the

Earth into her groin, belly, and heart, cascading upward through the crown of her head. The pulse of the Mother trembled inside her, rising from Earth's core. With every vibration, Lucia's hum transformed into the planet's oscillatory force.

In an instant, bright white light exploded through her body, streaming from her crown. She felt the oneness of everything and her place within it as a web of white smoke wove through her. The fibers seemed to originate in her groin, traveling upward through her chest and then into her head, creating intricate patterns that connected all parts of herself. Finally, the smoky web stretched beyond her skin, reaching outward to touch everything around her.

Crows cawed from a nearby bare tree, their calls resonating in the crisp air as they watched her intently, creating a protected atmosphere around her. She felt their presence, experiencing the world through their eyes and wings. Grounded as the ancient stones surrounding her, she remained fluid as the ocean tide, a solid anchor yet able to move with the flow of life.

In a heartbeat, her energy scattered into a thousand winds, igniting with the sun's Blaze—as expansive as the solar system. Suddenly, she recognized the fragility of her physical form against the vastness of all existence.

Suddenly, a hawk screeched above her, the sound slicing through the air like a hot knife through cold butter. Her heart, once solid, softened and melted, touched by the sharp, unyielding blade of that cry. In that moment, Lucia dissolved into the air, floating toward the horizon, riding the bird's voice. She felt no separation from the world around her; she embraced a profound sense of independence. The humanity within her marveled at the possibility of such extremes.

A mixture of awe, curiosity, and wonder filled her psyche as she recognized the importance of actualizing her true self each day she walked this Earth. She became fully human and fully divine, conscious of the meaning woven into her existence.

Lucia understood her responsibility to nurture the Earth just as it nurtured her and everyone else on the planet. She sensed an intricate network of influence, where every action and interaction rippled through life's web. The world needed her just as she needed it. Interdependent and yet connected, each person, plant, and animal contributed something unique to the grand system of life.

A quiet voice whispered in the back of her head, "Nature guides you all, and the universe directs your paths, funneling each individual into the precise position required for full expression. That expression, in turn, propels other parts of this vast mechanism to function, creating harmony within intricate complexity."

Lucia chose to observe this intricate dance with clarity while also embracing the chaos and randomness that permeated the world. In the completeness of this existence, she found balance while recognizing that the pursuit of harmony included both darkness and light. Lucia thought, "Embracing life's rhythm encompasses not only joy and illumination but also loss, struggle, and pain."

Lucia realized that immersing herself in the cycle of life required accepting its rhythms. Fighting, denying, or hating those cycles brought more profound suffering than any destruction. "The Buddhists really had this right," Lucia thought.

Feeling her legs begin to tingle and ache, she glanced at the sun's position and realized she had been sitting for at least two hours. Stretching her body, she savored the silky dirt beneath her.

As Lucia rose, she ran her hands over the warm rock wall, a refuge that had cradled many families and offered shelter during cold desert nights. Laughter and tears echoed in her ears. She saw mothers cradling their children and children holding their dying parents, each moment brimming with beauty. The cycle of life imbued every experience with meaning; to love entailed grief, and to live necessitated death. However, growth sparked a desire to seek what was missing, and longing led to becoming, which in turn fostered unity. In Lucia's image of this ancient culture, every thread of their existence felt extraordinary.

Her memory drifted back to her time in Mexico, where she felt an unbreakable bond with generations of women, deeply aware of their struggles. The balance of life had faltered, and it was time to restore harmony. Women, alongside all marginalized communities, carried lessons of struggle and resilience. They found strength in one another, flourishing when they lifted each other up. Yet Lucia was acutely aware that some had lost their way amidst suffering, clawing at others in their desperation for escape.

She realized it was essential to remember each person's unique role in the narrative, notably as the patriarchy declared space only for a few successful figures—often white men. Lucia suspected that a great awakening stirred among them, recognizing the power of change lay in mutual support, not in climbing over one another.

Lucia shook out her body, her limbs vibrating with energy as she began her descent down the trail. She galloped down the hill, laughter spilling from her lips as she engaged with her surroundings in playful jest, reminiscent of her joyful spirit at the tail end of her last hike.

When she reached the car, a buoyant feeling enveloped her, as if her head floated freely above her body. She embraced this sense of freedom and whimsy. Traversing the crevasse of cracked Earth, she wore a broad smile; her heart lit with joy. Lucia understood in that instant that childlike abandonment is part of the balance that she is seeking.

A few miles down the road, she spotted a sign for Slide Rock. Blaze had mentioned it, but she remained unsure of what to expect. The parking area seemed a little chaotic as children burst past her while she stepped out of the car, their laughter echoing as they chased one another up a path until their raucous energy faded into the distance.

Curiosity drew her toward the sounds of ridiculous delight, leading her to the water's edge, where she witnessed people joyfully sliding down a natural waterslide. This smooth, rushing river provided a marvelous gift from Nature that both tourists and locals relished. It offered the perfect environment for sliding down without the need for a raft; Nature would show the way.

Climbing to the worn path, Lucia reached the upper section of the slippery rocks, where excited patrons eagerly awaited their turn. Her heart fluttered, a familiar clench of exhilaration tightening her stomach, much like the thrill she felt as a kid before heading onto the big roller coaster at an amusement park. She hesitated, drawing in a deep breath just as an eleven- or twelve-year-old girl leaped ahead of her, shouting, "JUST DO IT, YOU WON'T REGRET IT, IT'S SOOOO FUN!" The girl launched herself down the rushing water, her gleeful scream echoing in the air.

Without another thought, Lucia leapt forward onto the slippery rocks as soon as the little girl cleared her path, her heart racing with excitement. The smooth, moss-covered rocks glistened under the dappled sunlight as the water cascaded down with a gentle roar. As she soared through the air, her stomach surged into her throat, a thrilling mix of exhilaration and fear.

She splashed into the cool, clear pool at the bottom, sending ripples dancing outward and droplets showering her like tiny pearls. With a burst of energy, she quickly climbed back to the top, her laughter mingling with the delighted squeals of children waiting in line for their turn. To her surprise, she realized she was the only adult embracing this adventure; the others lingered at the edge, hesitant and unsure, perhaps fearing that indulging in such childlike play would be too frivolous.

But Lucia didn't care—this was a slice of pure joy. Each twist and turn of the natural slide sent her heart soaring, and she felt a freeing rush as the water raced around her. The cool mist on her face and the sun warming her back reminded her of carefree summer days spent by the water as a young person. In that moment, she felt utterly liberated, losing herself in the laughter and the thrill of the ride, letting the pressures of adult life wash away with each exhilarating plunge.

As the sun slipped below the horizon, it brought magnificent closure to the playful escapade. Leading Lucia to drive through the canyon to find a modest hotel near Sedona. After grabbing some snacks from a convenience store, she checked into a budget hotel on the outskirts of town. And then she slept—without dreams, without the noise of thought. She awoke clear-headed, comfortable, and secure within herself. Her heartbeat steadied, calm and rhythmic, and she felt prepared to move on. Rising with the sun, she followed its light back up and out of the canyon.

Chapter Twelve
SITTING IN PRESENCE

The willow, which bends to the tempest, often escapes better than the oak, which resists it.

- Walter Scott

An invisible tether pulled Lucia back to the ocean, drawing her away from the parched desert. She had taken what she needed from the sunbaked land, which cradled her as she expanded her consciousness, igniting her spirit from within. Oak Creek Canyon, one of the most stunning places in the United States, spoke to her heart, promising that she would return there throughout her life.

An inexplicable urge beckoned her toward California. Although previous flights had skimmed over parts of the state, a longing to drive along the coastal highway surged within, to stop in the town that shared her name, just south of Big Sur. After that, perhaps a return to Seattle awaited; Michael had been curious about her plans. Yet, vague thoughts of Seattle felt hollow, lacking the thrill of adventure. It resembled more a need to resolve an obligation than a journey fueled by genuine curiosity.

Fragments of her yearned to root herself somewhere along this winding path or perhaps return to Mexico in search of Ixchel. Seattle tugged at her heart—the rain, the mushrooms, the intricate layers of life woven there. A deep love for the city mingled with a simultaneous craving for all these places, creating tension within.

As she tuned into the weight of her choices, each option felt heavy, laden with uncertainty. At once, surrendering to the inner flow became essential; her path would unfold in time. Lucia was sure an answer would reveal itself, as perhaps the right direction still lingered on the horizon, hidden yet waiting.

Until something felt right, Lucia decided to follow whatever felt right in each moment. Now, those urges led her to the coast of California, where a friend offered to share her home in Morro Bay for as long as she wanted. The generous offer would save her money and give her access to the coast. So, she veered off her usual path and drove toward that sunlit shore.

As she navigated the lonely highway through the stark mountains, a thirsty landscape surrounded her. The beauty of that desolation captivated her now, an evident contrast to how she would have viewed it in the past—before the fierce flames of transformation ignited her spirit.

Not long ago, solitude and loneliness had plagued her. She was reminded of the discomfort of being alone with her thoughts, prompting her to fill her life with distractions: friends, endless scrolling on her phone, and work. When she drank too much, the façade always cracked; either tears flowed, or she lashed out at anyone who seemed to constrict her.

Her journey of self-awareness began from that discomfort, a palpable unease she carried in her skin. The necessary change had loomed over her like a storm cloud, threatening destruction if she remained dedicated to everyone but herself. Before leaving her husband, that simmering malaise became unbearable. It flared beneath her flesh, radiating into her bones, robbing her of sleep, and igniting irritation that led to unexplained medical issues.

Deep down, Lucia always sensed an undercurrent of universal flow within her, a connection to the Divinity surrounding her. Yet she had drifted away from herself, lost to the demands of survival. Society's expectations swept her along its current, justifying her sacrifices by claiming marriage and motherhood brought her happiness. But deep down, she realized that this life, veiled in well-meaning devotion, failed to nurture her own well-being.

Lucia faced a profound journey of self-care, one that stretched endlessly before her. Outgrowing the shell that once felt familiar required embracing the whole self, confronting both the darkest shadows and the soul's deepest desires. For years, Lucia lived beneath a blanket of low-level sadness, convincing herself that this was a brave embrace of darkness. In truth, there was only a search for control over pain, resulting in a murky worldview shaped by sacrifice and sorrow.

Her body protested this adaptation, often leaving her with the helpless sensation of being caught between a rock and a hard place. She recalled uttering that phrase countless times, expressing her dismay. Though she loved her husband, a gnawing unhappiness consumed her. Leaving him had never entered her mind, yet she grew wearier of the role she had settled into. Somewhere deep inside, she sensed that this existence wouldn't suffice; she craved a life imbued with meaning and substance.

For so long, when alone with her thoughts, she felt like a caged animal. Loneliness loomed, a fear she sidestepped by losing herself in the lives of others—through television shows, social media, books, and the stories of friends and family. The more she engaged with them, the more she bypassed her own needs, hurriedly moving from one distraction to the next, always filling the empty spaces.

Lucia had resisted the idea of drastically changing her life to rediscover self-love. The thought of relinquishing her comforting routines made her anxious. She clung to relationships that felt 'relatively' safe, terrified of the unknown that awaited her. What would follow if she ended her marriage or stopped obsessively supporting others?

Doubts mustered in her mind: what value would she bring to the world if she didn't pour herself into caring for everyone else? The fear that everyone would abandon her was haunting, an ever-present shadow whispering that change would mean losing everything she held dear.

The power Lucia felt in her youth had diminished over the years. Bones hardened, becoming brittle, while her flexibility slipped away. Malnourished from giving everything to others, her vitality had faded, leaving an emptiness that echoed through her essence. Dreams arose of others filling her up, for the strength to do so herself had vanished. For years, fantasies of someone tending to her wounds filled Lucia's mind, yet the overwhelming burden of self-healing seemed insurmountable.

Eventually, a flicker of motivation sparked Lucia's courage to confront those false beliefs. The notion that someone else could fill the void faded into memory. With dedication, the journey to self-restoration began, and a slow and steady process of reclaiming emotional and energetic nourishment began. Years passed, and as resilience strengthened, self-care transformed from an empty ritual into a source of rejuvenation. Visits to the spa or quiet moments spent caring for her skin finally offered nourishment where there had once been none. Those moments, previously too little and too late, bloomed into vital practices of self-love.

Consistent attention to her personal needs became paramount, and the establishment of boundaries allowed for a redefined existence. 'Shoulds' no longer dictated life's choices, and a newfound freedom emerged, ushering in the replenishing vacation she had sought for so long.

On the way to the coast, vacant roads felt like a warm embrace. The world buzzed with life—both around and within her. Embracing self-acceptance, she reveled in the vibrant journey undertaken. Awash in the dynamic force of existence, a deep desire to share this newfound joy surged forth. Yet, a quiet understanding settled in until others filled their own wells, they could not grasp this possibility.

Her recent connection with women from all walks of life ignited a yearning, stimulating a hunger to provide a haven for others to rebuild their strength. Lucia longed to provide a safe container to those who had never been afforded the space to care for themselves. A promise emerged within her: acknowledging that the difficulty of the journey mattered less than the knowledge that it was worth every struggle.

The path unfolded in front of Lucia, free from the judgment of others' needs or deficits. Instead, it offered a willingness to meet people exactly where they stood. Recognizing the ease of remaining asleep and the challenge of awakening, a commitment to love others through life's complications began to solidify in her heart. In her hopes of embracing each soul, she envisioned a gentle touch of reassurance, fingertips weaving through hair, guiding them toward maintaining boundaries and cherishing the peace and passions of their own lives.

Lucia embraced these principles wholeheartedly, and the experience felt invigorating. Yet, she recognized how easily her attention could drift from her wellness and how tempting it was to don the superhero cape when someone truly needed her. To maintain focus while caring for others, a complete shift in perspective was necessary—her lens had to continually include herself in the shared 'we' of the world.

The remarkable revelation for Lucia was that this practice of self-focus did not breed selfishness or detachment; instead, it cultivated a sincere, nurturing spirit. With a cup overflowing, newfound compassion emerged, free from a sense of lack. Self-focus had not permitted much space for other people's negativity, allowing a deliberate choice in where to direct her energy.

This approach revealed a more genuine calling, starkly contrasting with the draining habit of unquestioningly prioritizing others. Gratitude bloomed within this realization that a sense of wholeness created room for others while preserving personal vitality. This equilibrium arose from listening intently to her body—attending to what resonated with her needs and truth while discarding what felt constricting, exhausting, or off-key.

Now, solidity grounded her like never before. It was her time, ripe for unfolding potential like a lotus flower blooming from murky waters. She became her authentic self, projecting that essence into the world—a kind of magic in itself.

As she navigated through the mountains, her body spoke clearly, signaling when to rest, eat, or sleep. Lucia followed these cues without hesitation, instinctively aligning with what felt right, flowing with the energy coursing through her veins.

In moments of reflection, delightful memories of Ixchel surfaced, rich with experiences shared in Mexico. Tasting the past became a sweet indulgence, not an anchor. Memories transformed into little nuggets of goodness savored without distracting her from the present or weighing her down with longing. Hard memories served as teachers, reminding Lucia of the growth still needed. They offered crucial lessons but risked burdening the present if she dwelled too long in their shadows. Balancing their significance allowed her to honor the past while remaining rooted in the now.

Lucia had known many people who wallowed in dismay and plenty who avoided challenging emotions. She had fallen into these traps herself but eventually realized that neither approach fostered her growth.

Lucia recognized the need for positive self-exploration alongside confronting the hard truths—the conditioning, the false narratives, and the trauma responses—became essential to her growth, but also to her compassion for others. It was clear that in the past, avoiding discomfort had bred a bypassing mentality in her, leaving wounds to fester beneath the surface, like an infection waiting to break through.

When it finally erupted, it oozed pain onto everyone and everything. Ignoring the underlying issues allowed the bacteria to thrive, manifesting in ways that hurt her and others. Just as neglecting a disease stifled healing, so too did neglecting emotional turmoil obstruct personal progress. Committing to intentional work was crucial to addressing any problem within and in the life she lived.

Reflecting on past choices, Lucia recognized how often she had allowed wounds to fester, bypassed issues, and distracted herself. This cycle took a toll, not only on her but also on those she loved. Depletion stemmed from her failure to establish boundaries, and giving everything without reciprocation led to resentment. Though it felt like no one tended to her needs, the truth was she hadn't valued herself enough to ask for care or set requirements.

Stubbornness had often defined her as an asset and a liability. Capable of convincing herself of anything, she could become rigid once her mind was made up. Eventually, the importance of flexibility dawned on her. Someone had once spoken of bamboo's resilience, emphasizing how it thrived through its ability to bend with the wind and flow with the ground, rooted yet mobile. This balance, capable of connecting heaven and Earth, resonated deeply. Lucia aspired to embody that same resilience.

Now more powerful than ever, a sense of strength coursed through Lucia's nourished bones. Still, challenges loomed ahead, and she knew she needed to learn more about facing discomfort and remaining present amid unease. The temptation to slip back into old patterns and behaviors lingered. Practicing the art of being in the world alongside others without losing her sense of self became paramount. A natural reflector, she understood that without continuous learning and self-awareness, she risked mirroring the desires of others, convincing herself they were her own.

Lucia felt a tug to embrace a more experiential life, taking necessary breaks from her philosophical musings. She yearned to live fully, to explore both the world and her-self, tapping into her intellect only when needed. The realization dawned that this chapter was beginning; her journey had only just emerged. An infant at this new way of living—open, authentic, connected—she sensed a delightful insecurity in her budding expression, overshadowed by a swell of excitement for whatever would come.

Questions about future challenges lingered in her mind, not as sources of worry but as mysteries of the universe unfolding before her. Suffering and difficulty lay woven into the fabric of existence; avoiding them proved futile. Acceptance brought forth the understanding that these trials would shape her path. All that remained was the hope of navigating them with presence and authenticity. Proper preparation meant building resilience, readying her for the inevitable hardships.

As she drove toward the imposing rock off the shore of Morro Bay, a deep, meaningful sigh escaped her. The sharp mound loomed out of the ocean like a sleeping giant, a steadfast guardian of the town. A decision crystallized: a visit to the monstrous rock jutting off the shore of Morro Bay as her first stop offered a final sense of solitude before heading to her dear friend Tressa's house. Lucia thought, "It's best to forge a friendship with the town's protector from the moment I arrive."

After navigating the narrow strip leading to the parking lot at the rock's base, Lucia stepped out and stretched. People scattered among the smaller boulders, some standing, others seated, all captivated by the water's dance. While approaching the bay, her gaze caught sight of playful creatures swimming on and beneath the wet surface. At least fifteen otters frolicked, some floating on their backs while others' adorable antics seemed tailored for their audience's amusement.

Lucia sat and watched the otters' antics for about 45 minutes before wandering down a path that wound around the gigantic stone centerpiece. At the end of the path, the landscape opened into a vast landscape of neatly stacked rocks balanced in harmonious towers. Lucia remembered that someone had told her they were called Cairns.

She recalled her further reading about cairns as markers guiding one through life. Lucia took in the sight of thousands of the formations before her, each tiny temple standing as a testament to nature's artistry. A laugh escaped her as she reveled in the simple beauty of the perfectly balanced stones. A couple of tourists shot her strange looks, but amusement dulled her awareness of them.

Minutes passed, and soon, laughter bubbled up uncontrollably, an infectious joy that made her cheeks ache.

People around her watched, and eventually, they began to join in Lucia's laughter, creating a collective euphoria that drifted over the waves and into the sunset. Lucia pictured their shared joy transforming into molecules that permeated the air, spreading well beyond the confines of the beach, reaching distant souls who, too, might join them with a chuckle at the absurdity of existence. Perhaps this awareness could sustain them in those moments when the world felt like it was unraveling.

After savoring the sight of seabirds hovering above crashing waves, Lucia turned back toward the car, eager to share her experiences over the past months with Tressa. Lucia finally found herself navigating the windy driveway that led to her dear friend's stone house.

Tressa, a rock climber with whom Lucia had fallen in love decades before, had a unique way of capturing moments in time. Tressa had even taken the photographs at Lucia and Andy's wedding. Their connection felt palpable, akin to a soul family bond, and Lucia could hardly wait to exchange stories of her journey with Tressa, sure her raven-haired friend would understand.

Pulling up to Tressa's beautiful, sprawling home, Lucia felt an unsettling aura hanging in the air, almost tangible. The grand structure, with its sturdy wooden beams and immaculate flower beds, usually exuded warmth, and charm, but today, it seemed to reflect Tressa's inner turmoil. Tressa, a vision of elegance with her flowing sundress, paced anxiously in front of the wide wooden porch, her phone pressed tightly to her ear. The sun cast a soft glow on her ebony hair, but her expression was strained. As Lucia parked and stepped out, she saw Tressa hang up, forcing a broad smile that barely masked the distress lurking in her eyes. The contrast between the idyllic surroundings and her friend's frantic energy created a palpable tension that Lucia couldn't shake off.

They embraced, exchanging pleasantries while Tressa glanced toward the kitchen. "Are you hungry?" she asked, leading Lucia inside. In the center of the table lay an elaborate charcuterie board, meats, cheeses, nuts, and olives arranged just so, as if plucked from the pages of a food magazine.

Lucia took a deep breath and asked Tressa what was happening. Tressa revealed that her father had been in a rest home that now faced closure. She felt the weight of responsibility resting solely on her shoulders, burdened by the thought of bringing him home.

Her father had dementia, and the nearest facility able to care for him was over four hours away—a distance that felt unbearable. Tressa knew she couldn't let him live that far from her. The news fell like sticky sap from her lips as she shared that her dad had received a diagnosis of inoperable pancreatic cancer. Though he experienced little pain, doctors had given him just a few months to live.

The timing of the rest home's closure could not have been worse, and Tressa faced a rocky path ahead. Lucia listened carefully to her friend's fears and the whirlwind of "what-ifs" that swirled in Tressa's chaotic mind. Embracing her tightly, Lucia created a container of unconditional acceptance for Tressa's tears and raw anger, allowing her friend to vent her fears that life was on the precipice of irrevocable change. Often, persistent thoughts of offering solutions danced in Lucia's mind, but she silenced them, recalling an old friend's soothing voice echoing in her thoughts: "Sometimes, people just need to feel supported; you don't have to fix it."

They engaged in heartfelt conversation that stretched late into the night. As the soft morning light filtered through the window, Tressa appeared noticeably lighter, the heavy burden of her worries slightly lifted. "Thank you for letting me share all that," she said, her voice carrying a touch of relief. Then, curiosity sparked in her eyes, and she turned to Lucia, inquiring about Mexico, enamored by Lucia's vibrant and grounded presence.

"What helped you survive the divorce?" Tressa wanted to know, her voice a mix of concern and intrigue. Lucia offered snippets of her journey, but the moment called for listening rather than sharing. The feelings her friend expressed were not about her; this was about Tressa navigating grief in a space soon to fill with the process of death. Their shared silence became a sanctuary, a testament to shared experience over empty explanations.

In those moments, the urgency to present her own story dissipated, transforming instead into a deep compassion for Tressa's situation. Offering support did not feel like a sacrifice; it felt remarkably enriching because it was being given from a full cup. Lucia felt a genuine nurturing spirit flourish within her, perhaps for the first time, as she remained fully present, content to stand beside this extraordinary woman braving such a profound life change.

In the coming days, they spoke about Tressa's love for her dad, although also reflecting on his absence throughout her life—a selfishness that had lingered like a shadow. Tressa recounted her journey through the tangled emotions surrounding his neglect, revealing how she had wrestled with her feelings for years. Despite the pain, they gradually nurtured their communication, strengthening their bond over recent years. As his memory faded, he became more present in the moments they shared, a blessing in an otherwise heartbreaking decline. Remarkably, he never forgot who she was.

Amidst this bittersweet revelation, Tressa acknowledged the arrival of hospice nurses and caregivers. While their help promised relief, it also threatened her solitude, forcing her to navigate a new landscape of constant company. The thought of relinquishing her freedom weighed heavily on her; the life she once lived for herself began to slip away.

Lucia sensed an opposing trajectory in her own life, yet she recognized the fickle nature of circumstances—her time to step up for family might come unexpectedly. This truth echoed the inevitable passage of life.

The coming phase demanded that Tressa release the self she had known, shifting focus solely onto her father. She grappled with the realization that her needs would take a backseat as she bore the responsibility of guiding him through his final days. Though she had invested significant effort in reconciling their past, the prospect of providing such profound care weighed heavily, given their fraught history. With raw honesty, Tressa reflected on the challenge of embracing unconditional love—a destination that felt elusive and complex.

Lucia offered steadfast support, vowing to help Tressa find that place of peace. Together, they watched the ocean roll in, strolled down to restaurants, and ventured along the coast to observe the elephant seals and the old churches. Hours passed as conversation flowed effortlessly; eventually, the chatter softened into a comfortable silence, both women captivated by the beauty surrounding them. They embraced each moment, knowing that sometimes unspoken understanding held a power all its own.

Three more weeks would pass before Tressa's father moved in, and Lucia planned to help her prepare for his arrival. They needed to fix up the house, making it more accessible for hospice and arranging it for the comfort of Tressa, her father, and the parade of visitors sure to follow.

Lucia decided to leave before Tressa's dad arrived. As they readied the house, Tressa faced the emotional weight of this transition, and Lucia stood by her side, offering support. Surprising herself, Lucia found comfort in focusing on Tressa's needs. As this hardship was a monumental moment for her friend, being present for her felt right. While tending to Tressa, Lucia realized she was also nurturing her well-being; she felt her mind open up to compassion and clarity.

Recognizing that by serving those who truly needed her, she practiced Divinity, although Lucia understood the importance of also caring for herself at the same time. This dual approach held its own power, as profound as any personal growth. On one foggy morning, Lucia contemplated, "A wise person instinctively knows when to prioritize situations and needs. I hope always to possess that wisdom." But just as quickly, amusement struck; the idea that she might navigate this path flawlessly seemed laughable. Her best hope lay in having better judgment, more often than not.

Lucia observed that Morro Bay held a unique enchantment. An indescribable vibe flowed through the place. Once home to a nuclear power plant, nature had reclaimed its space. The townsfolk embraced this rebirth, creating a curious balance around the massive rock rising from the ocean. An earthy mysticism enveloped this special little seaside town.

The ocean here differed from the shores of Mexico, the bay in Seattle, or the rugged beauty of the Olympic Peninsula, where one could confront the vast Pacific directly. The expanse around Morro Bay evoked infinity, a profound reminder of nature's vastness. Lucia imagined surrendering to its depths, finding solace in the embrace of Gaia, the mother earth, and Yemaya, the mother of the sea. In this place, Lucia felt small yet essential. An unspoken understanding connected her to everyone else who wandered Morro Bay.

Lucia made a habit of visiting the sleeping giant, sitting among the cairns, and gazing out at the water—a beloved self-care ritual that proved immensely enriching to her. When she wasn't sitting with Morro Bay's natural wonders, casual conversations with locals about the simplest of topics filled her with a sense of peace.

Soon enough, plans would take her further up the coast, but for now, she soaked up the kindness radiating from the tiny town by the rock, savoring every moment shared in its gentle embrace.

Lucia had worked countless hours for Tressa to prepare for her dad's arrival. Yet when Tressa insisted on compensating her, it stirred an uneasy response. This help wasn't about money; Tressa knew that. But on the upside, the funds would allow for a few delightful stops along the drive up the coast, so gratitude lingered with Lucia's acceptance of the financial support.

One of the beautiful days in this haven led her to a charming bakery by the bay, where she sipped coffee alongside Napoleon pastries. Memories surfaced of a silly conversation with Michael in which she had asked him to describe her as a pastry. He had declared her a Napoleon, sweet and layered. In that space, it felt like a grand compliment. Now, comparing herself to a pastry seemed absurd, as if trivializing her depth.

Lucia no longer felt a desperate need for validation of her personhood. It dawned on her that those requests for others' descriptions stemmed from a craving for affirmation—a reflection of her inability to see herself clearly. The memory of a time fraught with the yearning to be understood resurfaced. She had longed for someone to see beyond her armor, to penetrate the social facade she had constructed. Inside, her strength clamored for acknowledgment; her deep knowledge fought for visibility.

Now, a sense of authenticity anchored Lucia. Self-actualization encapsulated this journey she had undertaken. Yet, reflecting on how frantic her search for understanding had been, it still stung. It had demanded so much energy. Words from others had seemed to be a way to tear her open, to nourish and stitch her back together; complete and vibrant. In these recollections, she felt a child's vulnerability, a stark contrast to her perceived strength. She had believed herself to be so tough earlier in her life, which, in a way, was accurate compared to her fearful childhood self. But that strength had masked a deep-seated weakness, a failure to substantiate her existence and misplaced trust in others.

An exhaustive fear of being wrong about herself once loomed large. Without others' confirmation of Lucia's worth, perhaps she was just another flawed human grappling with complexities or even a mental illness. For years, the only source of her significance had been the voice in her head—a possible false prophet. Searching for meaning had yearned beyond the surface, into the very essence of her being, where true magic lay waiting to be recognized.

Lucia's journey since the divorce unfolded as one of profound self-discovery, but in that, she realized how important it is to also consider others, not in spite of herself but in addition to herself. Finally grasping her true identity, she embraced the space to express herself in the world without effort. Growth came unexpectedly, revealing connections with people who genuinely saw her. Yet, in the end, those connections, including Kaya, weren't the source of her affirmation. It was the process of expansion itself that flourished within her. Even in her darkest moments, Lucia recognized her existence as valid no matter what—this rooted her as authentic and unapologetic. Embracing herself didn't feel selfish, absurd, or villainous; it felt real.

Reflecting on her path, Lucia acknowledged the fears she had shattered, the challenges she had faced, and the infinite road ahead. Resolutely, she promised herself never to stray from her true self again. No matter the obstacles, being authentic needed to remain her priority, and now she approached it with compassion for those around her. Overflowing with self-awareness and confidence, she found a wellspring to share with others while remaining vigilant of the signs signaling when her cup began to deplete.

Glancing up from her coffee, she noticed an older adult, frail and struggling with a walker, attempting to mount a stool. Without hesitation, Lucia leaped to his aid, inquiring how she might help. He replied, "Please?" softly and without further words. Without a thought, she placed her hand on his back, offering gentle support as the man navigated the height of the chair. Once she moved the walker within his reach, he thanked her; she nodded and returned to her seat, a sense of warmth enveloping her.

Moments later, the manager approached Lucia's table, expressing heartfelt gratitude. The manager had been unable to get to the man in need of assistance and appreciated Lucia's selfless action. The kindness moved the overworked woman.

At that juncture, Lucia realized she didn't need any reward for her actions. She observed a need and acted, instinctively answering the call to help. With her inner depletion resolved, attending to others felt effortless; no accolades or affirmations were required to validate her worth anymore.

Savoring her complimentary meal, she felt grateful for the manager's acknowledgment of the importance of looking out for one another. Afterward, she lost herself in a book, sipping coffee and simply being fully present in her own life.

A deep, masculine voice cleared their throat, startling Lucia from her thoughts. Looking up, she locked eyes with a striking, long-haired gentleman in his middle years, dressed in a trendy button-up shirt and fitted jeans. He quickly excused himself for the interruption, his intense gaze scanning her face with a mix of curiosity and intrigue. Confusion washed over her—why was he talking to her? He asked if he could join, and she shrugged, reluctantly agreeing. Glancing around, she noted that all the tables had been taken. "Oh, okay, he just wanted a place to sit," she thought, warmth creeping to her cheeks, wondering if there was something more beneath his request.

He introduced himself as Lucian. A laugh escaped her as she told him she bore the female version of his name. "Both versions mean light," Lucia said hesitantly as both of them seemed startled by this coincidence.

Lucian's gaze didn't waver. With a chuckle, he remarked, "I chose your table for a reason." Confusion deepened as the moment felt surreal. Lost in her thoughts, this unexpected encounter threw her off balance.

"You have a unique energy," he continued. "I can tell you've done a lot of work in different energetic systems. You seem like someone I want to know."

With a hint of overconfidence and a smirk, Lucia shot back, "Oh really? I'm sorry, but I didn't even notice you, and I'm very intuitive."

"I can tell you are. But you weren't paying attention while I was," the gentleman gently replied, his voice steady.

"Touché... Okay, well..." She paused, centering herself in this unusual moment. "Maybe, we should talk, then."

"Yes, that would be a start. But first, I want you to know I'm not hitting on you. I pay attention like you often do on days other than today. I remember that I never know who I might meet, and I trust my instincts when I feel drawn to someone's energy. Initiating a conversation is worth the risk when I notice that something feels out of the ordinary."

He took a breath, seeming to gather his thoughts. "I know I'm an older man, and I don't want to come off as creepy or unwelcome. So let me start again. I'm Lucian. I am genuinely interested in talking to fascinating people, and you appear to fit that description. I would love to have a conversation if you're open to it."

Surprised, Lucia nodded and smiled, realizing she had almost missed this opportunity. Her oblivious defensiveness nearly shut her down. However, she also acknowledged the countless men who had approached her over the years. Their intentions were clear, interested only in a physical connection, indifferent to her personality. With a sigh, she granted herself grace, focusing on this fellow light bearer.

He began with questions, keen and curious. "Where are you from? How did your spiritual path unfold? What is your relationship with the divine?"

Lucia stared at him for a moment, slack-jawed. Surprisingly, his direct, dive-right-in mentality intimidated her slightly, especially since he immediately assumed she was a mystical person. Kaya had 'seen' her, but she definitely wasn't used to that. Finally, she spoke. "I came from Seattle. I wasn't raised there, but I've lived there for many years. An undercurrent connected to the divine has always run through me. I consider myself a mystic, as the Divine has always made more sense than anything else in life. I've been drawn to religion and philosophy for as long as I can remember.

"If I had been born in a different time, I might have become a nun or something similar—dedicating my life to God. Spiritual marriage never seemed far-fetched. Yet, in this lifetime, I feel the need to experience my body, relational connection, my humanity, my sexuality, and to live fully.

"Recently, I underwent what many would call an awakening. It felt like waking up to something that had continuously resided within. This awareness isn't just of Divinity but of self. I perceive God, the Universe, and the Divine through me differently now. It feels integrated—my body and spirit are not separate. I am it, and it is me. The dynamic movement of my thoughts, emotions, and actions in the world connects me to the Divinity in everything.

"I've noticed that nature serves as a guide to living; the answers often lie therein. I can feel the cycles of life within and around me, woven into the fabric of the Divine, and I now see the connectivity between all things.

"I consider myself fortunate to understand the importance of being present and paying attention—not only to the environment, which I totally missed today, but also to my psychology. If I ignore my constrictions, traumas, stories, and issues, I won't be open enough to embrace the Divinity within or around me.

"I view every journey as unique and essential; this is just mine. I might be a mystic in the way some are artists or teachers; it's my calling, my path. But how that path unfolds remains uncertain.

"It feels as if I have recently been reborn into this awareness, and I need to learn to crawl before I can walk. Excitement mingles with nervousness inside me all the time. Thankfully, I've learned to slow down and listen to the wisdom inside while also seeking signs in the world to help me uncover opportunities. This exploration is new for me. I must remind myself to grant grace, knowing mistakes will come.

Blushing, she motioned to the stranger with the same name, shrugging at her oblivious behavior. Taking a deep breath, she realized she had spoken as if in an interview.

Lucian held her in focused compassion while listening to her story, his genuine curiosity and interest creating a comforting space. Unlike her experiences with Ixchel or as an apprentice of Kaya, this felt different. She sensed something deeper at play, a comfort in his desire to hear her inner story. Grateful for his questions about her passions, she found solace in finally voicing her internal adventures, which she had kept close since arriving in Morro Bay.

Lucian drew a breath that seemed to reach deep into the Earth. Speaking with intention, he said, "I love all of this. It resonates with my own experiences of God and the Divine. I could elaborate on many facets of what you just shared. Thank you for speaking so candidly; it felt like a direct expression from your heart. Few can articulate such thoughts clearly."

Continuing, Lucian dove into an explanation of his existence. "I'm from Santa Cruz, right here in California. I drive the coast regularly because this stretch between Morro Bay and Santa Cruz holds such power. My favorite spot is the southern part of Julia Pfeiffer State Park. A waterfall cascades straight onto a beach along the coastline, one of only a handful in the world. It's intense and beautiful there. You absolutely have to check it out. Funny enough, McWay Falls sits only twenty minutes north of Lucia. Were you named after that town?"

Lucia grinned. "My mother told me I was actually named after it... That makes sense, right? Here I am, a plain old white girl with this beautiful Spanish name. Are you named after that town, too?" Excitement laced her voice.

Lucian chuckled. "Yup! Lucian is a variation of Lucia. My parents traveled down the coast, and I was born in Lucia by accident—came early. They decided I had to carry the name of that little spot with the expansive ocean. It explains my fascination with this area."

A smile spread across Lucia's face at this shared connection. "I wasn't born there, but my mother took that highway-one drive when she was young. It was the only road trip she ever did alone. She stayed in Lucia, watching the ocean for days. Mom envisioned me there and knew in a flash she would name her daughter Lucia."

Lucia dreamily added, "I've already decided to head north to Lucia and stay by the water for a couple of days. Thanks for telling me about the falls; I didn't even know they existed. This will be my first time on Highway 1."

Lucian's eyes sparkled with genuine excitement. "Oh my goodness! You are going to love it! It's magnificent!"

They spent time discussing the coastline and Santa Cruz, and Lucian shared stories about his years living in Europe. He explained his decision to return to California before it fell into the ocean, elaborating on his love for Santa Cruz with its broody sunshine vibes. The town's proximity to so much—the Bay Area and Big Sur—enchanted him. He had inherited a house there, using it as his home base, and he enjoyed working locally, though travel often called him away.

Hours slipped by unnoticed as their conversation unwound. Finally, Lucian asked if they could meet the next day; he wanted to introduce her to a friend. She agreed, and they embraced before he dashed out of the coffee shop.

Gathering her things, Lucia returned to Tressa's, still trying to grasp the whole interaction. When she described Lucian to Tressa, her friend's excitement was palpable. "Oh my God, I know that guy! I met him at a dinner party. He's friends with Maurine. He was very cool; I liked his energy."

Lucia marveled at how small the world felt and mentioned the upcoming introduction to Lucian's friend, wondering if it might be Maurine. Tressa speculated it probably was, sharing that Lucian had mentioned working a case with Maurine, which confused Lucia since Lucian described the friend as an artist. Yet Tressa didn't feel the need to question it further, and so she let the matter rest.

Tressa embodied a present spirit, grounded and warm-hearted. In contrast, Lucia often drifted through life, her ether energy threatening to lift her away into the clouds. She sincerely appreciated the stability that friends like Tressa provided. Without their anchor, the vibrant ethereality could consume her. Tressa's presence served as a constant reminder of the importance of such connections, keeping Lucia tethered to reality and reminding her of the beauty in their friendship. In those moments, Lucia felt grateful for the balance Tressa brought to her whimsical existence.

Lucia felt Tressa's unwavering presence, a steadfast companion who embraced her for who she truly was, not for the expectations others imposed. This adventure had stretched on for what felt like an eternity, her independence morphing into an obstacle. It was time to lean into interdependence with those who loved her.

Finally strong enough to trust her worth, Lucia realized her relationships would enhance rather than overshadow her self-care. Empowered, she understood that while a good life awaited her, challenges would inevitably arise—and she would navigate them as best as she could.

That evening, laughter intertwined with tears as Tressa and Lucia celebrated their bond. Gratitude surged within her for Tressa, and a deep ache settled in her heart for the difficult path awaiting her friend and her father. They grasped the weight of supporting someone at the precipice of death. At her core, Lucia recognized that this would be Tressa's most daunting trial.

She wanted to stand by her friend's side, ready to offer support in the ways Tressa might allow, yet she sensed her friend's fierce independence would drive her to face each day alone, undeterred by circumstance. Tressa embodied determination, steadfastly dedicated to those she loved.

Their evening resonated with power. Two women united in confidence and raw honesty created something magical between them. Lucia finally shared more pieces of her adventure, Tressa handling them with beautiful reflections. Their shared love and joy might even have shifted the world's energy that night, rippling outward. Lucia couldn't shake the feeling that their connection stirred a longing in the hearts of women sitting alone, a collective yearning for a sisterhood inherent in every feminine spirit.

Chapter Thirteen
TO BE TRUTH

My wild spirit is my deepest truth, my greatest expression, and my highest love.
It cannot be contained. It defies rules and explanations and logic. I embrace my
untamed spirit and unleash her into a world that is meant to be filled with joy
and love and laughter.

- Adrienne Enns

The sun rose, casting warm light through Lucia's window as birds chirped and sang their morning songs. The faint clucking of chickens drifted down the street, a curious sound in a place like Morro Bay. With the tranquility of dawn surrounding her, Lucia drifted off again into images of comfort and care.

As she entered the soft embrace of dreamtime, visions of a swirling mass of butterflies enveloped her; thousands of them blanketed the sky in vibrant orange and black. Their wings created a dance of movement while they filled the air with life, as though they wielded the healing power of the very element that surrounded her.

Lucia swam through the butterflies as if time stood still. Their wings brushed against her flesh, imbuing her with a sense of connectivity that resonated through every fiber of her being. Suddenly, she felt a transformation taking hold, as if she had become a single caterpillar within their flurries of chaos. Her soft body crawled along a branch, drawn toward a succulent leaf that beckoned her closer. An irresistible hunger stirred, compelling her to consume the leaf, filling her form with its nourishment.

As she indulged, a cocoon began to form around her, firm yet comforting. In those moments of metamorphosis, Lucia felt a profound shift, a surrender to what felt like destiny. Fear crept into the corners of her human mind, whispering doubts about change, yet the instinct of the caterpillar surged within her, guiding the process of transformation. The world around her faded, leaving only the certainty of regeneration—a natural, perfect change promising a rebirth into something entirely new.

Lucia awoke shortly after emerging from the fragile shell that had encased her delicate body, now set free to soar through the expansive midday sky. As her morning wings unfurled, she took in the world around her, vibrant and alive. A glance at the sun's high arc stirred memories of plans to meet Lucian and his friend later in the day.

Thoughts of a stroll through flower-filled gardens ignited Lucia's imagination, drawing forth images of dancing bees flitting over vibrant beds of blossoms. These colors wove together to form a radiant tapestry within her mind, much like the dreams of butterflies that had captivated her the night before. For now, those visions would have to suffice; the sanctuary of a deep, claw-foot bathtub beckoned, promising a subtle ease into the day.

In that warm embrace, surrounded by the whispers of water and the gentle hints of floral scents from the gardens she longed to visit, she could almost feel the touch of sun-kissed petals against her skin. The allure of tranquility painted a stark contrast to her bustling thoughts, inviting her to sink into solitude and let the cares of the world dissolve.

After savoring the remnants of the powerful dream, warm water enveloped Lucia's body in a soothing embrace. The bath, infused with figures hidden in the steam, invited reflection.

Memories surged forth—vivid details of the ethereal butterflies wove into the fabric of her being, their iridescent wings tracing an exquisite design against the canvas of her mind. These delicate creatures hovered through the haze, igniting whispers of forgotten moments, every fragment a kaleidoscope of color and emotion.

Each soft ripple in the water mirrored the gentle dance of those wings, drawing forth a sense of calm and clarity that anchored her thoughts. In this tranquil haven, the outside world faded, leaving only the shimmering slivers of the dream to weave a tapestry of light and yearning.

The glorious moment of the chrysalis shattering lingered in her thoughts, releasing her into this vibrant existence. Waves of liberation surged within as the gentle ache of soft, powdered wings stirred for the first time, igniting an exhilarating thrill that urged her to embrace the waiting air.

A day brimming with promise loomed ahead, wrapped in echoes of possibility that infused her with a profound sense of wonder. With each heartbeat, the realization settled deep within—this dream marked a shift, a metamorphosis into a renewed version of herself.

Uncertainty cast shadows over how this new chapter would unfold. Yet, clarity shone brightly in her mind: she stood on the brink of a vastly different life, one that beckoned exploration of her fullest potential and the gifts she had come to recognize as uniquely hers. All the past efforts and trials endured had forged a pathway to her most authentic self, unlocking the key to living her best life.

With the sun kissing rays upon the horizon, each flicker of light felt like an invitation to take flight. The world awaited, vast and uncharted, ready for her to weave her story into its very fabric. In that moment of awakening, the air filled with the promise of transformation, and with a deep breath, she stepped forward into the embrace of the unknown, eager to discover what awaited in the unfolding journey ahead.

The feeling of being an infant in this renewed world enveloped her, a reminder that she was learning a new way of being. Rebirth had been a recurring theme in her life; with every evolution, recognition of self often faded, altered by time's relentless passage. Gradually, however, comfort emerged in the understanding that this process was as natural as the seasons altering the landscape.

In learning to flex with the changes—as bamboo sways but never breaks—she discovered an expanded sense of self. Confidence swelled within her; a core of power recognized in the wisdom harvested from past experiences.

As the bath ended, Lucia prepared for her meeting with Lucian, humming a tune that felt both familiar and elusive. It resonated like a lingering reverberation, perhaps from a repressed memory or even a distant past life. Excitement and a twinge of nervousness skipped through her as she anticipated what the meeting would unveil, the comfort of their previous conversations grounding her amidst the budding anticipation of a new journey ahead.

Lucia admired Lucien's directness; he seemed to instinctively grasp her worries before she even voiced them. Suspense bubbled within her as she prepared to meet the mysterious person, wondering if it was indeed the person Tressa had mentioned. This moment felt as daunting as stepping off a precipice, akin to the fool in a tarot deck—taking a leap into the unknown, trusting that fate would weave its magic. With a deep breath, that notion steadied her racing heart; she embraced the uncertainty, ready to plunge into a meeting that promised to alter the course of her life.

***

Lucia approached the vibrant house perched in the bosom of the gentle hills. Sculptures punctuated the landscape, drawing the eye to the striking features of the dwelling: purple shutters framed the windows, while green stairs led up to a bold red door. The windowsill glowed with yellow blooms, and the roof peaked in a warm orange, creating a riot of color that captivated anyone who looked.

The house itself, a soft lavender, blended harmoniously with the riot of flowers that filled the yard—each hue blooming with life. Hummingbirds danced through the air, weaving effortlessly among dragonflies, their movements a lively celebration of the scene. Rainbow windsocks fluttered at the entryway, adding to the sense of whimsy. This place, with its mosaic of colors and joyful sounds, felt like a sanctuary where time could stretch indefinitely, inviting Lucia to stay forever.

Lucian greeted her at the door and welcomed her inside. A witchy older woman occupied a fluffy velvet chair by the mantle, which brimmed with herbs and flickering candles. The air buzzed with an array of scents, each competing for attention, and Lucia struggled to focus on the enchanting figure. With a knowing smile, the woman introduced herself as Maurine. Lucia grinned as she realized it was, indeed, Tressa's friend.

Lucia's gaze swept through the house, eager to absorb its myriad details. In one corner, animal skulls adorned a makeshift altar, hints of ancient rituals murmuring in every piece. Soft, silky fabrics draped every window, door, and corner. The shifting colors with every glance created a mesmerizing dance of light across the space. Rainbows streamed from prisms nestled in the windows, casting playful patterns all around. Each room unveiled new textures and hues, while all sizes of goddess statues seemed to guard the atmosphere, watching over the eclectic collection.

With each blink, Lucia found herself drawn deeper into this captivating sanctuary, where every element whispered secrets of the unknown.

Maurine opened her arms to Lucia, enveloping her in the warmest, softest hug she had ever received. The wise crone exuded a comforting presence, her lengthy hair shimmering with silver and streaks of brown cascading over a flowing purple velvet dress. Bright aquamarine eyes sparkled with a vibrancy that captivated anyone fortunate enough to meet the older woman's gaze.

With a joyful spirit, Maurine led Lucia through her home, fingers intertwined in a gentle grasp as she shared tales of her artistic endeavors. Each room unfolded like a story. Lucia marveled at a breathtaking 3D painting of a water goddess, shimmering with colors that seemed to swirl in the light. In the corner of the sunny canary yellow kitchen loomed a dragon head, a whimsical testament to the woman's creative flair.

Her cottage embraced nature; herbs and dried flowers hung from every windowsill, their earthy fragrances mingling with the warm aromas of cooking. A rack of pots and pans, elegantly suspended from the ceiling, caught the eye, each one a piece of the artistry that filled this vibrant space. The bathroom, lush and verdant, resembled a jungle, and Lucia could almost hear distant birdcalls emanating from behind a colorful shower curtain that concealed the tub.

As they meandered through the rooms, a long-haired gray cat named Sorcia trailed closely, weaving around their legs, adding her own touch of warmth to the enchanting atmosphere. The house felt alive, a sanctuary of creativity and connection, where each corner whispered the stories of a life fully embraced.

After about an hour spent absorbing mesmerizing stories, vibrant art, spell materials, and the myriad of curious trinkets adorning the witch's house, the time had come for tea. The three of them gathered in a charming sunroom, surrounded by cascading vines, blooming flowers, and the fragrant spiral of incense. Sunlight poured in, casting a warm, golden glow that seemed to flicker around them, adding a touch of enchantment to the moment.

Lucian turned to Lucia, explaining how Maurine had enlisted him to collaborate on a project years ago in Santa Cruz. Lucia's brow furrowed in curiosity, and she glanced at Maurine, eager to know what kind of art had drawn her to that coastal town. With a playful chuckle, Maurine looked at Lucian and said, "You haven't shared the story with her yet, have you?" The atmosphere, rich with intrigue, hinted at tales yet to unfold, leaving Lucia hanging on the precipice of revelation.

Lucian sheepishly shook his head in response.

Maurine cackled a sound that echoed with playful mischief. "I am an artist, my dear, but my work extends beyond the canvas. I investigate phenomena ripe for research as I have also attained a Ph.D. in transpersonal psychology. I engage with people, listen to their stories, and determine which experiences warrant deeper exploration. My role lies within a scholarly research company connected to several universities in the Bay Area."

She continued, "I discovered Lucian one afternoon in a bustling coffee shop, deeply immersed in a stack of books on mysticism. He was pursuing his doctorate, conducting literary research around mystical experiences for his dissertation. The more he spoke, the clearer it became that he had traversed extraordinary realms in his life but remained largely unaware of the mystic within him. Yet beneath his humble exterior, it turned out he carried a wealth of knowledge that surprised even me." She laughed heartily, a sound entirely unconcerned with whether her merriment drew others in or left them behind.

Lucia listened intently, hardly able to believe the revelations unfolding before her. The idea that they conducted metaphysical investigations captivated her; she envisioned this job as a dream come true, a path that resonated with her deepest aspirations.

Lucian seemed to notice her intrigue as if the wonder etched across her features prompted him to elaborate. "I know this sounds crazy, but it is true," he explained, his voice steady yet energized. "I've embraced my identity as a mystic and discovered ways to apply my experiences to the practical world."

He paused, allowing his words to sink in before continuing. "I am also an official investigator and researcher. We belong to an organization dedicated to expanding how people perceive existence. We're theorizing, gathering research, weaving together thoughts and insights, all in pursuit of reformulating spiritual concepts—what most refer to as reality and the divine. Does that make sense?"

Lucia nodded, delight spinning within her. A whirlwind of questions surged in her mind, each one clamoring for expression, yet silence fell over her lips. A smile lingered as she struggled to settle the excitement churning in her chest. Thoughts danced at the edge of her consciousness, eager to escape, but for now, they would remain unvoiced; the moment felt too precious for anything to disrupt it. Instead, she focused on her physical reactions, hoping that the warmth in her smile and the light in her eyes conveyed her eagerness to engage further when the moment felt right.

"Maurine, what exactly did Lucian tell you about me?" Lucia asked, curiosity flickering in her eyes.

Maurine smiled softly. "He mentioned seeing you around town the past few weeks, drawn to your energy. Finally, he approached you and confirmed you were who he believed you to be."

Lucia's brows knit together without assumption. "Who am I, then?"

"A mystic," Maurine replied, her voice steady. "You possess the ability to change the world with your insights. I also sense that you have a deep understanding of people, which could guide you in the research aspect of our work."

Lucian watched her closely, gauging her response as if deciphering the layers within.

"Do you really believe I can do this? I don't have a doctorate, and my knowledge of research is limited." Doubt seeped into Lucia's voice, a hesitant tremor revealing her uncertainty. "I mean, you don't really know me. Is this...an offer?"

As she spoke, her brow furrowed, and her eyes flickered with a mix of curiosity and apprehension. The weight of the question hung in the air, begging for clarity amidst the unspoken expectations. The notion of stepping into a world so far removed from her current existence filled her with both trepidation and an unfathomable spark of intrigue.

Before Maurine could respond, Lucian nodded, conviction etched across his features. "I trust my instincts about people, and I sense something genuine in you. It may sound peculiar, given our limited interactions, but I believe intuition uncovers truths that go beyond mere acquaintance."

Maurine leaned in, her voice a blend of warmth and resolve. "However, the decision lies with you. This isn't about imposing our will upon you; it's about embracing your freedom and desire to embark on this journey. We can only open the door before you; it's entirely up to you whether you choose to step through."

The air between them thickened with unspoken possibilities, an invitation made all the more poignant by the weight of her words. Each moment hung suspended, charged with potential, while the path ahead shimmered faintly in the distance.

Lucian leaned forward, his eyes reflecting a deep fervor. "We are passionate about this work," he said, each word infused with hope. "We want you to join us, but we respect your choices. Patience is essential. In our experience, everyone needs the space to uncover their true selves. Often, we see potential in others that remains hidden, a spark waiting for the right moment to ignite. And that's perfectly fine; what matters most is that you live with authenticity and embrace life fully."

He paused, allowing the weight of his words to settle in the still air around them. The room, filled with sunlight filtering through the windows, felt charged with possibility. There was an invitation in his voice, a call to explore uncharted territories within oneself while also holding firm to the understanding that the journey is personal and sacred.

Maurine's eyes sparkled, catching the soft glow of the evening sunlight. In that moment, the atmosphere hummed with possibility, as if the world itself awaited Lucia's decision.

Lucia felt a tear welling in her eye, struck by how profoundly Maurine had mirrored her own emerging insights. Doubts meandered at the edges of her mind, whispering fears of inadequacy, yet she dismissed them as quickly as they arrived. The succinctness of Maurine's words stirred a mix of anticipation and uncertainty within her. Could she genuinely embrace this new chapter? In a moment that felt like an eternity but was actually an instant, these anxious thoughts faded, allowing her burgeoning strength and clarity to take center stage.

With a burst of conviction, Lucia declared, "Yes! I do want to go on this ride!"

Lucian and Maurine erupted in laughter, their joy infectious, as they enveloped her in warm embraces. The evening unfolded with animated discussions about how and when to embark on this thrilling journey. Amidst the chatter, Lucia shared the vivid dream that had visited her that morning, and in delightful synchronicity, Maurine and Lucian chimed in, "You have to go see the monarchs!"

They explained the wonder of thousands of Monarch butterflies that made their way south to a sanctuary near Pismo Beach during this time of year. The idea of mass migration painted a picture of beauty that resonated deeply within Lucia. They proposed a trip, and she readily agreed, her heart swelling with excitement at the thought of including Tressa.

The weekend excursion began to take shape in her mind, an opportunity not only for exploration but also a chance to offer Tressa a glimpse of beauty amidst the shadows of her father's illness. The mystical duo had no idea about the dream Lucia awoke to that morning; their synchronistic suggestion only strengthened her resolve that they had insights beyond their education.

It was a plan!

Lucia felt an overwhelming wave of fatigue wash over her, prompting the thought that it was time to return to Tressa's. The day had filled her with so much information and so many emotions, and the need to process it all loomed large in her mind.

Lucian watched her, his expression a mix of concern and encouragement. "Take a moment to consider your future working with us, and whether you'd like to stay in Santa Cruz with me or go back to Seattle," he suggested. "If you decide to stay, I can offer you the bottom floor of my house. You'd have your own bathroom and kitchen, but I'd need you to keep it clean and look after the cats whenever I'm away."

He continued, painting a vivid picture of the opportunities that awaited her. "Santa Cruz brims with access to groundbreaking research from the Bay Area. Numerous universities and institutes delve into the fascinating field of Transpersonal Psychology, which aligns perfectly with the work we do. Eventually, there will be travel involved, but that may come later. For now, the option exists to fly from Seattle or wherever else might call to you, working in chunks or online."

Lucian encouraged Lucia to embark on an internal inquiry to explore the possibilities that lay before her. "Consider what feels right. There's no rush, and we both want to honor your needs and desires. Your choices matter completely, and flexibility is key for us."

His sincerity wrapped around her like a comforting embrace, making her wonder about the paths available to her and the weight of the decisions still unmade.

With that, Lucia agreed to think it over. Embracing her new friends tightly as she descended the blue walkway, each step echoing a sense of anticipation. The luminous moon cast a silvery glow upon everything. At the same time, millions of tiny sparkles orchestrated a symphony of hope in the sky above, creating a mystical guide to what might be. Giddy with emotion and slightly dizzy, she settled into her car, allowing a few moments to slip by, though they felt like an eternity, as the evening spun around her.

Eventually, clarity returning, she drove toward Morro Bay's stone protector, yearning for the solace of the cairns and the rhythmic crash of waves against the shore. The nearly full moon infused the scene with ethereal light while the ocean sang a melodic refrain that tugged at her soul with every crest and fall.

Time slipped away as she allowed herself to drift beneath the sky's sparkling tapestry, the moon a steady presence overhead. A surge of silver energy enveloped her, offering a profound understanding that transcended specific thoughts, an awareness of all things intertwined. In that tranquil embrace, she surrendered to the moment, grounding herself in the earth as its heartbeat resonated with her own.

For an exceptionally long stretch, thought dissolved into silence. Lucia became a witness to every sensory experience unfolding within her body, mind, and heart—listening deeply to the subtle messages of her nervous system, tracing each sensation to its source.

A profound peace enveloped her; nothing required tending at that time. She perceived the succinctness of existence and recognized she was precisely where she needed to be, immersed in pure stillness. In the heart of this stillness, a small voice emerged within, whispering gently, "You've only just begun."

***

The following day, Lucia awoke with a surge of energy after a long, dark night. No dreams lingered in her mind; the restfulness of her sleep had been so profound that when Tressa peeked in, she wasn't sure if Lucia was breathing, hovering a mirror beneath Lucia's nose to check for signs of life.

In that quiet night, a part of her had vanished—specifically, the self-doubt that had shadowed her thoughts. Now, it lay buried and would never resurface. She embraced self-analysis and criticism as necessary companions, keeping her grounded and aware. However, the insecurity that had questioned her abilities no longer held a place in her life. Lucia felt lighter, ready to embrace the world with newfound confidence.

Tressa prepared a delicious breakfast of a cheese herb omelet accompanied by fresh local fruit; the bounty she had procured the day before at the farmer's market. As they savored their meal, the conversation turned to Maurine, whose remarkable qualities inspired admiration and curiosity. When the invitation to witness the migration of the monarchs came, gratitude swelled within Tressa for the chance to be included in such a unique experience.

Lucia expressed her intent to become a research assistant to Maurine and Lucien, trying to envision how that might unfold in her life. The thought of moving to Santa Cruz and sharing space in Lucian's house stirred a mix of fear and excitement. Tressa, concerned for her friend, questioned whether this leap felt like a promising path or a secure decision.

Understanding the undercurrents of anxiety in Tressa's words, Lucia responded with warmth. Her considerations mirrored Tressa's worries: Was it wise to cohabit with someone after only a handful of afternoons together? What would it mean to leave her life in Seattle and Michael behind? And what of her potential return to Mexico to reunite with Ixchel?

Lucia spoke openly about these dilemmas, revealing her introspection while revealing the full depth of her connections to

Michael and Ixchel. Since her arrival at Tressa's, Lucia had focused on nurturing their bond, keeping her love life mainly to herself. The layers of their friendship blossomed amid those previously unshared experiences; each word intertwined with uncertainties but strengthened by non-judgment and unwavering support.

The tangled web of relationships loomed large, and clarity felt essential. Tressa, ever the straightforward friend, cut through the haze. "You need to go to Santa Cruz! For years, you put Andy first, took care of your son, and even prioritized me when I needed it most. This time, you HAVE to do this for yourself!"

Listening intently, Lucia absorbed Tressa's words. How often had the instinct to nurture others eclipsed her own desires? Tressa continued, "You excel at making compassionate choices for everyone around you. I see you've been taking care of yourself through this adventure, but now it's time to make your decisions based on that resolve. If you want to see Ixchel and Michael and spend time together, hop on a plane and visit. You can have love with both of them and not sacrifice for either."

Tressa paused, allowing her words to settle. "For now, the Bay Area is calling. Working with Maurine and Lucian will give you a chance to share your gifts with the world. And believe me, those gifts are needed now." A knowing grin spread across Tressa's face as she exchanged a glance with Lucia.

Tears glistened in Lucia's eyes. The weight of Tressa's insight struck deep, resonating with something long buried. She nodded, her heart swelling with resolve. In that single breath, a decision crystallized: after savoring her time in Big Sur and the town that shared her name—Lucia would drive to Santa Cruz. The promise of new beginnings awaited, and it was time to embrace her own life beyond this journey.

***

The group climbed into Maurine's Jeep, excitement buzzing as they set off to witness the butterflies. Their laughter echoed, accompanied by spirited sing-alongs to the music and whimsical debates that swung through their conversations, filled with philosophical musings. The drive unfolded with a myriad of vibrant landscapes, a striking testament to life itself. Lucia realized that none of them would have traded that moment to be anywhere else on earth.

As they approached the sanctuary, they saw monarchs flitting gracefully about them, which revealed the day's promise of adventure. The warmth of the temperate air mingled with the sweet scent of eucalyptus trees and blooming flowers, rich colors bursting from every green stalk and vine, creating a scene that was nothing short of magnificent.

Lucia stepped into this vibrant realm and felt the air shift as monarchs began to swarm around her like a radiant halo. Stunned, the sight transformed into something extraordinary; orange and black wings enveloped her, hiding everything but the sheer joy radiating from her spirit. Her friends stood in awe, their gazes fixed on this surreal spectacle, marveling as Lucia became the center of a living canvas of butterflies.

Tressa's concern flashed across her face as she instinctively lunged toward Lucia, but Maurine caught her arm, reassuring her that nothing was amiss. This moment was sacred, a rare connection unfolding between Lucia and the alchemy of wings. Lucia surrendered to their delicate presence, arms held wide as they landed on her, cloaking her in their gentle embrace. Her eyes closed, and she immersed herself in the soft hum of their wings settling around her. The vibrations resonated deep within, harmonizing with the exhilaration that filled her steady breath.

A symphony of whispers surrounded her, people gasping and cooing at the sight that seemed to defy what they knew of the relationship between humans and nature. The "monarch whisperer," they called her, capturing the surreal miracle with their cameras while sharing their disbelief and delight in hushed tones.

For several precious moments, Lucia remained still, absorbing the energy they offered, a silent communion of spirit and nature. Then, as swiftly as they had descended, the butterflies took flight, all at once sweeping away in a swirling flurry. The sudden absence nearly toppled her; Tressa, Lucian, and Maurine quickly guided Lucia to a nearby bench, where they offered water, grounding her at the moment. Even Maurine appeared shocked, her voice a soft murmur of astonishment, affirming how right they had been about Lucia's gift. The air still echoed with the remnants of magic, a vow that the day would linger in their hearts long after the butterflies had vanished.

Lucia found her footing and firmly stated that she felt incredible. Monarchs continued to twirl overhead, enveloping the trees and dancing around her in a ballet of synchronicity. The butterflies, with their playful flutters, filled the group with delight, prompting laughter that rang out as music supporting the performance. Everyone embodied enchantment, reminiscent of children encountering butterflies for the very first time.

After a while, hunger led them to a charming seafood spot nestled by the water. The atmosphere was relaxed, infused with the salty breeze and the distant sounds of waves lapping against the shore. Conversation flowed easily, though many found themselves caught in the spell of the moment, exchanging jokes and exclamations of wonder over the enigmatic beauty of the monarchs that graced them with otherworldly inspiration. Laughter spiraled into the evening air, ridiculous yet perfect in its simplicity. Their hearts brimmed with joy as the group drove home, basking in the warmth of shared smiles.

As the car ride settled into a comfortable rhythm, punctuated by the soft strains of music, Lucia broke the tranquil silence. "I've decided to move to Santa Cruz," she declared, her voice steady with purpose. "But first, I need to spend a week at Lucia. I must engage in some deep conversations with the Divine, and that place calls to me strongly.

"I feel like going to Santa Cruz is right for me, and I would love to take you up on the offer to stay with you, Lucian. As long as I have privacy and don't feel trapped if I need space," Lucia said, her voice steady and hopeful.

Lucian replied earnestly, "You will have absolute freedom here. There will be no obligations or control on my part. You can do what you wish; this will be your space. I want you to make friends and invite people over whenever you want and come and go as you please. I want you to feel like this is a place where you can truly be yourself."

A smile blossomed on Lucia's face, brightening her features. "And I promise that I will help with the cats and keep the place clean," she assured him, her tone light yet sincere.

Lucian grinned in response, extending his hand to seal their agreement. Their hands met in a firm handshake, a gesture that grounded their promise to each other.

They all laughed together, the warmth of the moment wrapping around them. As the music swelled, they turned up the volume, allowing the melodies to fill the air while they sang along, voices blending in a cheerful harmony that carried the promise of new beginnings.

***

With Tressa's dad arriving later in the week, the house was ready; its small corners polished and surfaces clean, prepared for the barrage of hospice care workers who would accompany Tressa's father. During quiet evenings, Lucia chose to spend time with Maurine, satiating some of her curiosity about the witchy woman in the soft glow of twilight. As dusk painted the world in soft hues, their conversations unfolded, deepening the bond between them like the lengthening shadows that heralded the evening.

Each night became a thread woven into the fabric of that week, creating a simple yet profound tapestry of friendship against the backdrop of the life that awaited Lucia. The vibrant energy of shared laughter mingled with stories told under the fading light, constructing memories that would linger long after the sunsets faded. She felt like Maurine was one of the most genuine people she had ever met, and she knew there was so much to learn from her. Maurine made it clear that Lucia could visit and stay with her whenever she wanted and that she would be in and out of Santa Cruz often to collaborate with her and Lucien.

On those final nights with Tressa, the warmth of connection eclipsed the impending distance of time and the complexity of these new relationships, wrapping around them like a familiar blanket, inviting and secure. Each exchange, each shared glance, stitched together a narrative that celebrated both the present and the promise of the future, making the ordinary feel extraordinary.

As the sun dipped low in the sky, Lucia knew it was almost time for her to leave. A knot of unease twisted in her stomach at the thought of leaving Tressa alone with her dying father. Maurine had promised to check in on Tressa, and Tressa welcomed the offer, agreeing to let her gather volunteers to help in areas where hospice services fell short.

Lucia's concerns lingered; she knew Tressa often neglected to care for herself amid the swirling demands of regular life. And it was deemed even more difficult for Tressa to ask for help in situations as extreme as this one. But Maurine, a steadfast presence, had already rallied a group of women eager to support Tressa. They would prepare meals and take shifts every afternoon to ensure Tressa found moments of respite. Everything was in place: hospice would provide nurses, assistance with bathing, spiritual support, and even some light housework to ease the burden.

With the understanding of these arrangements, lightening her heart, Lucia understood she needed to relinquish any sense of control. Trusting in the support system that had come together, she took a deep breath and prepared to step away, knowing that Tressa would not be alone in this effort. The love and care of others surrounded them, creating a network of strength in a time that demanded it.

As Lucia bid farewell, a sigh of relief escaped her. Maurine had truly stepped up, rallying her army of women, while hospice promised essential support. Yet during their conversation, Tressa made it clear that she didn't want Lucia to linger. Grateful for all Lucia had already done, Tressa felt confident the resources gathered would guide them toward a positive outcome. Lucia needed to continue her journey.

With tears glistening in their eyes and hearts wide open, they embraced tightly before parting ways. Lucia climbed into her car and drove one last time to the sleeping giant. There, she sat watching the otters play, silently thanking the land and sea that had cradled her while she supported a dear friend. Above her, a hawk hovered, its screech echoing like a mantra. The bird then landed on a sign above as it dropped a single feather, intently staring at Lucia as if it affirmed that she was making the right choice.

A soft giggle escaped Lucia's lips as she accepted the gift. With that blessing, she climbed back into her car and set her sights on the uncharted path ahead; with purpose clear, her heart soared with the hawk into her budding life.

***

Thoughts of nature's healing power filled Lucia's mind. It struck her how intricately connected humanity was to the world around them. Yet, a troubling separation had taken root over time, a mentality driven by the need to dominate rather than coexist. This division may stem from an instinctive fear of nature's vastness and indifference toward human fragility, or it may have emerged from a patriarchal structure that thrived on ownership. The thoughts reignited her fierce inner resolve to help shift this paradigm, anticipating she could bring this wisdom into her upcoming position.

Stopping by the beach north of Morro Bay, where elephant seals basked in the sun, Lucia felt a swell of awe wash over her. Hundreds of these massive, playful creatures—a curious blend of grace and clumsiness—flopped around in the sand, their sleek bodies glistening in the daylight. Watching them, so at home in the ocean yet oddly graceful on land, reminded her of the wild spirit that thrived beneath the surface.

As memories washed over her, she recalled a Christmas spent in Hawaii, snorkeling in quiet waters where a monk seal had drawn her attention. The immense seal had busily dug at something hidden on the sea floor. Instinctively protective, Lucia had intervened when a group of young men splashed too near, threatening them with local fines for disturbing the sea life.

The monk seal surprisingly swam beside her as she turned to swim up to the shore. It was as if he were saying thank you for watching out for him. He maneuvered up onto the beach and lay there for the next few hours. Lucia even got a picture of him; she called him her Christmas seal. It was one of her favorite memories and significantly influenced her perception of animals and nature. She had always been more comfortable in the ocean than on land, which was also evident when her ex-husband frequently called her a mermaid.

The memory struck her as a reminder of her duty—to honor the fragile intersections of life where humans and nature converged, to be a guardian rather than a conqueror.

Lucia stood on the shore, embracing the call of the ocean and the weight of her purpose anew.

Watching the seals play and cuddle on the beach grounded Lucia. An undeniable connection to the earth surged through her spine, awakening a sense of belonging. The warm sun ignited her spirit, while the cool sand seemed to anchor her feet to the land. The wind filled her lungs as she gazed in awe at the mighty sea mammals, their sleekness forms a testament to nature's beauty. When a feeling of completeness washed over her, Lucia strolled back to the car, the tranquility of the moment lingering in her heart.

As she navigated the twisting highway above the eroding cliffs, the ocean unfolded like a vast canvas, mesmerizing in its infinite blue. Each lookout beckoned her to stop, to pause and absorb the majesty surrounding her. Waves crashed below, their rhythmic sound a soothing balm, and the salty breeze whispered secrets of the sea. Feeling fortunate to witness such splendor, Lucia soaked in each view, the raw power of the landscape filling her with a deep sense of gratitude.

The winding road beckoned, guiding Lucia ever closer to her destination. What should have been a brief hour-long journey from San Simeon stretched into a contemplative three-hour drive. As the ocean unfolded alongside her, she immersed herself in the rhythm of the land, the caress of the wind, and the sun's golden embrace. With each stop along the rugged cliffs, she felt her spirit lift as if it might soar into the emerald waters below. Approaching the edge, she found solace in the moment, offering quiet prayers to the great Mother, her heart swelling with gratitude for the abundance surrounding her.

Arriving at the Lucia Lodge, she let the brisk wind guide her towards the entrance. The receptionist greeted her with an infectious smile, and excitement lit up her eyes. "Lucia!" she exclaimed, the name rolling off her tongue like a cherished melody.

Lucia could hardly contain her enthusiasm, recounting how the lodge had once welcomed Lucia's Mother long ago.

The woman's name was Crystal, and there was no doubt that she fully emulated it. She wore a large, wrapped quartz around her neck, a beautiful purple charoite pendant that hung right at her heart, and big silver hoops almost half the size of her curly-haired Amazon head. Crystal spoke melodically and had more energy than most could dream of having. Lucia liked her; she was genuine and obviously had a big, open heart. Although she hadn't been around back when Lucia's Mother stayed at the lodge, tales of those days sparkled in Crystal's anecdotes, weaving a connection between past and present that created a feeling of grounded buoyance.

Lucia enjoyed Crystal's bubbly personality for at least thirty minutes before excusing herself and slipping out the door, making her way to her room's sanctuary.

The space was bright, with a large picture window framing a view of the water and a porch adorned with a soft lounge chair, where Lucia envisioned spending countless hours. Comfort brought clarity, and in that light-filled room, thoughts could flow freely.

Lucia considered how many of her friends favored moving meditations over stillness, embracing the rhythm of their bodies. Lucia had tried to find the same solace, but movement often scattered her focus like leaves caught in the wind. However, walking and hiking grounded her in the present, blending body and environment. She longed for a balance of both—active exploration and tranquil reflection—during her stay.

Savoring snacks from Morro Bay, Lucia reclined in the lounge chair, her gaze drawn to the waves crashing against the cliffs. Nearby, a hummingbird feeder hovered in the air, inviting tiny creatures that illuminated like living jewels. Watching their mesmerizing flight filled her with indescribable joy while the symphony of the cliffside lulled her into a gentle slumber.

In Lucia's dreams, light pirouetted through clouds, illuminating a vibrant landscape that sighed with gratitude. Lush green hills basked in the warmth, shadows trailing behind like children holding their Mother's hand, tugged along through the bustling streets of a lively city.

Sparkles shimmered from the earth, reflecting dewy highlights of moisture and growth. Lucia strained to decipher their source, but the elusive lights danced just beyond her sight in a sweet, ticklish manner. Abundant beauty enveloped her in a soft embrace, drawing her deeper into its allure.

Warmth resonated within Lucia's sleeping mind, igniting sensations akin to discovering a home for the first time. Strangely, solitude wrapped around her, a companion she had long feared. With no other humans to dictate her path, she reveled in the freedom to feel what she wanted and act upon it; simplicity blossomed in this uncharted territory.

Safety cradled her within the arms of land and sky, the sun's heat wrapping around her like a warm blanket, and the life-giving droplets resting on each blade of grass. The elements converged into a Divine melody. In this sacred space, Lucia sensed a profound connection—her essence mirrored the earth's heartbeat, her soul inseparable from the vibrant pulse of life surrounding her.

Lucia's dream revealed how people had distanced themselves from nature, forgetting that the power of all things lies within the meanings assigned to them. In this separation, they had also turned away from Divinity, choosing to dominate instead of coexisting. They sacrificed the essence of life for the sake of convenience, neglecting the Divinity woven into their very cells. The dream painted a stark picture of individuals allowing others to dictate what should be meaningful and powerful in their lives, while the truth lay before them all along.

Suddenly, intense turquoise eyes framed by warm brown skin filled her vision, surpassing all else. A forceful presence emerged, and a penetrating feminine voice resonated within her mind: "The sacred reveals itself only to those who seek. So, do not cease seeking, dear one. No matter how challenging life becomes, nurture your curiosity; let it guide you toward discovery, for therein lies your passion. Do not be tempted to direct those who have not found their way yet; it is their journey to unfold. You exist to inspire and to honor yourself and everyone you encounter."

Lucia jolted awake to the roar of waves crashing against the cliffs below. The voice from her dream echoed insistently in her thoughts. Compelled to capture its essence, she seized a pen and began to write, letting the words flow onto the page with an urgency that bordered on the primal. The ink filled the paper as she sought to engrain the message in her muscle memory. When the page ran its course, she paused, inhaling deeply from her belly, her gaze fixed on the vast expanse of the Pacific Ocean.

Confidence mingled with uncertainty as her mind teetered on the edge of understanding. The meaning of the dream seemed clear, yet she hesitated to cling to a rigid interpretation. Instead, she chose to attune to the feelings stirred within her by that mighty presence. This entity had infused her with unexpected empowerment, distinctly different from Kaya's or Kali's energies. Resolved, she released the need to identify the voice, creating space for the spirit to reveal itself in its own time.

Lucia spent long hours on the deck, immersing herself in meditation and stillness for three days. Each moment gently unfolded as she stretched her body, walked the pathways, and engaged in quiet conversations with the animals she encountered. The birds, riding the wind, became companions in her observations of the world around her.

On the fourth day, an impulse led her to Julia Pfeiffer Burns State Park. The drive was serene, and she found McWay Falls just off the highway, bathed in the soft light of early morning. Only one older couple crossed her path, offering a nod of acknowledgment as she hurried down the trail.

The hike surprised her with its ease, each step drawing her closer to the ocean's embrace. A pathway wound through a tunnel, opening to a magnificent view that took her breath away. The vast expanse of blue met the sky, and the gentle roar of the surf created a harmony that felt like a conversation with nature itself. At that time, Lucia felt a deep connection to the beauty surrounding her, as if the world had paused to share its secrets.

Lucia stepped softly onto the ground; her gaze fixed on the magnificent expanse of teal water stretching before her. As she reached the end of her path, awe washed over her, leaving her stunned momentarily.

Before her lay a waterfall cascading directly onto a breathtaking sandy cove cradled by rugged rocks. The blue-green water danced along the shore, rolling in foamy white waves. Beyond the rocky embrace, the ocean deepened into a rich azure, a hue that seemed to harbor every mystery humankind had ever sought and all those yet to be imagined.

The surrounding forest whispered secrets in the gentle breeze, and Lucia felt a magnetic pull toward the wild beauty of the scene. It was a place where the world felt infinite, and time itself paused, caught in a moment of pure magic.

As the sun ascended, casting a golden halo over the undulating landscape, Lucia felt a profound sense of privilege in witnessing this daily metamorphosis. Each crevasse, carved by time and tempered by the elements, whispered secrets of Mother Earth's hidden treasures, revealing tales of indigenous journeys.

Finding her perfect perch upon a rugged outcropping, she nestled in to observe the tides' rhythmic ballet—an elegant ebb and flow that caressed the shoreline with its gentle embrace, extending all the way to the cascading waterfall, where water danced in shimmering arcs of rainbow mist.

This ceaseless cycle unfolded the sandy beach like a storyteller revealing a tale as tiny shells and delicate shards of driftwood emerged momentarily, glistening like jewels in the morning light, only to be tenderly reclaimed by the advancing wave—a quiet reminder of nature's eternal rhythm and its ever-changing beauty.

The movement of the water mirrored her own internal shifts, a reminder of the constant twists and turns of life. Throughout the day, visitors came to marvel at the falls, their questions swirling around them like the mist rising from the water.

When they assumed her intimate knowledge of the area, she smiled and confessed it was her first visit, a moment she wanted to soak in for as long as possible. Each visitor responded with surprise, exclaiming how it seemed as if she had grown up in this enchanting land. Deep down, a knowing stirred within her; it felt undeniably like home.

As the sun began its descent, painting the sky in vivid, warm hues of orange and pink, Lucia decided to linger a while longer. The gentle breeze rustled the leaves, adding a soft melody to the evening air as she pulled out the assortment of snacks she had meticulously packed earlier. She savored each bite—crispy apple slices and rich, dark chocolate—along with the cool, refreshing water she had thoughtfully brought, feeling it wash over her like a gentle wave.

The setting sun drew an audience, and soon, she found herself surrounded by a diverse group of people, their faces illuminated by the golden glow. Each person, whether a child giggling in delight or an elderly couple sharing sweet whispers, was captivated by the carnelian sphere sinking into the horizon. In that shared moment of awe, with the sky transforming into a canvas of color, they each felt an unspoken connection to the beauty of the world—a reminder of life's simple joys—and to each other, bound together beneath the expansive, starlit sky.

The cirrus clouds swept around the dropping ball, creating an aurora of multiple dimensions. Each layer had a different shade of orange, yellow, pink, and purple. The tangerine layer of the sky turns into ginger and marigold, highlighted by lemony honey melting into the vista ahead of them. Somehow, there were fluffs of violet with mauve mixed into the glowing halos of pink. This perfect recipe was the most inspiring sunset that Lucia had ever witnessed.

Lucia wanted to carry the image of this place with her for the rest of her life. She hoped that this vibrant scene would serve as a refuge in the years to come, a sanctuary against the losses that would inevitably accompany her on her journey.

The day was marked by a fiery sky and the enchanting cascade of the waterfall, potentially serving as a lifeline to support her when her strength should falter. Each moment spent in this sanctuary wove itself into her being, creating a thread of solace for those times when she would find herself unable to walk alone through the shadows of life.

***

When Lucia stepped away from the sacred place, a knowing settled within her—a promise to return whenever she felt lost. That haven revitalized her spirit and could awaken her essence once more. Back at the lodge, she dialed Michael's number, and for hours, their conversation flowed. They shared what filled their days, recounted their recent experiences, and delved into the importance of embracing this new opportunity. The discussion meandered through their feelings for one another, culminating in the anticipation of his visit to Santa Cruz as soon as she settled.

Though bittersweet, their exchange felt necessary, and Lucia allowed herself to confront the heartache that came with not returning to Seattle. Reflecting on the past, she realized the need to release any attachment to outcomes regarding Michael. The journey ahead required acceptance of the unknown; whatever would unfold, she would embrace.

A few days later, Lucia reached out to Ixchel, their conversation blooming sweetly for just an hour before Ixchel had to attend to her brother. The fatigue in her voice hinted at the toll of watching him suffer, and Lucia felt a wave of compassion wash over her. The weight of Ixchel's responsibility hung heavy in the air, yet even through her exhaustion and grief, a spark of excitement flickered for Lucia's arrival in Santa Cruz and the new adventure awaiting her.

Though their time together came to a sudden end, a shared understanding lingered between them. Ixchel would reach out again when she found the space. At the close of their call, she offered a heartfelt affirmation that wrapped around Lucia like a warm embrace: "My sweet one, they see in you what everyone will recognize in time. You are special and spectacular; don't you ever forget that! You deserve everything your heart desires, my love."

These words sent tears cascading down Lucia's cheeks, a release of emotion fueled by Ixchel's unwavering belief in her. As the call ended, Lucia made a silent vow, clutching the kindness of those words deep in her heart, promising never to forget the light Ixchel had seen within her.

***

Lucia no longer sought to transcend the life unfolding before her or the shadows of her past. Instead, she embraced the present, ready to immerse herself in every moment and uncover whatever lay ahead. Being human felt like a precious gift, one she vowed never to squander again.

Inspired by the endless possibilities that stretched before her, a thrilling excitement surged within like a gentle tide rising with the moon. Wonder and awe entwined in a delicate embrace, beckoning her to explore the myriad experiences yet to come. A profound gratitude for the remarkable blessings that had graced her journey filled her heart, propelling her toward a new chapter rich with promise and the whispers of dreams yet to be realized. The prospect of collaborating with the enigmatic Lucian on this mystical investigative journey sparked delight within her. Every time the thought flitted across her mind, a radiant energy ignited her entire being, signaling that something extraordinary awaited just beyond the horizon.

Lucia drove along the coastline, the cliffs rising sharply beside her as she ventured into the unknown life that awaited. With determination, she had pulled the ripcord on a journey toward living her most authentic and sacred existence, embracing a choice that allowed no retreat. The world stretched out before her, vast and inviting. This moment marked her transformation; she was stepping into the empowered woman she had always carried within.

As the car glided around each bend, the salty air filled her lungs, mingling with the thrill of possibility. Waves crashed against the rocks below, echoing the heartbeat of change. Each mile driven brought a new sense of clarity, an exhilarating reminder that she had the power to shape her destiny. It was her time to rise, to claim the life she had long imagined.

Lucia felt her wings unfurling behind her as she glided over the enchanted sea. The fire of Kali Ma ignited a deep curiosity and fierce passion within her, empowering her to burn away what no longer served her purpose. Mother Gaia anchored her to nature's profound lessons and the grounding of self, even amidst the heartache that seemed to echo through the lives of women everywhere. From Yemaya, Lucia received extraordinary gifts of nurturance, transformation, and unconditional love. Finally, the butterflies taught her the alchemy of the spirit.

Once a humble caterpillar, she had woven her chrysalis and emerged reborn, learning to embrace the expansive sky above. Each twist and turn of her life had transformed into this moment of liberation. Lucia discovered the alchemy of wings, a testament to her journey woven from the delicate threads of joy and sorrow. Each fragile wing, printed with the hues of her trials and triumphs, carried the weight of transformation. A dance between shadow and light unfolded, transforming every hardship into flight and lifting her toward a new horizon. With each beat of her wings, the world unfolded before her, rich with possibility and filled with synchronicity.

ABOUT THE AUTHOR

Website: dawncelestemcgregor.com
Social Media: TikTok, Instagram, Facebook
@dawncelestemcgregor

Dawn Celeste McGregor, Ph.D., is a trailblazing transpersonal psychologist, educator, and author who fuses mysticism, empowerment, and social justice into her life's work. Armed with advanced degrees in Transpersonal Psychology from Sofia University, her groundbreaking research explores awe, the alchemy of grief and gratitude, and the reclamation of sexual agency in middle-aged women—all underpinned by her passion for dismantling societal conditioning that stifles personal autonomy. A professional psychic and relentless advocate for LGBTQ rights and embodied feminine wisdom, Dr. McGregor transforms lives through her dynamic workshops, writings, and visionary leadership. Her novel, The Alchemy of Wings, is a stunning testament to her ability to inspire liberation, celebrating resilience, self-discovery, and the electrifying power of authenticity.